A

BODY

IN THE

YARD

A
BODY
IN THE
YARD

The Frank May Chronicles

Lawrence Friedman

A QP Mystery

QP BOOKS
New Orleans, Louisiana

A BODY IN THE YARD

The Frank May Chronicles

A QP Mystery, published in 2018 by QP Books, an imprint of Quid Pro Books.

QUID PRO BOOKS (Quid Pro, LLC)
5860 Citrus Blvd., Suite D-101
New Orleans, Louisiana 70123
www.qpbooks.com

ISBN 978-1-61027-389-3 (paperback)
ISBN 978-1-61027-387-9 (eBook)

Publisher's Cataloging-in-Publication

Friedman, Lawrence.

A body in the yard / Lawrence Friedman.

    p. cm.

Series: *The Frank May Chronicles* (#12)

ISBN 978-1-61027-389-3 (pbk.)

1. Lawyers—California—Fiction. 2. San Mateo (Cal.)—Fiction. 3. May, Frank (Fictitious character)—Fiction. I. Friedman, Lawrence. II. Title. III. Series.

PS357.F744 2018   813.'1'8857—dc22

20187122935

CIP

for Leah, Jane, Amy, Sarah,
David, Lucy, and Irene

A

BODY

IN THE

YARD

1

The day Freddy called me on the phone to tell me about the death of Sybil Glass—indeed, the murder of Sybil Glass—had already been an awful day for me. Many things, of course, can spoil a day. Car trouble, for one thing. A day with car trouble is never a good day. But I didn't have car trouble. I had plumbing trouble, which is also very bad. Our downstairs toilet was clogged; I tried to solve the problem the usual way, with my usual tool, a rubber plunger. No luck. Meanwhile, disgusting water spilled all over the floor. And this was a morning when I desperately wanted to get to the office early. The girls—my daughters—were fussing and quarreling, and were late for school. My wife, Celia, was also running late, and I was rushing about, trying to remember the name of the plumber we used and why it wasn't written down where it was supposed to be, and didn't the neighbor recommend somebody else? In the end I called and called and finally got through to a plumber and of course they couldn't send somebody out right away, or even the day after the right away day. This was, on the whole, a miserable situation. I cleaned up the bathroom floor as best I could, sighed, and went off to work.

That was how the day began. In addition, it was raining. It was January, and the rain was falling hard, from a bleak, ugly, unfriendly sky. We love rain here in California—in theory. We love it because we're supposed to love it. Actually we hate it. We're either in a drought, or coming out of a drought, or in danger of getting a drought; as a result, everybody is supposed to be very careful about water, which is a precious resource. And, in addition, we are supposed to pray for rain. The trouble is, sometimes you get what you pray for. In this case, rain. And, indeed, it was a dreary, steady, chilling rain, a dark rain, rain coming from big, bloated clouds, rain in the middle of the morning, where it spoils things, instead of rain in the middle of the night, when nobody much cares, except, I suppose, burglars and people who stay up much later than they should.

And my umbrella wouldn't open properly after I parked the car. Before I could manage to get the umbrella to do its duty, I was drenched to the skin.

All this happened even before I got the phone call from Freddy. My client Freddy. Young Freddy. He had his faults, Freddy did. But I liked him. Freddy called because his day was worse than mine. Immeasurably worse.

But first I had better introduce myself. My name is Frank May, and I'm a lawyer. I practice law in California—to be exact, in San Mateo County in northern California and, to be even more exact, in the city of San Mateo. I'm a solo practitioner, which means I don't have any partners. I'm in the general practice of law, but I specialize in wills, trusts, probate, estate planning—that kind of thing. I'm in my late forties. I still have almost all of my hair. I'm married, to Celia, and we have two teenaged daughters. I have a house ... and a mortgage. Celia teaches high school. All very normal, even humdrum, except for the fact that life keeps playing a joke on me, an unfunny joke I must say, and the joke is that somehow I get involved, without intending to, in ... well, the sort of thing Freddy was calling me about. A murder. Why this happens to me is one of life's eternal mysteries.

Freddy's call came in the afternoon. Sylvan Platt had called in the late morning, and asked if I wanted to have lunch with him. We're friends, and we have lunch from time to time. Sylvan is a fellow-lawyer, and a real foodie. Sylvan is relevant to this story, but at this point I had no way of knowing that. And I had to say no to his invitation. I had a ton of paperwork to do, some of it personal, some of it professional. And then there was the rain. I preferred grabbing a bite down the street, where I could be exposed to as little rain as possible. "Another time, Sylvan," I said.

It was about 2:30 in the afternoon when Freddy called. I could tell from his voice that he was agitated. At least the rain had stopped.

"Frank," he said, "Frank, I hate to bother you, but something terrible has happened."

"Something terrible, Freddy? What is it? Are you okay?"

"I'm okay, Frank. It's just ... well, you won't believe this, but you remember that woman, that nasty woman, the one who said she was my mother? Called herself Sybil, but maybe that wasn't her name. You met her, Frank."

"Sure thing, Freddy. How could I forget?"

"And you remember, Frank, that we hoped she would somehow go away?"

"Right, Freddy."

"And ... you remember she said she could prove she's my mother, that she had evidence, documents? Oh Lord. I didn't really want her for a mother, I really didn't, Frank. I just wanted her to be gone. Well, she's gone," he said.

Here I have to break in and tell you that Freddy had been adopted, when he was just a baby. The women who was killed—Sybil was her name, or what she said was her name—claimed to be Freddy's birth mother. At first, we didn't believe her. We thought she was an imposter, out to get Freddy's money. I'll explain more about this later.

Freddy had taken an instant dislike to her. As he put it, when they finally met: "She waltzes in, and gives me this oh, I'm your mother shit, and I'm supposed to do what? I mean, hug her and kiss her and say, oh, I love you, you're my long lost mother, this is a new life for me? I mean, no way. I wasn't buying that, not for a second. Besides, she was repulsive. She had clammy hands. She had a mean look on her face. I just didn't like her, Frank. I mean, really."

And now, here was Freddy telling me she was gone. At first I didn't know what he meant by "gone." I said: "She's gone? That's good, Freddy." What I thought was, maybe she really was a fraud, and she thought we were going to expose her and decided it was time to slip away, to Brazil or Timbuktu or Wichita, Kansas, wherever she pleased, and try some other crooked way to make a living in a different venue.

"Well, not so good," Freddy said. "Actually, she's dead."

"Dead, Freddy? Oh my. That's awful, I guess. What happened?"

"Well, that's the thing," he said. "I don't really know what happened. But, Frank, here's what I have to tell you. I mean, it's not like she died, you know, of a heart attack, or something normal like that. Somebody killed her. Actually killed her. Shot her, and stashed her body on my own property. You know my place, Frank. It's got all this land, trees, acres and acres out the back, up a hill, you've seen it, it's basically wild. I've got a gardener, he comes once a week, he's terrible actually, I keep meaning to fire him, but I never get around to it. He's a real jerk, and we can barely communicate because he doesn't speak English. I mean, Frank, a lot of people love to garden and all that. To me, it's a pain in the ass. If I had my way, I'd just forget the whole thing. Anyway, this gardener guy, I mean, he's not important—he doesn't do the wild part, he just does the stuff in front of the house; nobody goes up there—and then there's this other guy, his name is Desmond, he's a neighbor, he's got a house just the other side of all this wild stuff, and he's a mushroom person, he likes to pick mushrooms, and with all this rain, there's a zillion mushrooms, and he came onto this part of my property—I mean, it's not like it's forbidden, I met him once or twice and I told him, 'Sure, whenever you feel like it, pick mushrooms....'"

"Freddy, what do mushrooms have to do with this?"

"Nothing, Frank. I mean, I don't pick them myself, suppose they were poisonous, they could kill you, but this neighbor, this Desmond, he was looking for mushrooms, and he was prowling around back there, and he found this body—it was way in the back, near the property line, sort of covered with leaves and stuff. And naturally he called the police or 911 or something. I wasn't home, I was away, but I came back the same day, and the rest was, I mean, utter chaos, Frank."

"And the body, Freddy, it was Sybil?"

"I nearly puked when the police made me look at this body. 'Did I know her?' they asked me. They asked me a million questions. Like, 'What was that body doing there?' I told them I didn't know a thing about it, somebody put it there. 'Well, didn't you notice somebody doing something out there?' I said, no I did not. Frank, I was away for a couple of days, I went to Santa Barbara, I'll tell you about it later; and somebody could have done this thing while I was gone, I mean, at night, in the dark, nobody would notice.... And they asked me, what was my relation to this woman? Frank, what was I going to say, 'Yeah, this woman, she's supposed to be my mother, but she's not'? I mean, like I'm Oedipus and killed my own mother. Didn't he kill his mother? I don't honestly remember. They were sleeping together or something. I mean, I wouldn't have touched Sybil with a ten foot pole. Of course I didn't kill her. Maybe they think I did. I mean, this is a fucking nightmare, Frank, pardon my language."

I tried to be sympathetic. "Terrible, Freddy. Really awful. I'm so sorry you have to go through this." I could hardly absorb what he was saying. Freddy was an excitable guy, but this was excitement at another level altogether, as you can imagine. My mind was racing around. In some ways—I hate to admit this—but actually, Sybil's death simplified things. But I didn't say this out loud.

"Frank," he said, "you've got to help me. This is big trouble. Big, big trouble."

"I can see that, Freddy. But how can I help you?"

"People say things about you, Frank; and I believe the things they say. I really do."

"People? What people? And what are you talking about?" But I knew what was coming. It was that old story—this crazy reputation I have, of solving mysteries. It's true, I've been involved in more than my share. And it's also true that sometimes, through luck really, nothing to do with the "little gray cells," I was able to help out. Mostly just by knowing the cast of characters. But the idea that I have a skill, an aptitude, it's just not true.

It was no surprise that Freddy thought of me as some kind of great detective. After all, it was an old friend of mine, Zelda Valdez, who recommended me to Freddy, told him I was just the lawyer he needed for his financial affairs; and Zelda was firmly convinced, thanks to a number of situations I won't go into here, that I had these skills, these detective skills. Which (in her opinion) I kept secret, out of modesty; and maybe for other reasons. Zelda, by the way, is a novelist. She writes mostly romance novels.

Of course, I told Freddy I would help him, if he needed help; I could make recommendations. But I vigorously denied any talent for solving mysteries. And more: I vigorously denied *wanting* to solve mysteries, or even to get involved in them.

I am fairly sure he didn't believe me. He said he did, but there was no conviction in his voice. In any event, this strange and awful woman, Sybil Glass, was dead. This began a new phase in the life of Freddy Lucas. And in mine. But I had better go back and fill you in on Freddy Lucas and his tangled affairs.

2

About Freddy: first of all, his name wasn't Freddy. His actual name was Alexander Winterbottom Lucas. He was in his mid-twenties. He had dark blonde hair, and watery blue eyes. He was neither tall nor short, had regular features, a nice smile, and a dimpled chin. People liked Freddy. Women liked to mother him. Others seemed to prefer a very different and more exciting role; Freddy was not exactly celibate. He was pleasant, even charming, rather self-absorbed, a bit immature, but very likeable, on the whole. Good-natured. Generous. And he loved to talk. At any rate, ever since he could remember, people called him Freddy. That's what he said when we met: "Just call me Freddy." I thought it was odd to be called Freddy, when your name was actually Alexander. I supposed it was because somehow he looked like a Freddy and acted like a Freddy—not at all like somebody named Alexander Winterbottom Lucas.

I met Freddy one bright day when he came to my office. First, he had called, telling me he needed a lawyer. It had to do with his great-aunt's estate, and with money. That sounded good to me. I like clients, especially clients with money. I asked him who had recommended him. He said, "This woman I know. Zelda Valdez. Tall woman, skinny, hooked nose, wears black clothes, looks like the Wicked Witch of the West. Met her at a yoga thing."

"Oh," I said, "so you do yoga."

"No; God no. I tried it, but I didn't like it, and I quit right away. My friend Derek does yoga, so I thought I'd try it.

Couldn't stand it. But this Zelda, as I said, I met her, she was deeply into it, and she tried to talk me into sticking with the stuff; I said no, but we had coffee and talked and we got to be friends. She said she was a novelist. Wow. She told me about a book she was working on, something about a pirate and a nun, crazy stuff. She showed me some of it, I read it, I told her I loved it, and she gave me a big fat hug. I love Zelda, but this book, I mean, was one of the worst things I ever read. But I'm nice to people, that's the way I am."

We made a date, and he appeared in my office, wearing khaki pants, a plaid shirt, and flip-flops on his feet. "I hate shoes," he said. "Who invented shoes?"

Since I had no idea who invented shoes, I said nothing.

"Here's my problem," he said. "I need some kind of estate plan, I guess. A will or whatever. I mean, I'm young, and I'm not about to die, but you can't ever tell, can you? Car accident or something. Or cancer. Every time I go to the doctor, I worry, you know, there's blood tests and so on. I can't help thinking, do I have cancer? Lots of people have cancer. Even young people. So far, I don't have cancer. Anyway: everybody tells me I need a will, and to get a will I need a lawyer, so here I am."

"Well, you've come to the right place," I said, and immediately realized what a stupid phrase this was. But Freddy settled further into his chair, crossed his legs and went on talking.

"Zelda said you were great," he said. "I don't have a lawyer, right now. My aunt Clara, she had a lawyer, and I'm sure he wants my business. His name is Gideon Grambling, he's in San Francisco, and I absolutely can't stand the man; when I shook hands with him, it was like shaking hands with an iguana or something; and he was downright nasty about everything. Clara could handle him, but I thought no, this guy is not for me. Besides, he's in San Francisco, and I live in Los Altos Hills, no way am I going to go all the way to San Francisco, just to see a guy who nauseates me, you know what I'm saying? And parking in San Francisco, it's a total major nightmare."

"You've got a point," I said. I also knew Gideon Grambling, from prior situations, and I agreed with Freddy: He was completely obnoxious. For one thing, a dreadful snob. "I have lots of friends," Freddy said. "Derek, he's kind of a best friend, if there is such a thing. Anyway, he said, 'Freddy, I love you, man, you're fun to be with, and you're a good guy, you wouldn't hurt a fly; but let's face it, you're sort of worthless.' Funny thing is, he's right about me being worthless. In one sense. But when it comes to money, hey, I'm not worthless. In fact, I'm going to be seriously rich."

That was music to my ears.

"Derek, this friend of mine, he's a law student. Goes to Stanford. Must be awfully smart; it's like impossible to get into that school. I said, 'Derek, you're a different kind of worthless. All you want to do is make money.' He said, 'Yeah, so what? Freddy,' he said, 'I need a lot of money. That's why I'm in law school.' This Derek, maybe he's jealous of me. About the money. I always had enough money, because of my aunt, and a lot more is coming my way, so why should I knock myself out, going to law school or business school, or, frankly, getting a job? Maybe that's what's wrong, I don't have to do anything I don't want to do, so I don't do anything. I went to college, I mean, everybody goes to college these days, and I suppose I learned something, but I don't know what. I tried to take these computer courses, but it didn't work out. There were all these intense guys in the class, with their laptops, you'd think those things were attached to their bodies; I just didn't fit in. Right now, I'm sort of drifting, if you know what I mean. I'm trying to write a novel. It's not going too well. I do play tennis a lot. I think when you have a lot of money it kind of curdles your character. Derek said I don't have any character. But like Derek also said, I'm a good guy. And harmless. So why should I change?"

I could think of some reasons already, but I just let Freddy talk.

"Anyway, the reason I'm here: I'm going to have a lot of money, and I don't know what to do with it. I went to this seminar, and they said I should have a will. And Derek and my other friends, they said that was right. A will or a living trust, whatever that is. I started thinking, who should I leave my money to. When I get it. Right now, I don't exactly have it."

"This money: you inherited it?

"Well, I certainly didn't earn it, and I didn't win the lottery, or start some company or whatever. The money, it's from my Aunt Clara. Actually, she was my great-aunt; and she raised me, and she was filthy rich, and now she's dead. She spoiled me rotten when she was alive, and she's going to spoil me even more, just by being dead. Pretty ironic, right?"

I nodded my head, yes. This was more and more interesting. A young, rich client was nothing to sneeze at. I'd be willing to put up with a lot to get a stable of clients of this type. Freddy seemed to think it was important to tell me his whole life history. Not that I cared. At least not then. Later I did care. When this woman, Sybil, turned up dead.

I don't want you to get the wrong impression. I'm not mercenary, I'm not cold-blooded. I'm not a reptile, like Gideon Grambling in his palatial offices in San Francisco. I'm a decent person. I think. Some of my clients are a pain in the ass. Others are nice, or even lovable. Freddy, it turned out, was one of the lovable ones—though in some ways, he was definitely a pain in the ass.

It wasn't entirely his fault. Fate had played tricks on him.

"This seminar," he said, "it was, I have to tell you, so boring you could die. I actually left early. But it did start me thinking. They said different people had different needs. In their estate plans. They recommended this and that; and it depended on your family situation. But that's where I don't really fit in. Actually, I don't have much of a family. You could even say, I don't have a family at all. I'm adopted. I mean, I had biological parents, the stork didn't bring me, but I have no idea who they were. I have all sorts of fantasies about them. Maybe adopted kids always do. Anyway, I was adopted by this couple, they were scientists, both of them, I guess they couldn't have children, Max Lucas and his wife, Kathryn Lucas. Maybe they never had sex, who knows? They were kind of strange. Max had a big moustache, that's what I remember. Kathryn, she was nice, I guess. I think they loved me, but they were odd ducks. I barely remember them. They disappeared in the Brazilian jungle, honest to God. He was studying beetles. She was studying ants. That's how they met, they loved insects. I guess they loved insects more than they loved me. They left me with my aunt Clara and a nanny and went off to the jungle, and that's the last anybody ever saw of them. I was six years old at the time."

"Your aunt raised you?"

"She did. Actually, she was my great-aunt. I mean there I was an orphan, and people felt sorry for me, but they shouldn't have. I barely knew Max and Kathryn, and honestly, I was more attached to the nanny, and I would have been heart-broken if she died, but she didn't. Actually, I had a good life. This nanny, she was English, and she smelled of onions when she kissed me, I don't know why. But I liked her. I had a lot of nannies. Mostly they were okay. And I loved Aunt Clara. She was fat and full of fun, really, I mean, old as the hills, but still, full of piss and vinegar, if you know what I mean. She dyed her hair some ridiculous color, basically, it was some kind of orange. Whatever. She was Kathryn's aunt. When Clara was young, I guess she was quite something. A real black sheep. Went all over the world, had lovers, did stuff. When she was in her 30's or 40's or something like that, I suppose she decided to settle down; she married this man, Homer Fisk—I never knew him, but he was filthy rich, and he was much older than she was, and I guess he was crazy about her. Anyway, very conveniently, he died after a while, maybe the strain was too much for him, who knows, the sex or whatever. He left almost all of his money to Clara. He was a widower. Had one daughter, from the wife who died, I guess, but they didn't get along and had some sort of gigantic quarrel. He cut her out of his will and she went off somewhere, and that was that. So Clara got the money. Well, except for some stuff to charity, and friends and whatever. And a big slug of money to his cousin, a doctor named Pascal LeBeau. But mostly to Aunt Clara. She told me all about the will. Oh yes, and if Clara died before he did, which of course she didn't do, the money would go to this cousin of his, Pascal LeBeau, this doctor. He's still alive now, pretty old though, and he's retired. Not that it matters."

Clara Fisk. The name rang a bell. Had I read her obituary? I think so; at least I had a vague memory of seeing an item in the paper. I remember there was something odd, something unusual about that obituary, something that made me notice it. Normally, unless the dead person is a client, I don't pay much attention to obituaries. I made a mental note to look up the newspapers or to google her, and find out more about the late Clara Fisk.

"She died, like I mentioned, a few months ago," Freddy said. "I miss her, you know? She was quite a character. I lived in her house, always lived there, since I was six years old and my adoptive parents went to the jungle and never came back. Great big house. I loved it. Like I said, I miss her, she and I got along just great, we used to laugh and joke. I mean, she was as old as Methuselah, but she said, 'Freddy, inside this wrinkled body, it's still me.' Anyway, she left me all that money. I don't have it yet, but her lawyer, he says I'll get it very soon."

"Have you seen the actual will?" I asked.

"Yes. Not that I read it. I mean, it was pages and pages long, and it was Greek to me. As I told you, she had this awful man, Gideon Grambling, he was her lawyer. I can't stand the guy, he's so sanctimonious and he talks jargon. A total creep. My friend Derek, I told you he was a law student, so he knows something about this stuff, he said to me, if you don't like that guy, go ahead, get your own lawyer. And Zelda said: 'Frank May, he's your man.' So here I am."

I made a mental note to ask Grambling for a copy of the will. I asked, "You haven't gotten any of the money?"

"Not a cent. This Grambling creep, he asked me whether I needed money, and he babbled about some sort of arrangement for an advance, but I told him I wasn't exactly starving, and I wanted to tell him to shove it, but I'm a polite guy, you know?"

"Okay," I said, "but what are you living on?"

"Oh, Aunt Clara, she used to give me money, and she set up a bank account for me, and bought me stocks and bonds, and so on. I'm in good shape. And I'm living in her house. I think it goes to me, under the will, but anyway, that's where I am. That's where I grew up. I told you, it's in Los Altos Hills, and it has acres and acres behind the house, and you can hardly see the next house on either side, or in the back. Which is the way I like it. The neighbors, not that I really know them, are not my kind of people, to be perfectly honest. They're actually Republicans. You know the type. Country clubs and so on. Aunt Clara hated them. Well, not all of them. There's this one guy, Desmond, lives in some huge house, just behind us, he's alright. But the rest of them, forget it."

I told him I'd be happy to help him, that I would get hold of a copy of the will, and see to it that his interests were protected. As for his own will, sure, we could talk about that. Did he have any ideas? Who was he thinking of leaving his money to?

"Well, that's a question," he said. "I mean, I don't have a wife or kids. I don't really have *any* relatives. I mean, not close relatives, and not anybody I know. I must have had a mother and father, but God knows who they are. Or were. Anyway, my friend Derek, he's in law school like I told you, working his ass off. I mean, he knows something about this stuff. I talked to him, like, what would happen to me when I died? And he said, 'Well, the money goes to your relatives.' I said, 'Derek, I don't have any.' 'But you do,' he said, 'everybody does.' I said, 'I was adopted.' He said, 'Well, then you have *legal* relatives, maybe they're not blood relatives, but they're considered relatives.' And that's what bothered me. My adoptive father, Max, he's actually got a mother who's still alive. She's 96, and she's totally demented—she's got Alzheimer's, she's in a home for people like that. God forbid my money would go to her. She wouldn't know what to do with it. And if she died, which she's going to do pretty soon, I suppose, there are some cousins, but they live in New Zealand—I never saw them in my life—and one uncle in Dallas, Texas. The less said about him the better. So, I do need a will just to cut these people out? You know what I mean?"

"I do know. And of course, it's up to you."

"I started thinking, maybe I should leave some of the money to my parents. My real parents. The biological ones."

"But you don't know who they are, do you?"

"Not a clue. Maybe I should hire a detective. You don't do work of that kind, do you, Frank?"

"Absolutely not."

"Whatever. You know, a lot of adopted kids run around looking for their mother and that sort of thing. I never did. But I do have fantasies about my parents. Me, I can have fantasies about two sets of parents, can you believe it? Like: my mom and dad, I mean, the adoptive mom and dad, I have this kind of daydream that they come out of the jungle, they were captured by some tribe, and they lived with them for a zillion years, and now somebody found them, like they were all naked and just like the Indians, or maybe my dad is like Tarzan, well, no, he'd be too old, but maybe my mom died, and he lived with some native woman, or maybe he died, and she was a captive, you know, a prisoner; and the chief slept with her, and she had a baby, male baby. And now that baby, *he's* like Tarzan, he doesn't speak English, and he swings from the trees, but he's my brother, well, sort of. Or maybe it's a baby girl, and now she's grown up, and she's beautiful and naked and so on."

I could see that Freddy had a vivid imagination.

"Okay, that's one set of fantasies, I know it's silly, especially the Tarzan part, I mean, they couldn't have children, I suppose, so why would they suddenly become fertile out in the Amazon jungle, only maybe somebody gave them some kind of herbal thing, you know, the natives, they know stuff, and lo and behold, she became pregnant. Okay, here's another fantasy, it's about my birth parents, my mother mostly. Here's the scenario: she was really young when she had me, and she felt she had to give me up, but now she's searching for me. She was a prom queen, high school prom queen, and she had a boyfriend, a real stud from the football team, and she had the hots for him, and one night, in the back seat of his car—it was a Mercedes, in my fantasy, it's a Mercedes, black Mercedes—and he takes her virginity and she's all guilty and stuff, *and* she's pregnant, you know, one time only did they have sex, but now she's pregnant. And he says to her, honey, I'll take care of the baby, I'll do the right thing, but then he's killed in a car accident, he has a car crash in this black Mercedes. And she's too far gone for an abortion, and her parents are these old-fashioned types, and she wears loose clothes, and nobody knows she's pregnant, and she goes to this dance, and in the middle, she says, excuse me, because she's gone into labor, and she has the baby in the bathroom, and wraps it up, and takes it and leaves it inside a church or something, and then she goes back and keeps right on dancing. I know this sounds crazy. Hey, you don't mind my talking, do you? Do you charge by the hour? I guess if you do, you don't mind whether I talk my head off."

"Well, Freddy, I don't mind if you talk. I do charge for my time, though, I have to tell you."

"Isn't the first hour free, or something like that? Whatever. I've got the money, so what the hell. Anyway, I do need to do this will thing."

I said, "I have to have some idea of your assets…. I need to see your aunt's will; and talk to Gideon Grambling. I need to have some idea how much you're going to inherit. That's the next step, Freddy."

He had a kind of charming, almost childlike smile. I said I would call him when I had the information, and he said, "Fine, no problem." He shook my hand and left. That was the first time I saw Freddy. I was pleased with the prospect of working with him. Little did I know what was in store for us.

3

I now had to get in touch with Gideon Grambling. I never relished that idea, but business is business. The problem I faced, each time, was actually connecting with the man. His receptionist screened all of his calls, and she usually told me he was "in conference." Which was a lie, I suppose. I told her that I was an attorney, and that my call concerned the estate of Clara Fisk. That seemed to make some difference. Gideon called me back later that day.

"Hi Gideon," I said. "You're handling the estate of Clara Fisk, is that correct?"

"May I ask, uh, the purpose of your call, Frank? Yes, I do represent the estate."

"Her nephew is my client. Alexander Lucas. They call him Freddy. He is, I am told, one of the principal heirs. I need to see a copy of the will, and to find out how much money is involved."

Gideon spoke to me in his usual condescending and frosty way. He mentioned specifically that he was the executor of the estate, and also that Mrs. Fisk had specifically named him, in her will, as the attorney for the estate. Of course, I know what was on his nasty mind. He wanted to make it abundantly clear that, even though I represented Freddy, there was no way I was going to pry the Fisk estate out of his greedy hands. Not that I wouldn't like to represent that estate; but I knew better than to try.

"Mr. Lucas has seen the will," he said. "I sent him a copy. He seems to have forgotten that."

"I'd rather not bother him, Gideon. And, yes, I suppose he's seen the will, but he might have lost it. He's not exactly sophisticated when it comes to legal affairs, if you know what I mean. I'm not sure he paid attention. So just send me a copy; you've got my address. And, while I'm waiting, can't you tell me, more or less, what the will provided?"

He began by telling me how busy he was, a client was coming in five minutes or so, one of the "leading figures in San Francisco society, and I don't like to keep her waiting."

"Five minutes, Gideon. Really."

"Very well. I knew the attorneys for her late husband, Homer Fisk. To be more precise, I took over the business from Fisk's attorney, who passed away. Fisk died years ago. When he died, his widow became a very rich woman. She also, later, became my client. I must say, she was in some ways unpleasant. And very stubborn. I did prepare her will. She left small sums to a woman who cleaned her house, or acted as a maid, a few smallish gifts to charity, and a fairly large gift to her husband's cousin, Dr. Pascal LeBeau. The rest of the estate, and it's extremely sizeable, was divided into two parts. One part is left in trust, to be managed by a bank, and the income goes to her nephew, Alexander, for life. On his death, the money goes to his children, if any; and if he has no children, then in part to certain charities and the rest of it to her late husband's cousin, Dr. Pascal LeBeau."

"Okay, that's half. And the other half?"

"The other half, similarly, is to be managed for the benefit of her nephew, for life, and he is to receive the income. But then she added a rather strange clause."

"Strange?"

"Well, certainly unusual. If, during the lifetime of her nephew, Alexander Lucas, his mother appears, and is alive, and makes herself known, then this half of the estate will pass to Alexander's mother."

"His mother? Adoptive mother, I suppose. He was adopted, as of course you know, adopted by Kathryn Lucas, Clara Fisk's niece. Did the will say his 'adoptive mother,' or give her name, Kathryn Lucas?"

"No, she did not mention a name."

"Then, Gideon, isn't there a certain, well, ambiguity? Could she have meant his birth mother?"

Gideon said, in a tone that showed considerable annoyance: "Frank, you think I didn't see that? I pointed it out to her. I told her it was ambiguous, I said, surely you're not thinking of the birth mother; but she insisted on leaving it that way.... Which is very strange. I told her, 'Mrs. Fisk, you're asking for a possible lawsuit; and you're ignoring my professional opinion.' I'm very proud of my draftsmanship. I've been a lawyer for twenty years, I've handled estates for some of the most eminent people in the Bay Area, and down the peninsula, complex estates, and I'm proud of my record, proud of the way I framed all these arrangements. I told her she was asking for trouble. But she was adamant, she said, 'I want it that way.' And of course, she was a client, and she had her way. I suppose it doesn't matter. Neither of these mothers is likely to appear. At least I hope not."

"Interesting," I said. "But my client, at any rate, will get all the income, unless this woman shows up, which won't happen I suppose. And even then, he still gets half the income. What's the size of the estate?

"I haven't had everything appraised, and I haven't filed the inventory, so it's difficult to give an exact amount...."

"Please, Gideon, humor me. I don't need to know how much, down to the penny. I just need an estimate; I won't hold you to it."

"I would say, 50 to 100 million. Something in that neighborhood...."

"That's quite a neighborhood, Gideon. I wished I lived in that neighborhood."

Freddy was, in other words, a very rich young man. This was good news. I was very happy to have him as a client. And, of course, I never expected any mothers to turn up, of any sort.

That's where I was wrong, of course. Many women did turn up, and one of them, Sybil Glass, had a very serious claim. She also later turned up dead.

4

The day after my conversation with Gideon, I called my friend Sylvan Platt—I've already mentioned him—and set up a lunch date. Sylvan has a nose for good restaurants, especially new restaurants. I don't always share his rather elevated tastes, but eating with him can sometimes be a culinary adventure. Since his wife had turned anorexic and left him, food played an even greater role in his life. On the phone, after we'd arranged the time and place, I told Sylvan that I had a new client, "a young guy, Freddy, he's the heir to a rich lady who died, Clara Fisk was her name."

"Oh, really?" he said, "I seem to remember something about her."

We ate in an Indian restaurant, which Sylvan praised to the skies: "It's a poor country, billions of people, a lot of them practically starving, I suppose, and sleeping on the street. I've never been there myself, and I don't think I want to go, you can get sick there. But they have a genius for food. I love the curry at this place." It was, I have to admit, quite delicious.

After we chatted about this and that, I told Sylvan what I knew about Freddy (nothing confidential, of course), and I mentioned his aunt's will: "She left the boy a huge pot of money. And she did it the smart way—in trust. No way can he squander the principal. He's a bit flaky, a nice guy, but clueless. So that was the right move, I think. There was one funny clause, though, in the will."

I told Sylvan about the clause, and asked him what he made of it.

He paused, with a fork in mid-air. "Here's what I think: she had some kind of thing about this niece. She imagines she's maybe still alive; you know, it's pathetic, but when people are missing, their loved ones keep harboring hopes that someday they'll come back. They never do, though."

"I get that, Sylvan," I said. "But why the ambiguity? Why not just say, 'If my niece Kathryn is still alive,' or something like that."

"No idea. Maybe she knew something she wouldn't tell Gideon. Maybe something about who Freddy's parents were. Maybe she had an idea. Maybe she helped arrange the adoption, you know, maybe it wasn't through regular channels. But of course, that doesn't answer the question, or why she kept this a secret, if she did, all these years. Gideon is not somebody you'd confide in, anyway. A total creep. Well, I don't think it matters. The niece is surely dead—the one in the Amazon jungle—and the mysterious birth mother, well, that's another story."

I said, "Maybe she's dead, too, Sylvan. Because, if she was alive, and if Clara Fisk knew she was alive, why didn't Clara Fisk say so? And if people knew who she was, wouldn't she have appeared long since? At least I think so. But who knows."

"Oh, I wouldn't count on that."

"Wouldn't count on what?"

"On the mother not appearing. I mean, not the real mother. But women are going to come out of the woodwork, saying, 'Oh, I'm the guy's mother.' That's because there's been so much publicity. The smell of money, it attracts people, the way a dead animal attracts vultures. Check it out. Look," he said, taking out a printout of a newspaper account, "when you told me about this Freddy guy, and Clara Fisk, I got curious and I looked her up, don't ask me why, I was just interested, and I remembered reading something about it at the time."

The newspaper article, from *The San Francisco Chronicle,* was an obituary of Clara Fisk; it mentioned that she was the widow of Homer Fisk, that she was extremely rich, and lived on "an estate" in Los Altos Hills. But the headline was "Leaves Part of Fortune to Dead Woman," and it stated (inaccurately, of course) that Ms. Fisk's niece, presumably dead, was the heiress to "about twenty-five million dollars."

Sylvan said, "Twenty-five million dollars. If that doesn't attract a whole army of mothers, I'll eat my hat."

"You don't wear a hat."

"Good point, Frank. Now it's time for dessert."

5

Gideon did in fact send me a copy of Clara Fisk's will, and I read it over carefully. It was thirty pages long, but most of that was what we call "boiler plate," that is, standard clauses of little or no interest to anybody but lawyers, and only rarely of interest even to them. I use these clauses myself, and I won't bore you with what they are or why they're there. At any rate, the gist of the will—who gets the money, and when, and how— had no surprises, at least not after my conversation with Gideon.

I called Freddy, told him I had a copy of the will and that I would be happy to discuss it with him and answer any questions he might have, and so on. Freddy seemed profoundly uninterested in the whole affair, except the question, when would he actually get the money, and how much. "Not that I'm starving, Frank, I mean, I don't want to sound greedy, but I might want to buy a Tesla, or whatever. Derek said, 'Why don't you buy a boat? Now that you're a rich bastard, you can have a boatload of chicks in bikinis, or you can do deep-sea fishing,' and he was only half joking. I said, 'Derek, I get seasick in a bathtub, why would I want a boat? And I went fishing once in my life, it bored me to death.'"

I interrupted this river of words to ask Freddy whether he had been approached by any candidates for Motherhood of Freddy. I reminded him that a successful candidate would come into a huge pile of money. He said, "Well, yes, they've been pestering Gideon, it couldn't happen to a nicer guy, I mean, he's managing the estate, so they go to him with their stupid claims. They're all fake of course; but still, I guess it's costing me money, because he has to spend time on this kind of shit, and Gideon's got this big swanky office, and this snotty receptionist and God knows what else, and I just know he's going to charge me an arm and a leg. I don't care about the money, not really. I'm a rich guy, right? But he irritates me no end. Can I do anything about it, Frank? I mean, can I fire him or something?"

I explained that his aunt had named Gideon the attorney—he was mentioned in the will. I told him that, despite this, he had a perfect right to get rid of Gideon, but was that really wise? I said, "Freddy, I'll be honest with you: I can't stand the guy myself. But he's a perfectly competent lawyer, and my advice is to leave well enough alone. And let him handle all these women, if there really are a lot of them. Do any of these so-called mothers get in touch with you directly?"

"Not so much. They don't come after me, I guess; maybe I'm hard to find. I don't have a landline anymore, just my cellphone, and these women don't know where I live. So Gideon is stuck with them. Well, all except one. This one woman, she calls herself Sybil, somehow she found my cell-phone number, God knows how, and she called me, and I said, 'Who is this?' and she said, 'Oh Freddy, this is your mother, Sybil' and I just hung up on her. But she called again, and I hung up again, and I said, 'Stop bothering me,' and she said, 'Oh, my boy, I can understand your reaction, after all these years,' and that sort of crap. And then I saw her, I think it was her, this lady was hanging around in front of my house, and I just went out the back door and avoided her. Hey Frank, is there some way of getting rid of her?"

"Well, I guess you could call the police if she keeps showing up. Tell them she's harassing you. Or stalking you or some-thing. But, Freddy, if you just keep on saying no, if you hang up on her, ignore her, shut her out—if you never give her any encouragement, I guess she'll have to give up in the end. At least I think so."

I switched the conversation to Freddy's affairs. "Your will. Have you given it any thought? No rush, of course."

"I've got some ideas. Should I come to your office?"

"Sure."

So there he was, on a bright day, in the middle of the afternoon, sitting in front of me. He was wearing what looked like a Hawaiian shirt, chino pants, and flip-flops on his feet. I had the impression his hair was not quite the same color it had been the last time I saw him.

"How have you been, Freddy?"

"Oh, so-so, Frank. Well, the good news: I got a check from Gideon, with a long letter explaining why he was sending it and what it represented. I mean, I couldn't make heads or tails out of the letter, it was written in this kind of legal sludge and it gave me a headache; but anyway, I could see this was my money, and that I'd get more, he said 'quarterly,' whatever that means. I wanted to ask him some stuff, but the thought of calling him gave me stomach pains. Anyway, the money. It was quite a lot of money. I deposited the thing in my checking account. Was that the right thing to do, Frank?"

"Absolutely," I said. "It's your money. And I'd like to see the letter so I can read it and tell you want it's all about."

"If I can find it. I spilled coffee on it. Maybe I threw it away. But I'll look for it. Anyway, about my will. Here's what I was thinking: I told you, I don't have any relatives. I mean, not real ones. Not anybody I care about. So I thought, I could leave money to some worthwhile cause, if you know what I mean? Like, saving the whales. Except I don't give a shit about whales. Derek gave me some suggestions. The environment or poor people or something. Nothing really appealed to me. So then he said, 'Max and Kathryn, you know, your parents, they were experts on insects, beetles and ants, so there's this organization, the Foundation for Invertebrate Life,' and I said, 'Stop right there Derek, if I see a beetle, I step on it, and as far as ants are concerned, they got into my kitchen, and I had to throw away some rice and pasta and they got in the sugar bowl, it was totally disgusting, so forget it.' How about some organization, something that works on the mental health of orphans—that's me—or adopted children, that's me too, like 'Save These Kids' or something with a name like that? Frank, could you find out if there's an organization that works on this kind of issue?"

I said I would see. Something along those lines. I asked, "And you want to leave them all your money?"

"No way. I mean, maybe 10% or something like that. Derek said, 'Hey, Freddy, you're rich, you don't need all that money; how about something for me?' And I said, 'You think I'm crazy? Leave you money, and the next thing I know, I'd be lying dead in a ditch; no sir!' and he said, 'Freddy, you think I'd kill you, my best friend?' And I said, 'For money, you'd kill your own grandma,' and he said, 'Sure, if I had a grandma, but both of mine are dead.' Anyway, I'd also like to do something like Aunt Clara did, you know, set up something for my mother, I mean, my mothers, if any of them show up. Personally, I think they're both dead or as good as dead, but still, why not?"

I told him this was certainly possible. He could set up a foundation in their memory. But why just the mothers? "I can understand that your aunt was thinking of her niece, but you had an adoptive father, Max; and you must have had a birth father too."

"Well, I don't know these people, any of them, I mean, not really. Max, well, I hardly remember him, he had a big moustache, and it tickled me, and I didn't like the way he smelled, but maybe I'm not remembering it right. I don't really think I liked him. Not his fault probably. It's all just fantasies, you know, what happened to these people. I think mostly about these mothers, you know, about the birth mother, and she's crying and stuff about her lost baby. Fathers, they don't give a shit. Maybe my birth father, he was some rat who ran out on my mother? I came up with a different story, like he was the football stud who died in a car crash, but, hey, I can change my fantasies every day if I feel like it. Most likely he was some guy who screwed his girlfriend, got her pregnant, and then said, 'Honey, it's your problem, not mine.' Somehow, I just don't care about these fathers. And Kathryn, I think about her, she's a prisoner in this village in the jungle, and she keeps thinking,

'Oh my Freddy, will I ever see him again?' Anyway, I'm leaving out the fathers, is that okay? I mean, I can do what I want."

"Whatever you say, Freddy. You're the boss. It's your money."

So we talked about how to do this, and I explained the mechanism very carefully. I could tell it went in one ear and out the other. I suggested a plan: to accumulate the income, say, from half the estate, for twenty-one years, and it would go to either mother if she appeared. I pointed out how unlikely it was that *anybody* would claim this portion of the estate. Freddy could live to be 80, or 90, and of course then it would be out of the question for some mysterious mother to appear. I suggested that this clause would lapse if Freddy reached the age of 60. He seemed to agree, perhaps out of sheer boredom. I told him, "I suggest you do that for half the estate. But it could be the whole thing, too."

He seemed to be thinking. "Maybe half is enough," he said, fidgeting.

"And then what, Freddy? And what about the other half?"

He seemed unsure. I pointed out that he might have a wife and children and that he could leave them the money. But if he had no descendants?

"I guess I should leave that part to some charity, or something. Maybe that thing for orphans. I don't know. Let me think about it. Hey, look: how about this—some of it, maybe 25% to this lady who has a cleaning store, on California Avenue, she does my shirts; and another 25% to the barber who's got the shop next door to her, he's the guy who cuts my hair, when I get it cut, which isn't too often."

"It could be a lot of money, Freddy. Millions of dollars, probably. Is there some reason why you want to leave it to these people?"

"Why not? I mean, they're nice. The lady in the store, she's from Burma or China or some place, she's all alone in the world, she's got relatives, but they're in New Zealand, she's really sweet, and she sews buttons on my shirts. The buttons keep coming off. Don't ask me why. And the haircut guy, he's next door, and he seems pretty nice, always says hello, and he's from Cambodia or Vietnam or one of those awful countries, he tells me how glad he is to be here in California, and I said to him, don't I know it. I like the way he does my hair. He doesn't charge much. Anyway, I get a kick out of thinking how surprised they'd be, suppose I died pretty soon, and you call them up, and said, 'You know, you're getting millions of dollars,' it would be like they won the lottery, too bad I'd be dead and I wouldn't be around to see the look on their faces...."

Freddy really was a sweet, quirky guy. I secretly liked this idea. I didn't know these two people, the woman who did his shirts or his barber; but I had my own barber, in San Mateo—he was divorced, had two wretched children, and had had a hard life. I thought it would be nice, if I was a billionaire, to give him a million or so.

I wanted to continue the discussion, but Freddy said he had to go. I said, we could talk some more later on.

That was Freddy. Of course, he was going to cause me a lot of trouble and grief—but that lay ahead. And in any event, it wouldn't be his fault.

6

Freddy called me a day or so later. I thought it would be about his will, which had been left hanging, but he said he wasn't ready. He replied, "Got to think about it. Anyway, it's not why I called."

"Okay, Freddy, tell me: why *did* you call?"

He said, "Frank, I'm good for your business, you know? I've lined up another client for you."

"Really? I like getting clients, Freddy, but can I ask, who is it?"

"It's my aunt's buddy, Dr. LeBeau. Her husband's cousin. Can you come over tonight? He's going to be here with his granddaughter. She's nothing much, but I like her. Do you want dinner? I get it delivered from restaurants, there's a service that does this. No way am I going to cook my own meals. Maybe with all this money I'm getting, I can hire a cook. I like the idea of a cook: I could say in the morning, 'This is what I want,' and he'll just do it. Do the shopping, too. But I don't want the guy living in my house. If it's a guy. Sexy woman, that would be different. But sexy women don't do much cooking."

I told him I would come. In point of fact, my wife Celia hates it when I miss dinner at home. But this was legitimate business. So, at seven o'clock, I drove out to Los Altos Hills; I was curious to see the house anyway.

Many of the people in Los Altos Hills are seriously rich, and they have the real estate to prove it. Aunt Clara's house was set back a short way from the road. It was a sprawling house, in mock colonial style, two or three stories—it was hard to tell from the outside. There were some huge trees in the front yard, and a small flower garden. As I found out when I got inside, it was a big, comfortable house, not quite a mansion, but extremely nice, spacious, attractively furnished. What it did have that was unusual was acreage. In the back of the house, there was a swimming pool, completely fenced in, and beyond the fence was a hill, which stretched for some distance—I'm not good at estimating distance—and was, as Freddy told me, completely wild: "My gardener is a real jerk, I'm just too lazy to fire him. Anyway, he never goes in the back. It's all Mother Nature there, you can't even see the next house."

The gardener doesn't figure in this story. The back acreage does. That's where Sybil Glass's body was found. But of course that lay in the future.

The living room was pleasant and roomy—comfortable. The taste was somewhat old-fashioned, but good-looking. "Aunt Clara bought all the furniture," he said. "Ugly, isn't it? But she liked it."

Dr. LeBeau was in the living room, and when I came in he got up and shook my hand. The doctor was a tall, bony man, with a small white moustache. He was slightly stooped, and he had a noticeable tremor; could it be Parkinson's disease? But his grip, though a bit clammy, was firm, and there was something strong about his face and his demeanor. His granddaughter was short, and quite plain—mousy looking, I would say, a bit overweight, with a round face. He introduced me to her, "This is Melanie," he said, "my beloved granddaughter." She smiled and looked a bit embarrassed.

"Hey, let's eat," Freddy said.

We went into a dining room, a nice big room, very brightly lit. Melanie scurried about, making sure there were knives and forks and the like. The meal was served buffet style. "This food company," Freddy said, "is called 'Food for Thought.' I'm trying them out; I used to use another company."

The main course was some sort of chicken, smothered in a greenish sauce, and sitting on top of a mound of kale. It came with small purple potatoes, no doubt something the Incas ate up in their mountains, and they tasted like, well, potatoes. I have to admit that the meal was pretty good. Dessert was a richly marbled cake of some sort, with a butterscotch frosting. Melanie brought us coffee. Freddy did most of the talking during dinner.

Afterwards, she cleared the table, and Dr. LeBeau and I went into a small study off the living room. He pointed to a desk and two chairs; I sat down near the desk.

"So, you're Freddy's famous lawyer," he said.

I thought: *famous?* What is this all about? "Hardly famous," I said. "I try to do a job." I immediately realized how lame that sounded.

"Never mind," he said. "I've had a lawyer, of course, in the past: Simon Richards, did you know him? He died last year, so I need somebody new. Do you want to take notes?"

I did. There was a yellow pad on the desk, and I began writing down what he said. Basically, he wanted to leave money to Melanie, but in a trust, "So nobody else can get their hands on it." He said, "I've got money of my own, quite a bit, you know, from my practice, and Clara left me money. But you know that."

"Is Melanie ... your only heir?" I asked. "I mean, do you have children? And other grandchildren?"

"I do have other children," he said. "And grandchildren. Melanie's my favorite because she lives around here and she's good to me. Clara loved her, too. Clara was the love of my life, by the way. I want you to know that. That's why she left me money."

"I see."

"You don't see, but never mind. Maybe it was guilt on her part. She knows I don't need the money."

"Guilt? Over what?"

"She ditched me. I wanted to marry her. She married my cousin Homer Fisk. It was because he was so goddamn rich. Then I got married myself, had kids; but it didn't last. It was always Clara. She was the one and only. You didn't know her. Clara was ... a powerful personality. When I asked her to marry me, she told me she loved me, but she said she loved money too. Granted, my cousin Homer was a nice enough guy. Sweet. But so much older than she was. You know what? She always loved me anyway. She came back from her honeymoon, they went to Venice and Rome, and the Greek Islands, and first thing she did when she came back was come to see me. 'Well, how was it, Clara?' I asked her. 'Was the money worth it?' And she laughed. 'Yes, it's worth it,' she said, 'but barely.' And then, what do you think? We made love. And you know what? All the time she was married to him, she was with me too. I don't have to draw you a picture. Years and years. I miss that woman terribly. I'm an old geezer, but I'm not dead yet. I loved her. I love Freddy, too, but I won't leave him any money because he's rich enough as it is. Melanie needs the money; Freddy doesn't."

"And Melanie's parents? Are they alive?"

"Her dad is. Maybe the mom too, I have no idea. Her dad is my son. I have three sons, actually. One of them is a neurosurgeon in Miami, he's very rich, and one of them lives in London, he's in some sort of hedge fund thing, and he's also rich. The two of them hate each other. I can't stand their wives and ex-wives, and I barely know their children. Maybe I should leave them some token amount, just so they won't sue the estate. Anyway: the third son, the youngest, he's Melanie's dad, and he's divorced. His name is Philip; he's always struggled, been in and out of rehab—it's a tragic situation. He's in Cincinnati, God knows why. Sometimes he works. Melanie is an only child. Philip will never make it, not really. I think he's bipolar, or worse. I set up a trust for him, and I could add to it, and maybe I'll do that; but right now, in my will, I need to take care of Melanie. To me, my family is Melanie, and Freddy. And Clara, but she's dead."

We talked for a while. I asked whether he had a will already. He said yes, but it was a million years old, and he needed a new one. We also talked about a living trust. I told him it was a better device, more efficient, cheaper, and so on. He listened carefully, and seemed to understand everything perfectly. I told him I would draft something, and get back to him. We also talked about how much this was going to cost.

Then we went back into the living room. Freddy and Melanie were there.

"Hey, should we go, Melanie?" Pascal said. "Or maybe I should go and you and Freddy can stay and talk, you two lovebirds."

She blushed. "Grampa, don't say that. You embarrass me. Did you get done what you wanted to do, the business with Mr. May?"

"Yes, dear," he said. "We talked about my will ... what happens to all my stuff after they shove me into a grave. I want you to be comfortable, Melanie. I don't know how much longer I have."

She said: "Grampa, don't say that. I hate it when you talk like that."

"Well, facts are facts," he said. "We don't live forever. Not even me."

She gave him a hug. I could tell she was crying. Then the two of them left. I felt it was time for me to go, too, but first I said, "Freddy, what have you been saying about me, behind my back?"

"What do you mean?"

"What's this business, 'famous lawyer,' and whatever else you told Dr. LeBeau."

"Hey, don't get upset, Frank," he said. "I didn't mean anything by it. It was nothing special. Just singing your praises. Pascal, he kind of looks after me, you know what I mean? I never had a real father; and he's always been there. He's okay, but he said, 'Freddy my boy, you're going to be very rich,' and when Clara died, right away he said I should see a lawyer, and I said, 'Well, there's that creep Gideon Grambling' and he said, 'You can't stand him, Freddy, and I'm not sure he has your interests at heart, he's a cold-blooded fish.' And Derek told me the same thing, I need a will, I need a lawyer. So then I talked to Zelda, and I got you. Then I told Pascal about you, I said, 'I've seen this guy, Frank May, he's my lawyer now.' And I guess he looked you up, and he called me, and he said, 'Look, Freddy, you're going to be filthy rich, and don't you need somebody better'—pardon me—I mean, don't be angry, God, Frank, I talk too much; Pascal, he meant well, he said, 'somebody from a big firm,' and I said, no way, this guy is great, this is Frank May, he's the best in the whole area, everybody knows that."

"I wish."

"And I told him, well, 'He's not just a lawyer. Anybody can be a lawyer. He's also a terrific investigator.'"

"Freddy, really!"

"And he said, 'What's that all about? And anyway, what do you need an investigator for?'"

"And what did you say?"

"I said, 'Well, maybe I need him to check up on things,' I mean, I had nothing in mind really. Not then. Now I do. Like these people who claim to be my mother."

"And what did he say? Dr. LeBeau, that is."

"He said, 'You're right,' and he said he smelled trouble ahead; but he didn't explain what he meant, and ... well, that was that."

I went into my usual litany; that I wasn't an investigator or a detective, and that the whole idea was ridiculous, and so on. He nodded, but I doubt he listened. After that, I went home and went to bed.

Dr. LeBeau had said he smelled trouble. At the time, I ignored this remark. But it didn't take long for trouble to develop. Big trouble.

7

The trouble came from Freddy, naturally. It was not about his will. Freddy liked to call me, mostly about the estate and the money. Whenever I asked him about the will, he said he wasn't ready to think about it. Dr. Le Beau was different. I drafted a will and a living trust for him, and certain other documents. We talked about the documents, we made some changes, then he came to the office, signed them, took the originals and left me copies, and that was that.

A few days later, Freddy called again, and said he wanted to see me because he had "Some stuff I've got to get off my chest. That's what lawyers are for, aren't they?"

"Not exactly, Freddy," I said. "I'm just a lawyer. If it's a legal problem, sure. If you just want to talk, okay, I understand. But if you want to get something else off your chest, as you put it, that isn't any of my business, I'm really not your man, Freddy."

"I know it, Frank, I do. Give me some credit. I mean, I've got a therapist. I go to see her every week, she charges a lot, believe me, but Aunt Clara always paid the bills. Not sure I need this woman, but I like the chance to talk. About my sex life, for example. Sexual hang-ups. Doesn't everybody have sexual hang-ups, Frank?"

"I wouldn't know," I said. For a minute, I was afraid I was going to hear all about Freddy's "sexual hang-ups," but I was spared that.

He said, "She tells me some interesting stuff, you know, about me, and why I am the way I am, and about my sex life, but really Frank, that's not what I want to talk to you about. Want to come over again, like, in the evening? We could have a bite and talk; I hate to waste your time during office hours."

"Freddy, you're not wasting my time. You're a paying client, remember? I'm delighted to see you, morning, afternoon, whenever."

We fixed a time, and he showed up at my office. He was late, by the way. A good half hour late. He made some excuse about parking: "There's no place to park around here, Frank. You have to do something about it. I nearly parked in a handicap spot, I was getting so desperate. But, my luck, they'd get me, and the fine is gigantic. Anyway, I finally found something two blocks away."

He started a riff about the parking situation generally, but I stopped him and said: "Freddy: let's talk business. What's on your mind?"

He said, "Two things actually. First of all, it's about these letters and calls and stuff, the women who claim to be my mother."

"I thought Gideon was taking care of those things."

"Oh, he is, and he bitches about it constantly. But he says he feels he should turn some of them over to me, 'for my assessment,' as he put it. And then, somehow, some of these ladies have gotten ahold of my address, and I'm getting calls from a bunch of them, too."

"I think you can ignore them, Freddy," I said.

"Yeah. I will. I'm doing that. Most of the time. I mean, they claim to be my mother; or they know who she is, and they can let me know. If I pay them, of course. Some of the letters, though, are really nutty. Like this one lady, she lives in Oregon someplace, she says she had a baby years ago, and the baby died, or that's what they told her. But she always thought, it was stolen, it was still alive. Now she's seeing this woman, Madame Estrella, and this Madame Estrella, she's got magical powers, she can see the future and that sort of thing, and the lady told her her baby wasn't really dead, not at all, its soul just passed into another creature. And she said, 'Oh dear, what sort of creature? I wouldn't want my baby to be a cockroach or something,' and the lady said, 'I can communicate with the other world and find out' and then she said, 'Your baby went into the soul of another baby,' and the lady who lost her baby said, 'Thank God he's not a cockroach, but can we find out which baby?' and guess what, it's me."

Some of the other would-be mothers were just as wacky. Or simply improbable. Women who gave babies up for adoption, and they're sure it had to be Freddy, and would he send a picture? Or one woman who said she had been trapped in a village in the Amazon, and she just got out, and she was an amnesia victim, but when she read about Freddy, it all came back to her: Freddy was her child. Her husband, she said, was dead. Squeezed to death by an anaconda: "That was when my mind went blank, watching him with that awful snake."

"But one of these women," he went on, "is really persistent. She says she really is my birth mother. She calls herself Sybil Glass, and she says she has proof, positive proof, that she's my mother, my actual mother. I mean, how can I believe her? And if she's my mother, where's she been all these years?"

"You talked to her?"

"Well, I did. At least she didn't give me that jungle shit. She kept calling and I told her, 'I'm going to change my phone number,' and she sounded like she was sobbing. I mean, give me a break. She says, 'Oh, you're my long lost boy.' I hung up on her. But then she wrote me a letter saying she could prove she was my mother, she had documents, she said. I wondered, what kind of documents? Anyway, I didn't pay any attention. And then she burst into my house—how she got the address, I don't know—she rang the doorbell, and I answered it, and there she was, and she flings her arms around me and kisses me, and says, 'my dear boy' and all that shit, and I told her, 'Would you please go.' But she wouldn't go, and she said, 'Let me show you the papers, the stuff I've got, you're my son' and I said, 'I don't care what you've got,' and I pushed her out, I mean, literally, and she was crying and making a disturbance, and I said, 'You come again, and I'll call the police.' But then she calls on the phone, and of course I hang up. Should I call the police, Frank? Is there something I can do?"

"Well, for now, don't do anything. If she's got proof, like she says, she won't hide it; maybe the best thing is to say, 'Either you prove your case, or just go away.' I assume she's a fake."

"Well, I guess she's a fake. They're all fakes, I bet. Still, Frank, after all, I did have a mother. You know, I must have had a mother. So maybe—okay, I know it's a long shot—but maybe she's the real thing. I hope not. If I'm going to have a mother, I want something better than these women. One of them calls herself Lizbeth, she's one of the most persistent. I don't know how they find me, I really don't. This Lizbeth, she has gray hair, but it looked real dirty, tumbling all about; she looked more like a bag lady, and, frankly, she smelled bad. I have to admit, this Sybil Glass person, she was different. Dressed properly and all that. She made all these motherly noises, but she seemed like a cold, calculating creature to me. Frank, shouldn't I do *something*? Something to get rid of all of them. This Sybil though, she's tough as nails."

"It's a real problem, Freddy," I said. "Maybe you could get a restraining order." I explained what that was. "Or you could hire a bodyguard."

"Wow. You think so? Well, maybe. Kind of exciting. Rock stars, they have bodyguards. Movie stars, too. You really think I need a bodyguard? But I wouldn't want him hanging around all the time. That's the trouble. Look, Frank, how about this: I'll tell this Sybil woman, 'Okay, you say you can prove you're my mother, you say you've got documents. Well, if you have documents, just show them to my lawyer, he's handling this. His name is Frank May,' and so on. Can I do that, Frank?"

I hated the idea, of course. But people do dump things on their lawyers. I had to remember what an excellent client Freddy was. Reluctantly, I agreed.

He seemed delighted, like a kid with a new toy: "Oh, that's great, Frank. I'll tell her right away. I've got a phone number. She wrote it on a piece of paper and practically shoved it down my throat. I'll say, 'Please see my lawyer, he's in charge,' I'll tell her you'll evaluate her claim or some crap like that, and that'll get rid of her. I hope."

I had a bad feeling about the whole issue. It seemed likely to me that Sybil Glass was a fake. I imagined she read the news about Freddy, and Clara, and the money, and it either got her greed molecules going, or her fraud molecules, or both, and she hatched some sort of plan to convince him she was his long-lost mother. Maybe just mentioning a lawyer would scare her off. Sometimes it does. I hoped, essentially, that nothing would come of this. Little did I know that some things *would* come of it, including murder.

8

As I said, when I agreed that I would handle, or try to handle, Sybil Glass, Freddy seemed utterly delighted.

"But you said you had two issues, Freddy," I said. "What's the other one?"

"I did say that," he said. "Okay, here's the deal. About six months before she died, Aunt Clara said to me, Freddy, 'Let's face it, I don't have long to live.' I said, 'Don't say that, you're a tough old bird, and you'll live forever,' but she just laughed and said, 'Freddy my boy, you're sweet, but no, I won't live forever.' Actually, I knew that. I was worried about her myself. She had a million things wrong with her, I mean, kidneys, and some heart thing, and arthritis, and I guess a bunch of other stuff I didn't even know about. She filled out one of those forms, about how she didn't want to be revived or something, and she said, 'Freddy, you'll decide,' which thank God I never had to do. Anyway, she also said, 'I've got a safe deposit box, and I want you to be able to get into it, if I'm dead or in a coma and that sort of thing.' So we went to the bank, and we did the paperwork—it was Wells Fargo, downtown branch in Los Altos—and she said, 'Freddy, here's a key. There's something in there I want you to have. But don't go and open the box while I'm still alive.'"

"You opened the box after she died, I assume."

"Hey, Frank, actually I opened it before she died. Like, if you gave me a box of candy, and said, don't eat any of it for a

40

week, no way could I not take a piece or two.... I was curious, I said to myself, What's the harm? I'm not going to steal stuff, I just want to know, what's in the damn box. I was having lunch in Los Altos, at a sushi place, and I was with Derek. I told him about the safe deposit box, I don't remember why, I mean, I don't remember how the subject came up. So he said, 'Well, aren't you curious, like, what's in it?' And I said, 'You know, I really am.' So he said, 'Well, why don't you find out?' So we went, the two of us, of course I was entitled to get into it, like I told you. Anyway, there was a diamond ring, really beautiful, must have cost a fortune, and a bracelet, I think that was pretty valuable too; I guess Aunt Clara liked jewelry at one time. And there was also a kind of big thick notebook, and it was labeled 'Diary' and there was also a sealed letter. I started to look at the diary, but it was handwritten, and she had a tiny handwriting, and I said, 'I'm not going to look at this, who cares?' Derek said, 'I'll bet it's interesting.' I said, 'Well, *you* can read it if you want.' He said, 'I do want.' Anyway, I figured, I'll let Derek have the diary for a while, then I'll put it back. Which is what I did. But I didn't open the sealed letter, because if Clara decided she wanted to look at stuff, if she went to the box, you know, or whatever; and if she saw the letter was open, well, she'd know I'd been there, so I just let it alone."

"You gave the diary to Derek? And he read it?" I should have told Freddy this was wrong, but I held my tongue.

"Well, I don't know if he read all of it, but he gave it back to me, and I put it back in the box. I said, 'What was in it, was it interesting?' And he said, 'Yeah, parts of it. Anyway, read it for yourself,' and I said, 'No thanks.' Meanwhile, my aunt—first, I have to tell you, I'm not a good liar, and I felt very guilty, and she could read me like a book, she said to me, that night, 'Freddy, you look like the cat that ate the canary, what's this all about?' So I said, 'Aunt Clara, I looked in the safe deposit box. Don't ask me why I did it, but I did.' And she said, 'Freddy, you know, I wondered whether you'd do what I said, and I thought, well, that's my Freddy, but listen, I love you, and I forgive you. Did you open the letter; that's the important thing.' And I said, no I didn't. So she said, 'Good. I don't care about the rest of it.'

And look, now she's dead, she's dead and gone, so I went to the box, and I took out stuff. I kept the ring and the bracelet, I figured they could come in handy if I was dating some girl and I wanted, well, to make a good impression, if you know what I mean—not that I'd really want a girl who'd give it up, just because of a bracelet, or something like that; not that any of these girls are exactly virgins nowadays, but anyway. Never mind. And I opened the letter, and I read it. It said she was leaving me all this money, and I was her closest relative, and she loved me, etc., but she wanted me to promise her one thing, she wanted me to read the diary. She had been thinking of writing her memoirs, but now she wouldn't have a chance, being dead after all, and she wanted me to read this thing in the safe deposit box, and make up my mind whether it's something you could publish or whatever."

"Did she ever write her memoirs?"

"I guess she started writing some sort of autobiography or something, but she didn't finish it, or she tore it up or whatever. Anyway, there's this diary. On the front page of the thing, she wrote, 'My Life as a Black Sheep,' by Clara Fisk. The letter also said, 'Freddy, take a look at it, and you decide. I know you won't do it yourself, Freddy. But you could hire somebody.' Well, she was right about that; I wouldn't know how to go about doing it, I mean, working with publishers and agents and whatever. And the letter said, 'Don't worry if parts of it are embarrassing ... or scandalous, after all I'm going to be dead, and I don't care, and you don't care, too, Freddy, who I slept with and what I did. I think we're two of a kind, Freddy, only I'm an old lady, and you're a young man. I'm leaving you plenty of money, Freddy, I want you to have a good life. And I've been good to you. So do me with this one big favor. Take a look at it, and if you think somebody might want to print it, okay.' And then there was something else in the letter, kind of peculiar."

"And what was that?"

"She said: 'Only one thing—the last section of the diary, it's kind of separate, you'll recognize it. That is not to be published. Under any circumstances. But do not destroy it. Keep it, in case you need it.'"

"What did she mean by that?"

"No idea."

"Well, did you read the thing?"

"Yeah, sort of. I mean, I started, and parts of it were pretty interesting, but it was all in this handwriting, she didn't use a computer or anything, and she had this tiny handwriting, like I said, you could get a migraine from it. And like I told you, Frank, I'm basically lazy, I can't help it, it's one of my worst traits, and I put things off. I asked Derek whether it's easy to publish something like this—I ask him about everything, well, at least things that might have a legal angle, since he's a law student—and he had read the damn thing, or parts of it anyway. He said, 'Probably no publisher will touch it, but there's self-publishing, where you pay money and they publish your book, they'll publish anything, any shit at all; provided you're willing to pay.' It still seemed too much like work to me. But I thought, maybe I'll try, because I made a promise. Now here's where you come in, Frank."

"Me? Whatever for?"

"It's like this, Frank: some of the stuff is pretty steamy, like, wow, it's all about her sex life, and she mentions actual names. So Derek said, 'You got to be careful, Freddy. Somebody could sue your ass off, libel and slander. You better show it to a lawyer, an expert.' So here I am, Frank. I'd like you to look at it to figure out if there could be any lawsuits and so on."

"I'm not an expert on that subject, Freddy. Not sure who is. It's a pretty specialized field. Newspaper companies hire experts on libel; publishers, too. But, okay, I know a little something about it, and if you want, I'll take a look at this diary. If I think I see a problem, I'll try to find out who I should refer it to."

"Thanks a million, Frank. And take your time, I'm not in any hurry," he said. And he reached into a big cloth bag that he had brought with him and handed the diary over to me. "Read it in your spare time. And let me know what you think. And oh, by the way, Derek said, 'There's another problem there, a big one. A great big one.' And I said, well, 'What is it?' And he said, 'I'm not going to say. Let your lawyer read it.' I said, 'Derek, hey, don't play games with me. Just tell me what's on your mind, or I'll punch you in the nose.' And he said, 'I'm not going to tell you, Freddy, and if you punch me in the nose, I'll punch you right back, don't be an asshole,' pardon my language."

"I'll be on the lookout," I said.

I took the diary home with me, and starting skimming it. Freddy was right about one thing: it was handwritten, and not always easy to read. It certainly was explicit. There were some pretty graphic passages in it. I had never met the late Clara Fisk, and probably would have dismissed her as a nice old lady. It's easy to forget that these nice old ladies, and nice old men, with gray hair, maybe tottering along the street, maybe pushing a walker, maybe they seem out of it, with a kind of vague stare—it's easy to forget they were once young and full-blooded, with sex lives, bad habits, exploits, God knows what else. This old man, who can barely walk, stumbling alone, with a blank look on his face: maybe he climbed mountains when he was young, maybe he went hitchhiking in Patagonia. And the old lady pushing a walker, who looks as if she doesn't know if it's Tuesday or the Fourth of July, maybe she slept with half the boys in some college fraternity. Every old person has a past. And that was certainly true of Clara Fisk.

And I couldn't help thinking of Celia's Uncle Harry, for example. He was 90; couldn't get around much, used a walker, had all sorts of medical complaints. And complaints in general. He was old, and exceedingly cranky. He had already been old when I met Celia, more than twenty years ago. But what was he like when he was young? Are old people really a different species? I saw a bumper sticker, once, on the back of a car, which said: "Inside every old person is a young person wondering: What happened?"

Clara's diary made me think of all this again. All the Uncle Harry's and Aunt Clara's of the world. Actually, "diary" was something of a misnomer. It was really a memoir, part of it in the form of a diary, but much of it had obviously been taken from diary entries and reworked. One long passage described how she met Homer Fisk. She had had a rich sex life before she met him, a whole daisy chain of lovers, of various shapes, sizes, and sexual tastes, but throughout it all, there was one constant figure: Pascal LeBeau. They had met when he was still a resident, working in a hospital in San Jose, and they had an on-again off-again affair over the years, which she described in full detail.

Clara often came for dinner at the LeBeau's and one night when she was there, she met his cousin, Homer Fisk, a widower with incredible amounts of money. "I wanted the money," she wrote, "and I was young, I was pretty, and I knew how to use my natural advantages. I found I could twist Homer around my little finger." After a very brief period, in which he obviously wanted her sexually, and she refused (for strategic reasons), he proposed, and they got married. "Homer wasn't exactly the greatest lover in the world—and he was past his sell-by date, if you know what I mean—but there was a little bit of pizzazz still left in him, and he tried awfully hard, I'll give him that." She went into some detail about their sex life, more detail than seemed necessary, if you asked me (which of course she didn't). Seemed Homer liked to wear a necktie when they had inter-course. No other clothes, but he just had to have a necktie on: "He had a whole collection of neckties. Some favorites, some not so favorite. I think he felt some of the neckties were better for sex than others." One blue and red necktie in particular.

Despite the neckties, he failed to satisfy her. "I continued having sex on the side. Mostly with Pascal. I had ended things with him, to get married to Homer. I admit, I did it for the money. Pascal got married too, a woman named Daisy Howard. They went off to Venice, for their honeymoon. They were gone for three weeks." When they came back, Clara wrote, Pascal made a bee-line straight to Clara's house, and, guess what, they made love. Pascal and his wife had three children; but that didn't stop him. Whenever he could get away from Daisy, he came to Clara. "I was home all day, Homer didn't want me to work. I wanted children, but this wasn't happening. I was trying to write a novel, but it was frustrating. I was extremely bored. I started having sex with workmen ... people who would come to the house, to fix things." She had a mad passion for a youngish man, a carpenter—Dylan was his name—who had long black hair and tattoos on his arms. He was building new cabinets for the kitchen. He and Clara had sex regularly, whenever he came by to work on the cabinets. "The job took much longer than expected, maybe because instead of doing the work when he came, we spent a lot of time in the bedroom. He was quite a sexual athlete. The bills mounted up. Homer grumbled about the cost. Little did he know he was paying extra because Dylan was having sex with me, and the sex took time away from the cabinets. I told Homer you had to pay a lot of money to get a quality job, and Dylan was the best there was, in the entire Bay Area."

The job finally got finished, and the cabinets were ready for use. Dylan, after all was said and done, had built some really beautiful cabinets. He left a bill on the dining room table, and got into bed with Clara: "Afterwards, I was lying on the bed naked. The light was dim. Dylan got out of bed and said he had to go, he had another call to make, and threw his clothes on, and I knew I'd never see him again. I felt so miserable. He never really cared for me. I was just a woman, and not so young anymore, a woman who threw herself at him." In another passage, she described how the gas company sent out a young woman because of some sort of power failure. "She had this blue uniform on, it said Pacific Gas and Electric, and she looked at me, in a funny way, and I thought, well, why not? We had a brief, passionate fling.... Homer never found out."

Bored and frustrated, she turned more and more to Pascal. By then he was divorced. "He said he had always loved me. And I realized I had always loved him. Him and only him. Whenever we could, we got together. And he was frequently at our house. He was, after all, Homer's cousin, and they had always been close; as Homer got sicker and sicker, he turned more and more to Pascal for medical advice. It was awkward, pretending Pascal and I were just friends. I felt the situation couldn't last. For his part, Pascal wanted me to leave Homer, and move in with him, maybe even get a divorce from Homer. Pascal said he wanted to marry me. I told Pascal I couldn't do that, it was unfair to Homer. Homer had always been good to me, I said. The truth was, I didn't want to lose Homer's money. I loved being rich. I would do anything to keep my hands on that money."

Yes, there was a great deal of sex in Clara's diary or memoir or whatever it was. I'm not sure any of it was libelous, but it was certainly indiscreet. I felt sorry for the late Homer Fisk, and his necktie-driven love life. Surely he was entitled to his privacy, dead or alive.

Indiscreet: but there was more. What really startled me was the last part, the part that Freddy was *not* supposed to print, but to keep for some unknown purpose. The reason why it was not for publication seemed pretty clear. You see, it plainly described a murder.

9

The passage had to do with the death of Homer Fisk. Interestingly, it seemed clear that Clara wrote it *after* the rest of the memoir; the ink looked different, and her handwriting was more spindly. I would guess she wrote it not too long before she died.

"The years had gone by," she wrote, "and Homer was a very old man. He was in very poor health. It was one thing after another—small strokes, problems with his lungs, his liver, his kidneys. He had a heart condition, too. Then he had a massive stroke, and I thought he would die, but somehow he survived. After that he could barely walk. He had trouble talking, and his whole left side was paralyzed. The poor man was in misery. We needed to hire round the clock nurses. He told me, 'Clara, I'm dying inside.' He really didn't want to go on living. He said to me once, 'Ask Pascal for some pills, something to put an end to this thing.' I talked about it to Pascal, and Pascal did give me some pills. But I kept them in the bathroom, on the highest shelf, where Homer couldn't reach them.

"Oh, I'll be honest: I wanted him to die. But he didn't. He was somehow hanging on. My life was pretty grim. I felt like I was drowning. I felt like I was a Siamese twin, hooked up to another body, but that body was dead, or half dead. I dragged myself through the days. Sure, we had money, we had help, nurses, everything. But I was just as much a prisoner as Homer was....

"And I had no privacy ... all those other people around; all those nurses, maids, doctors. It was a big house, but still. I know it wasn't right of me, but I kept hoping Homer would die. He was getting nothing out of life. The worst thing was, he clung to me more and more, he said, 'Clara, you're the only thing I'm living for,' and he wanted me around all the time. I would go out, and when I came back, he would ask me, 'Where did you go? What did you do?' Pascal was my only consolation. Pascal and ... our relationship. Our sexual relationship. Whenever I could, I flew to Pascal's side. My only happiness was the time I spent with Pascal.

"And then ... it happened. It was nighttime, and it was a weekend. The maid was off for the day. The night nurse hadn't come, and I told the agency, it was alright; I could handle the situation. Homer usually slept through the night, and I could take care of him. Besides, I said, his doctor will be here. That was Pascal. 'He'll look in on Homer,' I told them, 'and if we need anything, he'll be there. He's Homer's cousin, and he'll spend the night.' It was such a good excuse for the two of us to get together. It was a golden opportunity. And did we ever take advantage of this opportunity! Homer was in his room and we were next door, in the bedroom I had been using since Homer's stroke. We made love, hot and heavy, then we sat and talked. Suddenly I realized Homer was awake. He was making some kind of gurgling noises, and I had a kind of panic attack. Was Homer aware of what was going on under his roof?

"Pascal had fallen asleep. He was snoring in fact. And then I figured, the time has come, and I put on a robe, I went into the bathroom, and I got the pills; then I went in to Homer. He was awake, he was gasping for breath, and I gave him a glass of water, and he was mumbling something, I put my ear down to his mouth, and I heard him say something, like, 'This is no life, not for me, not for you.' I said, 'I know that, Homer.' And I said, 'Do you want to get it over with?' And he said, 'Yes I do. I don't want to suffer anymore. I've suffered enough.' I thought, should I give him the pills? But then I thought, maybe that wasn't the best idea, maybe there'd be an autopsy or something like that, and they might realize that it wasn't a natural death. So I took a pillow, and I smothered him. At first, he seemed to struggle a bit, but then he didn't.

"When I finished, I turned around and saw Pascal in the doorway in his underwear, watching me. I said, 'I have to call an ambulance.' Pascal came over and he felt for a pulse, and he said, 'He's dead, Clara. Forget the ambulance.' And then Pascal put his arm around my waist, and he started kissing me, and I said, 'Honey, are you crazy, Homer's dead, and you're starting in again?' But then he laughed, and said, 'Well, he can't complain, now, can he? And you're a widow, so whatever you do is okay, hey, before it was adultery, and now it's not' and he practically dragged me into the other room, and we had sex again. And again."

She described their stormy act of lovemaking, in full and excruciating detail. It was pretty weird. They were having sex, some thirty feet away from the dead body of Homer Fisk, Clara's late husband. I had to hand it to Pascal LeBeau. He had quite a repertoire, at least in those days. So did Clara, apparently. She made no excuses for what she did: "Did I feel guilty? Yes and no. Homer wanted to die. He had no life. This was an act of mercy. A mercy killing. Nobody made any trouble. Nobody was surprised that Homer was dead. He was half dead anyway. Old, sick, helpless. He was better off, wasn't he? And Pascal handled the death certificate. Heart attack—that's what I believe he put down. Nobody questioned it. Why should they?

"Why am I confessing this? I don't know exactly. To clear the air, maybe. It's not something I'm proud of. I just felt: I have to get this down on paper. Not for other people, but for myself. What I did and why I did it. So many people face this issue. They're trapped with the living corpse of somebody who used to be a loved one, and whose life has been pitifully reduced."

This segment ended there. There were a few, random later entries—written *before* this particular segment, I would guess, at least judging by the handwriting. A few statements about Kathryn and Max. Soon after Homer died, they had disappeared in the Amazon jungle. When they left on their trip, she took little Freddy into her house—the big house where she had lived with Homer. "I'll take care of him while you're gone," she told them. But they never came back. She wrote, "I was really rich now, too, and I liked that. Well, I had always been rich, ever since I married Homer—he was generous to me; he never denied me anything. But now it was all mine, to do with as I pleased. And I had Freddy, too; and I loved the little boy. I never had children of my own. Of course, I missed Kathryn, I loved her, and when she disappeared, it broke my heart. I paid for a search, but they never found her. My consolation was Freddy. He was now the only real family I had. He filled a big hole in my life."

After that, essentially nothing. Freddy's childhood and adolescence, and young manhood: all that was missing. And nothing at all about Clara's life in the Freddy period, as she passed into ripe old age. And nothing more about her affair with Pascal LeBeau. Obviously, they hadn't gotten married. Were they still friends, or more than friends?

This hardly mattered. What she *had* written: that was more than enough. It was a bombshell. I sat there, staring into space. I'm a lawyer, after all, and I was stunned by what I had read. The late Clara Fisk had murdered her husband. Murdered him. It was as simple as that.

10

At home that night, after dinner, I kept thinking about the diary. About what Clara Fisk had written. Why had she written it? To alert people to a social issue, an issue that many people face, with old, sick family members? I doubted it. She could have written an op-ed for *The New York Times*; that might have been more appropriate. And why reveal her mad sex with Pascal LeBeau while her husband's corpse was lying a short distance away?

Celia, my wife, said, "Frank, you're so preoccupied, what's the matter?"

"Oh, nothing," I said. "Client business. I have to think about, well, what to do about one of my clients."

Celia was knitting a scarf for one of her friends. This friend taught Spanish at the same high school where Celia taught. Celia put down her knitting and told me about events of the day, mostly involving the wretched vice-principal, a man she loathed. She went into great detail. Frankly, I was barely listening.

Clara Fisk. Her life as a black sheep. Clara and Pascal LeBeau. And our Uncle Harry. What would I be like when I reached that stage of old age? If I got there, I mean. Now Celia was asking my advice, about what to do, some issue provoked by the vice-principal. I mumbled something. It seemed to satisfy her.

I remembered vividly how, after lunch, that very day, I had gone for a walk. It was a beautiful, sunny day. There's a small park a few blocks from my office, and I strolled over there, and sat down on a bench. Flowers were in bloom. I saw a beautiful butterfly, hovering above some flowers. Fluttering, as if to show off its wonderful wings, all blue and white. I started thinking about butterflies. They start out as caterpillars—that's the strange part. They come out of eggs, I suppose. And then they're ugly little grubs, shapeless, squishy, munching on leaves, hideous, helpless; and then they spin a cocoon, and lo and behold, they're transformed into beautiful, graceful creatures. People are, in a way, the opposite. Young people are the butterflies; and then, at the end of life, they're transformed into caterpillars, ugly and helpless.

Is this unfair? Already, although I was never a total butterfly, I was on my way to the caterpillar stage. A bit overweight. Losing my hair. And my dear Celia was starting to turn gray. She was at that crucial time in a woman's life, when she faces a terrible decision: should I dye my hair? So far, for Celia, the answer was no.

And am I unfair to old people? Maybe they still have desires, hopes, dreams, maybe they still clutch onto life—as if they were still butterflies—and, deep inside, perhaps they still are.

I dozed off in my chair; maybe these heavy thoughts put me to sleep. Do butterflies sleep?

* * *

I called Freddy the next morning, at about 9:30, when I assumed he'd be awake. He answered the phone on the fifth ring, and sounded half asleep. I told him I wanted to talk about the diary, could he come see me? "Hey, how about lunch?" he said. "My treat."

I said, "Sure thing, Freddy." Of course, I would bill him for my time—a lot more than the lunch was going to cost. In a way, talking about fees with Freddy was exasperating; he seemed totally indifferent to the subject. Exasperating in one sense, delightful in another. I have clients who are worth a lot of money—they have stock in Apple and Google, they own real estate in Palo Alto and Mountain View—and yet they look on a lawyer's fees as if these fees were some sort of trinket in a middle Eastern bazaar. As far as they're concerned, only a fool pays the asking price. They go over the bill, and they haggle, item by item. Freddy was the opposite. He was about to become a very rich young man—not that he was poor at the moment— so why quibble? The whole subject seemed to bore him.

Of course, Freddy had never lacked for anything; he always got what he wanted because his Aunt Clara gave him everything. She had been exceedingly generous. Nonetheless, she had total control of the money. She gave him an allowance, she set up accounts for him ... but, in the end, it was her money, and her power over the money. That was then. Now Freddy was in control.

Freddy chose an upscale Japanese restaurant for our lunch. After we ordered our food, I brought up the subject of the diary.

"Hot stuff, wasn't it?" he said. "Like wow. Not that I read the whole thing. She was quite something, wasn't she? I mean, I always knew she wasn't your average old lady, you know, not prudish, she was somebody you could say 'fuck' in front of and she was always lots of fun, always willing to do things. But by the time I knew her, I don't suppose she had much of a sex life. Did you read the part about how she was doing it with a plumber? Or maybe it was a carpenter. But when I was growing up, I guess she was past that sort of thing. I mean, we had plumbers, we had carpenters and stuff, but nothing happened. I mean, maybe she wanted it, but they wouldn't. She was just too old."

"Freddy," I said, "be serious. Nobody would care about her sex life. But your aunt says, in plain black and white, that she murdered her husband. That's the part she doesn't want you to publish; and I agree. Frankly, I wouldn't publish any of the stuff. That's my opinion."

"Wow, that's heavy, Frank," he said, waving a chopstick in the air. "Okay, you know best. And she did say not to do anything with that part. I'm supposed to keep it, God knows why. But look, you say it was murder. Is that right, Frank? Anyway, who cares? First of all, she's dead. It's not like anybody could arrest her. And what do you mean, 'murder'? The guy wanted to die."

"Legally," I said, "what he wanted is just plain irrelevant. I'm not saying a jury would convict her, if there was a jury. I mean, probably not. I think juries go easy in these situations, mercy killing situations. If anybody prosecutes the person at all. But there's another problem."

"You know," he said, ignoring my last comment, "Okay. I get it. Anyway, the diary business: I was wondering before I looked at the stupid thing, why anybody would buy it? I mean, if we published it. But I think it could go absolutely viral, you know what I mean? All that sex, and even that death thing. Okay, I wouldn't do it, because of my promise. But you know, Homer was a well-known guy because he was so rich. And Clara, people knew about her. You should have read the obituaries, three whole columns in the *San Francisco Chronicle*. Somebody said the *New York Times* had a story, too."

"Look," I said, "I know all that. You can't arrest dead people. Sure. But the point is this: she killed somebody, legally it was murder, even if he was begging for it, which, by the way, apparently he wasn't. The real problem is that he left her most of his money. And if you kill somebody, you can't inherit their estate."

"No shit," he said. "I never thought of that."

"Actually," I said, "you really wouldn't have a problem here; I mean, practically speaking. In order to lose an inheritance, there has to be one of two things. First, an actual trial and conviction, and of course, that's not the case here. She's dead, so that's that. But there's another thing: somebody has to make a claim, and bring in evidence, and then the authorities would decide what to do—was this murder or not? Is it worth pursuing? And so on. And there's no such person, I mean, nobody making this kind of claim."

Freddy gave me a funny look. "Well, not exactly."

"What do you mean, not exactly?"

"I've been meaning to tell you about this, Frank. Okay, Homer Fisk, he had a daughter, Griselda, and they had this huge fight, and he cut her off, not a penny; well, this Griselda, she's got a daughter, name is Ella. She lives around here, but I never met her, not until recently, Clara knew about her, and hated her, she told me 'Watch out for that Ella, she's poison.' Anyway, somehow she got to know my friend Derek, and I saw her with him and she said, 'You're Freddy, I know all about you. You're the one who's got my money.' I said, 'What do you mean, I've got your money?' And she said, 'Your aunt, she stole the money. My grandfather left all his money to her, and now you're getting it, and it should have been mine.' I didn't know what to say, so I just said, 'Well, nobody said life was fair,' and she called me an asshole. But I have to admit, she's quite something, she's like wow. Sexy as all get out. But she scares me when she says things like that."

"Okay, Freddy: just stay away from her. Look, so long as she doesn't know about the diary, or what happened, there's no problem. And we're certainly not going to tell her. Anyway, it's been a long time, more than twenty years? I don't know exactly. Maybe, if you have a claim against an estate, you have to do it in a certain timeframe, or else you're out of luck. I could look that up."

Freddy nodded. He looked fairly glum.

"Freddy," I said. "Don't worry. Trust me. It's not going to happen."

"Easy for you to say," he said. "It's not your money."

"Look," I said. "There's another point. Suppose, just suppose, this awful thing happened, and the money couldn't go to your aunt. Where would it go? Well, the law says we'll act as if the person who did it—the killer—died before the victim. In other words, we'll pretend Clara died before Homer, not after Homer. What would happen to the money? I don't really know. For one thing, I'd have to take a look at Homer's will."

I'm not sure Freddy was still listening. He was lost in a depressive fog, thinking about all that money flying out the window. I assured him there was nothing to worry about. Homer's will might have said that if Clara died before he died, the money would go to her next of kin. That would be her niece, Kathryn. And from Kathryn to Freddy? It depended on how Homer's will was worded. Of course, I had no idea what

Homer's will actually said; I told Freddy I would try to find out. He shrugged his shoulders and said, "Go ahead." Then he left.

11

Unfortunately, the obvious place to start was Gideon Grambling. He was handling Clara's estate. Homer had died many years before, and Gideon had not been his attorney; he simply wasn't old enough. Still, he would surely know about the will and the estate, since he had taken over as Clara Fisk's lawyer.

I picked up the phone, and dialed his number. I hated calling Gideon; it was always a pain in the neck, and I knew I would be treated as if I was a worm, wriggling on the pavement, repulsive, and totally beneath his notice, or even his receptionist's. I tried several times, and left several message. The woman who answered the phone had a voice as frosty as ice. But finally I did succeed in reaching Gideon. "Gideon," I said, after some preliminary remarks, "I need to know what Homer Fisk's will provided."

"Frank, the man has been dead—what, twenty five years? Why on earth do you want to know? His estate, I believe, was handled by Maxwell Globus, and Globus, as you surely know, is deceased. A very distinguished attorney. I collaborated with him on some very significant matters. When he died, some of his clients went over to me. Members of leading families. At one time, I represented the absolute majority of the members of the board of the San Francisco Opera. At any rate, as you know, probate records are open to the public. If you're really interested...."

"Please, Gideon. Don't play games. I know about probate files. Yes, I could do it that way, but I thought, if you would be so kind as to give me the information I need, you could save me the time and the trouble."

"At the cost of *my* time and trouble," he said, with his own version of an icy voice.

With Gideon, as with some of my clients, I realize I have to swallow my pride, stifle my annoyance, and use patience and persistence. In the end, Gideon admitted that he had a copy of Homer Fisk's will in his files. He reluctantly agreed to send me a copy.

It was a long document, which was no surprise, considering how rich Homer had been. I was, of course, not concerned about the technical details; I simply wanted to know where the money went. And it went to Clara. The will did recite that Homer was deliberately leaving nothing to his daughter Griselda, "for reasons of which she is very well aware." There were gifts of money to one or two former employees of Fisk Enterprises; some money to a woman who, I later found out, was a maid in the household; gifts to various charities; and a gift of several art works to the Palace of the Legion of Honor in San Francisco, "on the board of which I have had the honor to serve." He left 20% of the rest of his estate "to my good friend and cousin, Dr. Pascal LeBeau" and the other 80% of the residue—and this was, as I know, an extremely large sum of money—"to my beloved wife, Clara, if she survives me."

As I had told Freddy, I really did not think Clara's inheritance was in any danger, certainly not at this late date. Still, if Clara was not in the picture, what then? The will provided that, if Clara failed to survive him, her share would pass, not to Clara's relatives, but to Homer's, to his "heirs at law," which meant his closest relatives, "except that, under no circumstances, shall my daughter, Griselda Fisk-Potter, inherit any portion of my estate." I asked Freddy to come see me, and when he came, I told him roughly what Homer's will provided, and I assured him once again that there was no problem. I asked him if he had any idea who, besides this daughter Griselda, might be Homer Fisk's closest kin.

"I know Dr. LeBeau is a cousin," I said. "And there's the granddaughter. He cut out his daughter, but he didn't mention the granddaughter. Maybe she hadn't been born yet."

"Wow. Dr. LeBeau, he got plenty of money from the estate, and he's rich anyway. Hey, Frank, do you think Homer would have left a nickel to the guy, if he knew this cousin was screwing his wife? But, anyway, I told you about the granddaughter. Griselda's kid. A real bitch, like I said. Ella Fisk-Potter."

"And who was Potter? Her father, I assume."

"I don't know the whole story. This Potter guy, I think he's the reason Homer cut off his daughter. I guess he was completely unsuitable, maybe she was pregnant, who knows. I think Potter is dead, or he's in prison, or something. Anyway, he's not around."

"So ... this Ella, she'd be the closest relative? Other than her mother?"

"I guess."

This seemed right to me. But I repeated what I had said to Freddy: she was not about to get anything. The whole matter was dead and buried, so to speak.

"But I don't trust her," he said. "She's a real snake. I'm afraid she might do something."

"Do something? Like what?"

"I mean, Derek knows her, and he says she goes around telling people that I owe her money, which I don't, and that she's going to sue me. Wow. Can you imagine? I don't want her suing me. Hey, Frank, you have to feel sorry for me, right? Like, I'm the poor little rich boy. I don't have any family, everybody's dead, and everybody else wants something from me—my money, mostly."

"Well, let's not get too excited, Freddy. Ella, she hasn't actually sued you; I assume it's just talk."

"Yeah. That's right," he said. "But you know, it's getting me all edgy. Why are they picking on me? I'm a good guy, Frank, don't you think so?"

"Money does funny things to people, Freddy," I said. "But, like I told you, I don't think Ella, or anybody else, has any kind of case."

"It's because I've got a great lawyer, right, Frank?"

I just smiled at Freddy, and switched the subject: "Let's get back to the diary. Okay, it's not going to hurt you, but the best thing is to do absolutely nothing. No publishing. Not that I think a publisher would be that interested in it."

"Hey, Frank, why don't I just get rid of it? Burn the damn thing."

My natural caution kicked in here. "I wouldn't do that, Freddy. Let's just sit tight. Keep it under lock and key. And, here's a question: Who else knows about the sticky part, you know, the part where Homer died?"

"Who knows about it? Well, Pascal does. He was there."

"Granted. But does he know about the diary?"

Freddy shrugged his shoulders. "No idea."

"Do you know if anybody else has seen the diary?"

"Oops. Derek. I showed it to Derek. Remember, I told you I showed it to Derek. I don't know if he read that part. I shouldn't have done that, right, Frank? But I did."

"Well, what's done is done. He's your friend. Can you trust him to keep his mouth shut?"

"I don't know, Frank. Derek's not exactly a saint. He could stab you in the back, I really think he could. Wow. Am I in trouble, Frank?"

I tried to reassure him. I told him to talk to Derek, as diplomatically as he could. Tell him that the diary isn't going to be published, and it would be best just to forget the whole thing. I asked, "Is there anybody else, Freddy? Either somebody who knows about, well, Homer's death? Or the diary?"

Freddy scratched his head. "Well, basically, I don't know for sure. I mean, she could have shown it to people, how would I know? She put it in her safe deposit box after she stopped writing it, but before that, who knows?"

"Was she close to somebody, I mean, somebody she might have shared this with?"

"Well, maybe Melanie knew about it. You met her, that's Pascal's granddaughter. She and her grampa are thick, and Aunt Clara really loved her. I mean, I don't think she would have looked at the diary, but maybe she knew about this thing, the way Homer died and all that. You know, she's about my age, and Aunt Clara always thought I should hook up with Melanie—get married to her—she was really keen on that idea. But you know what? Melanie, I like her, she's great, but she doesn't exactly light my fire, if you know what I mean. I told Aunt Clara, I said, 'It's not like in the zoo, you know, you put the male gorilla in the same cage with the female gorilla, and you expect them to have crazy sex, anyway, I think even in the zoo it doesn't always work, I mean, to us they all look the same, you've seen one gorilla, you've seen them all; but who knows? To a guy gorilla this lady gorilla might be totally repulsive,' and anyway, I said to her, 'Auntie dear, this isn't a zoo. Melanie's okay, but she's not for me.' Aunt Clara, she was sort of blind to all of that stuff, so she still thought maybe me and Melanie would get together. She never gave up hope."

I had to ask: "And Melanie, what does she think about you?"

"I don't know. Hey, Frank, I'm good-looking, no? Maybe she has a thing for me, but is too shy to say anything. But seriously, we're just friends. Anyway, now she has a boyfriend, Peter, who works with computers, or something, a real geek, wears glasses, and he doesn't have a chin, if you know what I mean, not exactly an Adonis, and he's Chinese, not that I've got anything against Chinese people, I think they're great; anyway, he's an American, born here I think, and he's not a bad guy.... He was studying engineering, I think, but then he switched. He and Melanie are both into something weird, Russian literature or something, can you imagine?"

I had a dull, sinking feeling in my stomach. Maybe Clara's secret was not such a secret. Pascal knew; and maybe Derek knew; and maybe Melanie knew; and maybe Melanie told Peter, her chinless boyfriend; and perhaps he told somebody, and the whole Chinese community in the Bay Area knew about it. But I realized my imagination was running away with itself.

And what was the danger, anyway? This was the stalest of stale murders. Worse than a cold case. It was frozen solid. And it was going to remain that way.

12

A lawyer has to be cautious. That's part of the job description. I told Freddy I needed to talk to Dr. LeBeau. I guess Freddy called the good doctor, who appeared in my office one afternoon, together with his granddaughter Melanie. I saw that Pascal LeBeau was using a cane, which I hadn't noticed before. He leaned a bit on Melanie when he walked; his tremor, which I *had* noticed before, seemed a bit worse.

I was not happy that Melanie had come along with him and I tried, as gently as possible, to suggest that I might want to talk to him alone. He said, "I don't keep secrets from Melanie. And I'm getting old and feeble, as you can see; I need her."

I was looking for some information, but I didn't want to let Dr. LeBeau know why I was asking him all these questions. I told him I needed to know certain things about Homer Fisk: "I know you were close to him, you were cousins, right?"

"More than cousins," he said. "Homer and I were, well, very good friends. And I was his doctor; not officially, but he trusted my medical advice, and I was happy to give it to him."

"He left his estate to his wife, Clara," I said, "but before that, I mean, before he was married to her, he must have had some other arrangement. I assume he had a will, or some comparable arrangement. Rich people always do."

He gave me an odd look. "Why do you want to know?"

"Doctor," I said, "you don't have to answer my questions. I have a reason for asking, but I also have a reason, at the moment, for not explaining why I'm asking. If that means you won't answer my questions, I guess I'll have to live with that. I'm just trying to save time and effort. I think I could find out what I want to know through other sources, including public sources, but it's easier this way."

I was bluffing, I have to admit. I had no idea whether I could in fact find out any details about Homer's estate plans. His lawyer in those days was dead and buried, and whether Gideon and other lawyers could or would tell me anything was dubious. As for "public sources," that was simply hokum. Homer's will and his estate file were public records, but any older wills or arrangements would obviously not be there.

"Well, I don't see why I shouldn't tell you what I know," he said. "I can't for the life of me think of why it's important, but what the hell. Melanie, what do you think?"

"Sure, grampa. Why not?"

"I always do what she says," he said, though in a way that plainly told me it wasn't true. "Anyway, I know something about his plans, the ones before he married Clara; he told me all about them because he said he was going to leave me a lot of money. That was a million years ago. There was probably a time the money was going to go to his daughter, Griselda, but then they had a terrific fight, well, you know that, and he cut her off without a penny. So he was going to make some new arrangements; I was going to have a big share, not that I wanted it—I forget how much my share would have been, I think it was half or less. The rest went to a bunch of charities. And then he married Clara, and you know what happened then. Basically, she got the money. Oh, not all of it. Most of it. I got some, too. I told him, Homer, 'I don't need the money.' But he insisted."

"What happened to his older wills? Did he tear them up?"

"I have no idea. I suppose he did. Does it make a difference?"

I thought it didn't. But I wasn't sure. I was acting out of an abundance of caution. All I had so far was rumors. Rumors that Ella Fisk-Potter, maybe on behalf of her mother, planned to bring some sort of legal action to overturn Homer's will and claim some or all of the money for herself and her mother. That would mean cutting Freddy out of the picture. I couldn't imagine, after all these years, that she had any realistic chance of success. Maybe she wanted Freddy to buy her off.

Still, murder is murder. If somehow she knew about the diary, if she knew that Clara more or less confessed to killing her husband, was it so unrealistic to imagine that she thought she had a claim? Griselda and her daughter were the only living heirs to Homer Fisk, as far as I knew. So that huge pot of money would go to them. Or Ella. Griselda's claim was a bit more dubious, because Homer had been so explicit about disinheriting her.

I didn't want to worry Freddy, so I kept these thoughts to myself. Wait and see. Freddy had other problems, more pressing problems. Mother problems. Dozens of alleged mothers, appearing out of nowhere, passionate to reclaim their son—and, of course, his money.

This should have been expected. The death of Clara Fisk was reported in the local newspapers; and, as Freddy had pointed out, it even garnered attention from the august *New York Times*. Clara was very rich; but not particularly famous. What intrigued the newspapers was her will, when that became known. They ran stories about this very rich woman whose niece had disappeared in the jungle, but who still thought she might be alive and, if the woman appeared, she would inherit a fortune. I went back to the online sources and collected a number of these accounts of Clara Fisk's will. They rarely mentioned the other possibility: that the birth mother of Freddy Lucas might also, under the terms of the will, claim the money. Most of the fake mothers claimed to be Kathryn Lucas, come back from the dead, and it was easy to show that they were fakes. There were only a few who claimed to be his birth mother. One of them, of course, was Sybil Glass, and since she had a serious claim—and also since she would end up dead in Freddy's backyard—she turned out to be a key figure.

13

The late Sybil Glass was, indeed, an unforgettable character. She came to see me, quite unannounced. I was sitting in my office, working on a trust document for a client. This man, Marcus St. John, had made money in some sort of hi-tech business. He was a shrewd investor, skillful, adroit, competent in almost every aspect of life, with one exception: relations with women. In that realm, he was a disaster. In addition to a string of affairs, he had had a whole series of wives. Number four, the current wife, was a former employee, twenty years his junior. She was also pregnant. There were several children from earlier marriages, of various ages and types, and the document was a tricky one to draft. I was deeply engrossed in the draft when Sybil Glass knocked on the door.

She was a woman, I would say, in her fifties. She was slender, with dark hair, dyed no doubt. She had sharp, rather dramatic features, and very notable green eyes. She was of medium height, dressed in a gray pant-suit. She had, I noticed, no wedding ring, but there were rings on her other fingers. She had a pearl necklace around her neck. Whether they were real pearls or fake was beyond my expertise. Celia, my wife, would have diagnosed them in an instant; and she would have told me, to the nearest dollar, what the pantsuit cost, and who made it.

"I'm Sybil Glass," she said.

At first I wondered: Sybil who? Then I remembered. This was one of Freddy's gaggle of would-be mothers.

She spoke in a firm, steady voice. "You look puzzled," she said. "Perhaps I had better explain who I am, and why I am here."

I said, "I think I know who you are, and why you're here."

"Do you?" she said. "I don't really think so. You think you know, but in fact you don't know anything about me. Not really. I understand you're the lawyer who represents Freddy Lucas. Freddy is my son."

"Yes," I said, "I do represent Mr. Lucas. If you have some sort of claim against him...."

"Not against him," she said, firmly. "Not against my own son. My claim is against the estate of Clara Fisk."

"In that case," I said, "you have to go to the lawyer for that estate. That's a man named Gideon Grambling. I don't represent that estate."

Here I wasn't being exactly honest. True, I didn't represent the estate. But I represented the major beneficiary, Freddy Lucas, and if she *was* Freddy's mother, that had a direct effect on his share of the estate. Sybil Glass was obviously no fool. She knew the lay of the land exactly.

"Gideon Grambling," she said, "positively refuses to see me. I've tried, unsuccessfully I might say, to discuss the matter with him. I got nowhere."

"Then I suggest you might engage a lawyer, if you're making a claim against that estate."

"I am in the process of getting a lawyer," she said. "And I want to correct your statement. I am not making a claim *against* the estate; I am claiming my rights, what's coming to me under the plain language of the will of Clara Fisk. That's not a claim against the estate, it's the opposite. I'm a beneficiary, just as much as Freddy is. My son Freddy."

"Look," I said, "Okay, I get your point. But, as I said, isn't that between you and Gideon Grambling?"

"Mr. May," she said, "please don't take me for a fool. Your client will get less money when my claim is validated. So I presume you will take a position against my claim, in the alleged interests of your client, Freddy Lucas, my son."

"What I will or won't do," I said, "is not anything I care to discuss with you."

"But you'll discuss it with my Freddy," she said. "With my son. And if you persuade him not to contest my claim...."

"Why on earth would I do that?" I blurted out. I added, more sanely, "I haven't discussed this with Mr. Lucas at all; and in any event, I'll do what my client instructs me to do."

She said. "Freddy is a big grownup baby. He'll do exactly what you tell him to do. And I want you to tell him to ... accept me. As his mother."

"But why would I do that? I have no idea whether you're his mother or not. To be honest, I'm a bit skeptical. The poor guy has dozens of women all claiming to be his mother."

"They're frauds," she said. "Complete frauds. But I'm not a fraud. I have documentary evidence, Mr. May. I have positive proof that Freddy is my son. I gave him up for adoption. I was very young at the time. Young and foolish. I turned him over to a couple who couldn't have children of their own. I thought they would give him a good home. But Freddy was my child, not theirs. And I've regretted my decision every day, every hour, every minute of my life."

Could this possibly be true? Some of the women who were plaguing Freddy—and Gideon—were no doubt delusional. Some were obviously charlatans. This woman seemed to fit in neither category. She seemed sure of herself—calm, reasonable in speech; even a bit cold-blooded. And, after all, *somebody* was Freddy's biological mother. And whoever that woman might be, if alive, if she knew about the Clara Fisk estate, the money would act as a powerful draw.

But I was certainly not in any position to say yes or no to her claims. I repeated my advice to her: "Put your case to Gideon Grambling; he'll get in touch with me, I have no doubt." And I told her again, she should have an attorney of her own.

I realized, of course, that I had told Freddy to send her to me. Perhaps I should have said, "Show me your evidence." But I didn't. I also realized that telling her to "put her case" to Gideon was something easier said than done. Still, I didn't feel I could go any further with her.

After she left, I called Freddy's cellphone. He didn't answer, and I left a message for him to get in touch with me.

The woman had sounded, well, plausible. I won't say convincing. I knew nothing about her background. If she was really Freddy's mother, if she had "documentary evidence," where had she been all this time? If her heart was still aching after all those years, why did she wait to make her move just now? The obvious answer was money. Sybil Glass, at least based on my short acquaintance, did not seem like the motherly type. She said she regretted giving up her baby; but frankly, that just didn't ring true. Not her type. What type then was she? The cold, calculating, and perhaps dishonest type.

I didn't want the job of assessing her claim. In fact, I wanted nothing to do with Sybil Glass.

14

I got in touch with Freddy, finally, after several tries. I told him about the visit from Sybil Glass. I advised him strongly not to meet her, not to answer her phone calls, if any, and to stay out of the picture entirely.

"But she says she's my mother, Frank. Wow. And she's got evidence, she says. I mean, what kind of evidence?"

"I have no idea, Freddy. Let her take it up with Gideon."

"But Frank," he said, "I don't want to deal with Gideon; he's like some sort of android, you know what I mean? He comes from a planet where they don't have human feelings, or something. Can't you take care of this? I mean, ask her what's the evidence and so on. Everybody's got a mother, everybody but me. You think it's just the money with her?"

"To be honest, Freddy, I do. Where's she been all these years?"

"Wow. Okay. I don't know. Maybe she's really my mother, but maybe she's also a famous criminal. That's why she stayed away. Maybe she's the head of a whole criminal gang. I mean, not thugs and that sort of thing, but master criminals. Maybe she's a famous jewel thief, you know—she worms her way into high society, then she steals stuff. Maybe she gave me up because, well, it didn't fit in with her lifestyle, having a baby. She's this big international crook, she's got a plot to steal the crown jewels of England, stuff like that. That would be exciting; I could relate to a mother like that."

"Freddy," I said, "don't get carried away. Please. I don't think she's an international jewel thief. And let the lawyers handle it, okay? Gideon Grambling, and whoever this woman hires."

Very soon thereafter, I met another candidate for Mother of Freddy. And this one, frankly, did seem delusional. She was entirely different from Sybil Glass in that regard.

I owed her acquaintance to my old friend Zelda.

I had a phone call from Zelda. She said, "Frank, can we do lunch? There are things I want to talk to you about."

"Sure, Zelda; my pleasure. But what things do you have in mind?"

"You know Freddy's my friend. Your client, Freddy. Freddy Lucas. And he's got these issues. I like him, though. This is all about Freddy. I met this woman, I'll tell you all about it, and she says she's got important information. Her name is Lizbeth. Lizbeth Hull. I think you should meet her. But I'll tell you more about it at lunch."

We met in Palo Alto, at an upscale Italian restaurant. Zelda ordered a salad. "I'm trying to watch my weight, Frank." I looked at her. She was thin and bony, and, poor thing, always looked like she belonged on a Halloween broomstick. I felt like telling her, in a friendly way, that wearing a long and coal-black dress, together with her hooked nose, skinny fingers, and pointy chin, made the broomstick look even more obvious.

Maybe she thought the black dress and the wicked-witch look made her beautiful. I always wonder about the way people shape how they look. Of course, they can't help the basics: the dimensions of the face, what the chin is like, and of course the nose—big noses, small noses, hooked noses, noses of every conceivable kind. You can have a nose job, I guess, but for most people, the nose you were born with is the nose that spends the rest of your life on your face.

So okay: these things, like noses, are a given. But what you do with them, that's what troubles me. Why does this young guy (for example) decide to cover his arms and legs with hideous tattoos, why does he stick some sort of metal thing on his ear, and in his tongue; and why does this overweight woman squeeze herself into skin-tight pants, which only draw unwelcome attention to the size of her butt, and why, moreover, does she choose pants that are a hideous shade of purple or green; and why does this other young woman deliberately choose a décor that would embarrass a bag-lady? Is it that people of this sort attract each other? Is it the fact that what strikes *me* as ugly, strikes certain other people as beautiful or sexy or intriguing? Possibly. After all, a male buzzard sees a female buzzard, which we consider the last word in ugliness; and at the sight of this female buzzard, the male buzzard is overcome with irresistible lust; and a male skunk sees and smells a female skunk, and thinks (assuming they can think) he never saw anything quite so sexy; and she smells like the finest French perfume; and the male warthog pants for the female warthog; and so on.

Zelda, fortunately, had no way of reading my mind. And I'm awfully fond of her; she's kind, she's interesting, she's empathic. I would never suggest that she change the way she looked or dressed or behaved.

Anyway, we chatted a bit about the weather, about politics, and then she got down to business.

"First tell me something, Frank. Is it true that this Kathryn Lucas, you know, Freddy's adoptive mother, if she turned out to be alive, would have a claim to a lot of money? Or would it only be the birth mother?"

"Not sure. Probably. The will, well, it was ambiguous. But if I had to answer one way or the other, I'd have to say, yes."

Zelda's face lit up. "Frank, I love these things. You get involved in such wonderful adventures. I don't know how you do it."

"I don't know either, Zelda. And to me, frankly, they're not interesting adventures. They're a colossal pain in the butt."

"Oh, Frank," she said. "I don't think you really mean it. You're awfully sly. That's the way you operate. Quietly. Secretly. It can't be a coincidence that you have all these strange and mysterious things, all this stuff happening to you. I mean, it could be your karma. But I think that, somehow, people know you have a skill and they seek you out."

I really had no way to answer her. She went on: "Anyway, I met this woman, fascinating woman, the one I want you to meet. You might think she's a little bit strange. She thinks Kathryn is alive. She's convinced of it."

"Zelda, where on earth did you meet this woman? And how does she come to tell you about Kathryn Lucas?"

"Well, it's an interesting story, Frank. I made a presentation in a bookstore, a local bookstore in San Carlos. They invite authors, various types of authors. A friend of mine works there, and she recommended me. She told them I was 'a well-known author of romance novels.' And they invited me to give a talk, and it was advertised: Zelda Valdez, the author, will talk about her new project, 'Love and Lust in the Amazon Jungle,' and this woman was there. She sat in the back row, but afterwards she came up and talked to me, and she said she wanted to get to know me, and I figured, why not, and so we went to a coffee shop and kept on talking. And it was there that I discovered she knew something about Kathryn Lucas."

"What an amazing coincidence," I said.

"Well, actually, I don't think it was a coincidence. She said she knew I was a friend of Freddy Lucas because she had seen me with him, and that's what drew her to my talk. I asked her, 'How do you know Freddy?' And she said, 'Oh, that's a long story, but I've been watching him, and I was outside this yoga place, and you both came out.' And we chatted some more, I couldn't get much more out of her, but I did tell her you were Freddy's lawyer and handling his affairs, and she said she wanted to see you."

"I didn't know you were writing about the jungle, Zelda. I thought you were doing zombies."

"I tried, but my heart just wasn't in it, Frank. I couldn't bring myself to write about zombies, I'm not really cut out for zombies, you know, romance is my style, and zombies are for horror writers—they're just too creepy for me. I've been married three times, so I suppose I'm an expert on romance, or at least romance that goes sour. I don't do zombies. I tried working on this book about Haitian zombies and voodoo and so on, but it just wouldn't go. So I turned to the jungle."

"Why the jungle, Zelda?"

"Well, it's not exactly about the jungle, but it takes place in the jungle. It's about Brazil long ago, maybe two hundred years ago. Historical romance fiction, that's where I made my money, and the zombies were giving me writer's block, so I went back to my old habits. This new book, it's like the ones before that sold so nicely. This one, it's the story of a pirate who falls in love with a nun, Sister Santa Cruz. She's young and beautiful, and she entered a convent because she had a child out of wedlock and her family disowned her, especially her father, a Spanish duke. And Rodrigo, he's the pirate who has an affair with her, and she leaves the convent, but their lives are in danger because he's a wanted man, and the Duke is their enemy, and they escape to the jungle, the Amazon jungle, to be safe and so on.

"Anyway, that's what I talked to the group about. How my heroes, Rodrigo and Sister Santa Cruz, take a boat up the Amazon, and there's danger everywhere, huge snakes, and wild animals, jaguars etc., and they both get terribly ill—some awful tropical disease, a raging fever—and the natives find them, unconscious and on the point of death, and bring them to their village deep in the jungle. And this is a village where they'd never seen white people, and some people think, 'Oh, these are gods' and that sort of thing. And there are complications because the chief of the village, Moomba, falls in love with Sister Santa Cruz, and meanwhile, his beloved daughter, Kalula—which means flower, in their language—she falls in love with Rodrigo. And the elders of the tribe tell Rodrigo and Sister Santa Cruz, that according to the laws of their people, their customs, anyway, it's the rule that the chief can have many wives, and whoever he picks has to submit to him, and Moomba also insists that Rodrigo must go with his daughter. So there they are, and what can they do?"

"Okay, I'll bite. What *can* they do?"

"Well, Frank, to be perfectly honest, I don't know yet myself, and I told the group, 'Ah, you'll have to read the book to see what happens.' Anyway, I told the people there, I said, the writing is going swimmingly, and I read some excerpts; but I said to them, 'I need to do more research about the jungle, make it more realistic, I've never been to the jungle.' And, like I told you, this woman, Lizbeth, came up after the talk and we went for coffee, and she told me she was fascinated by the jungle. She had never been there, she said, but she felt as if she had because she saw it in dreams—honest to God, she said that—and it was very real to her because her dear friend had disappeared in the Amazon jungle years ago, and so on. And I said, 'Who was that?' And she said, 'Her name was Kathryn Lucas,' and I thought, oh my God, this woman is talking about Freddy's adoptive mother."

"Did you tell Freddy about this?"

"No, Frank, I didn't. I thought it would be better to talk to you first. I think you should meet this woman, talk to her, and decide whether there's anything to it. She's a strange person, and I thought she was pretty intense. She reminded me of one of my characters, Mother Guadalupe, the mother superior, an awful person, she's sort of the villainess. I always try to think of a face, you know, so I can have an image in my mind, what the characters in my novels actually look like. Usually, it's some-body I know. You're in one of my books, Frank."

"Not a pirate, I hope."

"No, I used your face for Lord Bottomley, the man who impregnated Sister Santa Cruz."

"Gee, thanks, Zelda."

"Oh, Frank, it doesn't mean anything. He's about your age, and I thought, well, he's going to look like my good friend Frank. It's just something I do. Anyway, I hadn't picked out anybody in particular to be Mother Guadalupe, but when I saw Lizbeth, I thought, she's the one. This is Mother Guadalupe."

"Zelda, my dear, it's hardly a reason to talk to this woman. The fact that she looks like your idea of Mother Guadalupe. Besides, she sounds completely daft."

"She might be; I agree. Crazy. But harmless, Frank. Really. And maybe there's something there. She did know Kathryn, she said. Promise you'll talk to her, Frank. I said you would. She won't bite you."

Somewhat reluctantly, I agreed. I convinced myself that I owed it to my client, Freddy Lucas. Zelda said she'd make the arrangements. That's how I found myself, a day or so later, sitting in my office, across from Lizbeth Hull. I didn't know what to expect. Lawyers meet all kinds of people. But rarely the likes of Lizbeth. She was definitely one of a kind.

15

She was in her late middle age, maybe 60 or so, I would guess. She was heavy set, with a round face, a double chin, and gray hair that had not been combed in days, or brushed; at least it looked that way. I'd guess she hadn't washed her hair either; but this was not easy to tell. She wore a loose red and green dress, which sort of hung down on her body, and clashed with the gray and blue tennis shoes she was wearing. The laces were untied. She was carrying a brown purse, which had definitely seen better days; it was scuffed and torn, and seemed to be lacking a zipper. There was something slightly askew about her facial expressions, something slightly off, something a bit asymmetrical, and it made me think, oddly enough, of milk that had curdled a bit, or cheese that was turning moldy around the edges.

When she came in, she was out of breath for some reason, and when she plunked herself down in a chair across from me, she seemed exhausted, as if she had come from a great distance. She introduced herself and asked if I had some water. I didn't, but I told her I would get some, so I went into the common room of the suite I shared with other lawyers, and I got water from the cooler. She drank it down in one gulp.

She lowered her voice and spoke in a whisper: "There were things I couldn't say to Zelda. She wouldn't understand. I think you would. I can see by your face that you're a deeply spiritual person."

I made no response. In my experience, a person who talks about herself or others as "deeply spiritual" is usually deeply disturbed rather than deeply spiritual. But what do I know?

"I always knew I was different," she said, in a voice that sounded somehow—how can I put it?—conspiratorial. "I've had visions. Nowadays, I have visions about Freddy. I see him in my mind's eye. I can see his darling little face so clearly. Because, you see, he's my son."

Oh God. Under my breath I cursed Zelda, although it probably wasn't her fault. She hadn't told me this woman claimed to be Freddy's mother, only that she *knew* something about Freddy's mother. This was taking things to another level entirely. I wondered, how can I get rid of this woman?

She went on: "I can see, you don't believe me. I understand that. You know, even the most deeply spiritual people have doubts. The path they take, the path to enlightenment, it leads through a lot of darkness, you know? Never a straight path."

No one had ever accused me of achieving enlightenment. Or even that I was on the path to enlightenment. I said nothing, and let her speak.

"You see, in a sense, I *am* Freddy's mother. I really am. Not in the usual way, no. I'm still Lizbeth. My body is still Lizbeth's body. But Kathryn, she inhabits my spirit."

I thought: would it be wrong to humor this woman? Maybe it would be best to let her talk, nod my head, smile; and, at the right time, simply encourage her to go. Meanwhile, I mumbled something about the Amazon jungle, and pointed out that most people, since they hadn't heard from her for twenty years or so, thought that Kathryn Lucas was dead.

"Her body is dead," she said. "Her soul is not dead. She died in the jungle. Not a pleasant death. Sickness, the heat, the terrible conditions. Bad water. No food. Oh, she fought for life, but she couldn't survive. Then she gave in. But you know, life is only a phase. When her body died, when that phase was over, her soul, her spirit, had to find another resting place. That's why her soul moved into my body. So I *am* in fact Kathryn Lucas. She was reborn in me. It's part of a cycle. We're born, we die, we move on, one form, then another form."

I didn't quite know what to make of this woman. She had a look of total sincerity on her face. So total it was almost, well, psychotic. Personally, I think this sort of thing—souls traveling from one body into another—is absolute rubbish, but I guess millions of people in various countries believe in it; then there's the Dalai Lama, who is the reincarnation, supposedly, of the last Dalai Lama, who was the reincarnation of the previous Dalai Lama, and so on. I don't believe this for a minute, but the Dalai Lama is very popular, he travels a lot, and he makes speeches at places like Harvard in front of thousands of people, and the audience treats him as if he was a rock star. Amazing.

Lizbeth went on with her story. She described life in the jungle in great detail, "All those vines, choking every path, and it's very hot, and so humid, and there are bugs everywhere and monkeys in the trees, and so many birds, bright-colored birds, you know; and lizards, and crocodiles in the rivers, and the village, where she was with Max, poor Max—he died quickly, and they buried him, I don't know what happened to *his* soul—and she was left alone. The villagers were kind, she learned their language, you know, she was terrified of snakes, and there were snakes absolutely *everywhere*, big snakes, little snakes, great huge snakes that could swallow a pig, and she lost courage, Kathryn, because she knew she was going to die. I saw all this, so clearly, like a vision, not a dream.... And I tried to speak to her, you know, some kind of telepathy; but it didn't work. And then something happened. Something stopped. And I realized she was dead. Her body was dead. But then I felt something, I felt something come over me, and I knew, this was Kathryn's soul, entering my body."

Okay, I said to myself; millions of people believe in reincarnation, I'll grant that, but this is the USA, this isn't some Asian country, and this woman is seriously deranged. And I wondered, too, what she wanted from me. Surely she didn't think she was entitled to the money? I had this gleeful thought: she hires a lawyer, and pays him to make a claim for part of Clara's estate, on the grounds that she was Freddy's mother, that his adoptive mother's soul had entered into her unlikely body. Of course, that claim would get nowhere. Any lawyer would tell her that. Suppose she brought a lawsuit anyway? I could just picture the look on the judge's face.

Meanwhile, how was I supposed to handle this woman? Gently, I tried to tell her that she had come to the wrong place. "I don't have anything to do with Clara Fisk's estate, that's, uh, a lawyer in San Francisco, he's in charge. His name is Gideon Grambling, I'd be happy to give you his phone number."

She burst into tears. "You don't understand. It's not the money. It's Freddy. Kathryn and I ... we want so much to see him, our dear Freddy, our baby. Our souls are longing to see him. Maybe even from a distance. Would you help me do this, Mr. May? I'd be so grateful. And I know he'd be grateful too. I'm a poor woman, Mr. May; I'm going to be homeless soon, I can't pay my rent, and I'm afraid I'll be out on the street. Freddy wouldn't want that, would he? He wouldn't want his mother to be living on the street."

A cynic might say, aha, and jump to the conclusion that this was always her motive: money. That she was just another woman with designs on the estate of the late Clara Fisk. But surely a good scam artist could come up with a better story, a better claim than the one Lizbeth seemed to be advancing.

"I'm sorry to hear about your troubles," I said. "You don't have a job?"

"I had a job. I lost it," she said, sobbing. "I used to be a nurse, I had good jobs, I worked in a hospital, but they said I was, well, unstable. I think it was the head nurse, she didn't like me, I don't know why. They said I wasn't good for the patients. But I was, Mr. May. I loved the patients. I tried to help them. I can't stay here long, without a job. I get social security. But the rents around here, I just can't pay them."

This was becoming very uncomfortable. I tried to sound sympathetic, I suggested various agencies that might help her; this was cowardly of me. She would never ever get a nursing job again, or perhaps any job at all, not in her present mental condition. She seemed uninterested. I began to realize, this woman is not, in fact, looking for money. But then what did she want? I asked her: "Did you know Kathryn well? Kathryn Lucas? I mean, before she died."

She didn't answer, and my guess was, she had never met the woman. Or had she? Anyway, she started talking about Freddy: "He's a lovely boy. A lovely boy. That's why I want to see him. Kathryn was so proud of him. How he was growing up. Dead people can see things, did you know that? She saw him through my eyes. And now he's in terrible danger. That's another reason why I have to talk to him, Mr. May. I want to warn him."

"Warn him? About what?"

"That awful woman. She's evil, she's the devil."

"What woman is that?"

"She calls herself Sybil Glass. Believe me, she's a terrible woman. I wonder sometimes, is it true, that people can sell their souls to the devil? Because, if that's something real, that woman, that's what she's done. I believe that, yes I do. And everything she says is a lie. She's not his mother! She just wants the money."

She had raised her voice; and now she was half shouting, half wailing.

"She wants to harm my boy!" she shouted. "A woman like that doesn't deserve to live. She should be squashed like a bug! Like a bug!" And then she burst out in tears.

I wanted to get rid of her in the worst way; but I also wanted to know, what on earth did she have to do with Sybil Glass. Who *was* Sybil Glass? What was her background? What did this woman know about her? Maybe she had some genuine information. I asked her if she knew Sybil Glass.

"Oh yes, I know her, I know all about her, I tell you, she's an awful woman, and she'll harm him, I know she will."

And then she was sobbing hysterically. I handed her a tissue. This was becoming awkward. I did want to know more—about her and Sybil Glass; but the timing was very bad. I had a client coming in, he was due in ten minutes, and it would be utter disaster if this crazy woman was still in my office, shouting or crying or whatever. Maybe the best way to get rid of her was to humor her, at least somewhat. So I told her that I couldn't spend more time with her, I was sorry, but I had things I had to do; but that I was so glad I had a chance to talk to her, and I'd be sure to convey her message to Freddy. "And I'll warn him about Sybil Glass. Thank you thank you, for telling me about her. I'll tell Freddy to be on his guard."

"And you'll ask him if ... I can see him...?"

"Oh yes," I said. A total lie of course. I would in fact tell Freddy not to see her under any circumstances. But what I said seemed to calm her down, and she left.

I called Zelda that evening, and told her about the visit; I described it in rich, ample detail, and I added, sarcastically, "Thanks a lot, Zelda. You really did me a favor. This woman is either a crook or a nut.... Well, I don't think she's a crook. But she's totally crazy—didn't you see that? Personally, I never want to see her again."

Zelda apologized, "Oh, I'm so sorry, Frank. I was afraid of something like that, but I was sure you'd know how to handle her. I didn't realize she was so, well, confused. I did think her story was a bit off, but she seemed sincere, I mean, about Kathryn. I hope it wasn't a problem for you."

"It's okay, I handled it," I said.

"The poor creature," Zelda said. "But she gives me an idea. I'm going to put her in my book. Not just her face, I mean, it'll be the way she behaves. I'm still working on the plot. I'll make her a sort of medicine woman in the village, who believes the spirit of an ancestor has entered her body, and an ancestor of Rodrigo killed this ancestor, and she feels she has a duty to take revenge and kill him; that'll add to the suspense."

Well, at least Zelda would get some benefit from this woman: help for the plot of her latest book. And there was at least some small chance that Lizbeth could provide some sort of information that might help Freddy. Lizbeth seemed to know something about Sybil Glass, and maybe that could be useful. I was almost tempted to ask Zelda to follow up, find out what Lizbeth could tell her about the rival mother. Zelda loved to play detective. "I want to be your assistant," she said to me once.

I said: "Assistant to what, Zelda? Are you a member of the California bar?"

She said, "Oh, Frank, you know what I mean. Your detective assistant."

I sighed. I've told her, time and again, that I'm not a detective, and don't need an assistant. But if I ever wanted one, I would be sure to call on Zelda for help.

16

As I said, I almost did give in to temptation and ask Zelda to do some quiet snooping. What was the connection between Lizbeth and Sybil?

Lizbeth obviously hated Sybil Glass. Why? I had no idea. I puzzled over this, but only for a while. After she left, I had to get back to my day job—the job that puts money in my pocket. I had a succession of clients to deal with that day and the next. No time to think about those two women. Later, I would have good reason to remember what Lizbeth had said, or rather shouted. But at the time, I put it out of my mind, along with Freddy and his various mother-figures.

Of course, I gave Freddy a somewhat censored version of Lizbeth's visit. And of course told him to avoid her at all costs. This report was given to him in person; he appeared at my office, around eleven o'clock on a Thursday morning, yawning.

"These women are driving me crazy, Frank," he said. "I'm having trouble falling asleep, and then I don't get up until ten or so. And I'm gaining weight. I can't stop eating. Potato chips, for instance. I love potato chips. They're bad for you. I love salty food, Frank. Anyway, I'm behind on all my projects. Or maybe I don't have any projects. I need somebody to take charge of me, Frank. I need to make over my life. I'm just drifting. What should I do? Got any suggestions, Frank?"

I had none.

"Maybe I should go on the web," he said. "You can find anything on the web. Of course you can find girlfriends. People do that all the time. But maybe I should try to find somebody to take care of me. I'm not bad looking, am I, Frank? Don't answer that. I'd have to be careful; if I gave too many details, like, 'Hey, I'm nice, I'm a good guy, I'm handsome, I don't smoke, and I'm filthy rich,' I'd get a zillion responses. As it is, I have all these mothers to contend with. Well, not really. The only one that's really pestering me is this Sybil person."

"How is she doing that, Freddy?"

"Well, she's polite, she's calm, and she doesn't look crazy, but wow, is she ever persistent. Letters, emails, and she even came by again, and rang the doorbell. I was in my underwear, I peeked out, and there she was. I didn't let her in."

"You did the right thing. Ignore her, and she might just go away."

"Frank, what would happen, I mean, don't get this wrong, but what if something happened to this awful woman? Okay, let's assume, she really is my mother. I mean, people don't kill their mothers, they love them, right, isn't that the Oedipus complex? I remember that from school, how boys love their mothers: me, I didn't really have a mother, so that was sort of sad. Everybody else, they could talk about their mother. Kids always complained about their mothers. More than fathers. I mean, mothers made up a bunch of rules, and so on. But it made me depressed, sort of, anyway, I kept thinking, wow, I'm different from everybody else. Maybe to me Aunt Clara was like a mother. I guess she was, kind of. She spoiled me, and I did love her. If this Sybil creature really was my mother, and I killed her, that would be really something, right? Wow. It would get on the evening news and stuff. Of course I'm not going to do that, Frank, I don't go around killing people."

"Glad to hear that, Freddy," I said. "My advice is, don't kill anybody. For one thing, I don't think you'd be good at it, and for another, they'd catch you right away. Put you in prison. And I don't think you'd like the food at San Quentin. Or anything else about the place."

"The food? Frank, hey, the food would be the least of it, right? Wow, I wouldn't last a day. All those gangs, I read about the gangs, they run the place. You know, they're in the yard, the prison yard, so you're not safe. I saw a movie about this too. They're all tough guys, guys with tattoos all over, they could kill you and it wouldn't bother them for a minute, you know? I mean, I'd be scared to death. I'd probably get a knife in my back, for sure. Or they'd rape me. They rape all the white guys in prison. That's what I heard. I don't even want to think about what would happen to me, it's too disgusting for words."

"Right, Freddy, so forget about killing this woman," I said. "Not that you were serious. Anyway, it wouldn't do you any good—killing her I mean. She'd still get the money if she was really your mother. After all, if she is your mother, all she has to do is show up here alive, which she has, so it wouldn't matter if later on she died. She'd still be entitled to her share of the estate."

"Yeah, but if she died, I'd be her heir, wouldn't I, Frank? If she was really my mother."

"Remember what I told you. About the law. You killed her, there's a good chance you'd lose the money."

"Well, suppose she died in a car crash, that happens all the time, doesn't it? Or suppose she was in some other kind of accident. That could happen, right? Or what if I hired a hitman. They do that in the movies. I guess there really is such a thing as a hitman. Hey, Frank, do you know how to hire a hitman?"

"Freddy, what do you think? Of course not. You can't get a hitman off Craigslist. Be serious, Freddy. Anyway, she's not your mother. She's a fraud. That's pretty obvious, isn't it?"

We were having fun, joking around; what we said about killing Sybil was not meant to be taken seriously. Fortunately, nobody from the police heard our conversation. Because, as you know, somebody did kill Sybil. No car crash, no accident. Murder. And, to the best of our knowledge, no hitman was involved.

17

The next day, I had a phone call from my friend (and fellow attorney) Sylvan Platt.

"Frank, my boy, can I take you to lunch?" he said. "Today, if possible? My treat. We'll go someplace very, very special."

Sylvan was a real foodie, a genuine gourmet; he had a real sense for good restaurants—and he was, in any event, good company. It happened I was free. "Okay, sure, Sylvan. I'm totally available, but what's the occasion?"

"Frank, are we still going to be friends? I'm afraid I have some bad news, and I want to soften the blow by taking you to lunch."

"Bad news? Did somebody die? Somebody I know?"

"The opposite. Somebody's alive. But don't ask me anything else. Not now, Frank. Look: there's a terrific new Japanese restaurant, Bengoshi's in Menlo Park. Very pricey, but I don't care. How about it? Can you do noon?"

Noon was perfectly fine, and I was intrigued by the conversation. Whatever did Sylvan have in mind? Somebody alive? Oh God—was this another woman, another person claiming to be Freddy's mother?

The restaurant was very elegant, festooned with red and gold lanterns. A waitress wearing a sash came and bowed and said she was our server. I looked at the menu. The prices were exorbitant. Sylvan was, as usual, elegantly dressed, in a dark blue suit, with a tie that seem to shriek at you that it cost a lot of money. He was carrying a soft leather briefcase.

We settled into a booth. "Don't look at the prices, Frank," he said. "Just enjoy. I ordered ahead of time, a special feast. Do you like sea urchin?"

"I don't know. I don't think so," I said.

"Oh well; if you don't like something, you don't have to eat it. I tell you, the food here is absolutely exquisite."

"Look, Sylvan, I'm sure you're right about the food. But you're being so damn mysterious. This is a business lunch, no?"

"Absolutely. But who says you can't enjoy a business lunch? The food part, anyway. We can talk after the meal."

The waitress came up to the booth, bowing deeply, and carrying the first course on a dark blue tray. I have to admit, it was absolutely beautiful to look at. Each of us got a bowl, filled with what looked like ice, and on top of the ice was a smooth gray rock, which was, somehow, boiling hot. We had chopsticks (of course), and the waitress gave each of us a bamboo stalk, hollowed out, with one tiny piece of meat of some sort inside of it. "You take that with your chopsticks," Sylvan said, "and you cook it yourself, on that hot gray rock. Marvelous."

The dish did, in fact, look marvelous, but I had to wonder. First of all, how much did you have to pay for this Japanese food landscape, which consisted of a single bite and which, moreover, you had to cook yourself? I wondered, too, how many more courses it would take to fill me up. In fact, these courses—there seemed to be about a dozen—did not quite satisfy my hunger. They were all small, all exquisite, each one of them presented like a work of art. I avoided eating what I thought must have been the sea urchin dish. Maybe it's delicious, but I don't like eating things that wriggle and squirm while they're alive.

At least the sea urchin was safely dead. One of the other dishes, though, contained a tiny fish, which actually *was* alive, flopping helplessly on the lacquered plate. Alive, that is, until Sylvan started eating it, with his chopsticks. "Amazing," he said. I declined this particular delicacy, and passed my plate over to Sylvan, together with this poor dying creature; Sylvan put it out of its misery, eating with great gusto.

It was quite an experience. When we were done, Sylvan paid the check, and said, "Let's have coffee and dessert." We went out, and he directed us to an upscale coffee house, just off University Avenue in Palo Alto. There Sylvan ordered "Ethiopian coffee, it's fantastic," and also picked out an "outstanding pastry; flaky, with really good fruit, an old-fashioned tart, highly recommended."

In the middle of the old-fashioned tart, I said, somewhat meekly, "Look, Sylvan, this has been great fun; and thanks for the lunch. But what's this famous bad news you're talking about?"

"I have a new client," he said, sipping slowly on his coffee. "Sybil Glass."

"Get out of here! You don't! Honestly, Sylvan, why would you take her on? The woman is almost certainly a fraud."

"That's the point, Frank," he said. "Of course I was skeptical when she first talked to me. Who wouldn't be? But she's not a fraud. She totally convinced me. That woman is Freddy's birth mother."

"What makes you think so?"

"She's got proof," he said. "I've seen it. I'll show you what I've got. I made copies." He opened the briefcase. "Here's the first item. It's a certified copy of a birth certificate. It shows that she gave birth to a son; she named the boy Frederick Glass—by the way, that's where the 'Freddy' comes from, that's why young Alexander Lucas was always called Freddy. Anyway, Sybil is the mother, and the father is listed as 'unknown.' Sybil told me it embarrassed her to admit it, but she fooled around a lot when she was young. She was studying to be a nurse, and she had sex with a couple of residents, two interns, an anesthesiologist, a young proctologist, and God knows who else. I didn't want to pry. She says she isn't sure who the father was; and it didn't matter, since she was going to give the baby up for adoption. She had decided that already."

"Okay," I said. "So she gave birth to a boy, and she named the boy Frederick. I mean, so what? How do we know this baby was Freddy? I admit, it's something of a coincidence."

"Look at the date," he said. "The year is right—and, by the way, did you know that Freddy celebrates his birthday on August 12th? I found that out. Same as the certificate."

"More coincidences," I said, but with a bit less conviction.

"You're just saying that, Frank. I know this isn't good news for you. Freddy will lose some money, but he'll have his mother back, won't he?"

"I can't see him taking up with Sybil Glass," I said. "But I could be wrong. Anyway, is that all you have? I mean, the birth certificate?"

"Oh, no. That's just for starters. Here's a letter from Kathryn Lucas, to Clara Fisk. Just read it."

He handed me a copy of a letter. It said: "Dear Aunt Clara, a quick note to let you know the big news. The adoption is going through. We'll have the official documents soon. We're going to name him Alexander, after Max's favorite uncle. We love him already, and I know you'll love him too. He's as cute as the dickens." It was signed: "Your niece, Kathryn."

I was puzzled. "Sylvan," I said, "a letter to Clara Fisk? Where on Earth did you get it?"

"Frank, I'm trying to be honest with you. But about this letter, I'm not at liberty to say. Anyway, I want to show you two more documents."

The first was a letter addressed to Sybil Glass. It was only part of a letter—a page from what was perhaps a longer letter. The signature was consequently missing; but the context made it clear that it was a letter from Kathryn Lucas. It was dated, and the date (I checked on this later) made sense—it was when Freddy was six. It began, "Dear Sybil," and it told Sybil that Max and Kathryn had gotten a generous grant from the National Science Foundation. "We're on our way to Brazil, where we'll be studying insect life in the Amazon rainforest. This is very exciting for us. Freddy is in good hands—my aunt Clara will take care of him—and he has a very nice new nanny right now; her name is Ingeborg, she's a young woman from

Germany, she's used to children, and Freddy is fond of her. We've made all the arrangements. We expect to be gone six months, perhaps somewhat longer. Of course we will miss Freddy terribly, but this is a once in a lifetime chance, and Max and I felt we had to take it."

I found this letter somewhat surprising. It seemed to assume some sort of continuing relationship between Kathryn Lucas and Sybil Glass. Freddy had been legally adopted when he was quite little. That meant the end of any formal ties to Sybil, assuming she was Freddy's birth mother. Freddy was six years old, as I said, when his adoptive parents went off to the Amazon jungle. I asked Sylvan if he knew why Kathryn wrote this letter; it was certainly the first indication that Sybil Glass, or anybody else claiming to be Freddy's mother, had had any role in the boy's life. Freddy certainly did not know her. A six year old is no infant. But Sybil Glass was a complete stranger to him.

Sylvan just shrugged and said that Sybil had given him the letter. "I guess she kept it. I haven't a clue why she did that. Or why the letter was sent in the first place."

"But what is this letter supposed to prove?"

"Well, nothing much in itself. But it's just kind of, well, corroborating. On the point that Sybil was Freddy's mother."

"Did she give you other letters?"

"Only one," Sylvan said. "I saved that for last. This one is a killer, Frank."

"A killer?"

"Read it," he said, taking a Xerox copy of a letter out of his briefcase.

This letter was dated long before the fateful trip to the Amazon. From the date, I would guess that Freddy was about one year old. The letter was from Kathryn Lucas to Sybil; it was handwritten, very neatly and precisely. "Dear Sybil," it said, "I know this hasn't been an easy process. Not for you, or for us. But thank you so much for giving Freddy up to us. You can't know how much it means to have Freddy as part of our family. We love him dearly, more and more every day. And we will carry through on our promise, believe me, now that he is ours forever." And it was signed: "Kathryn."

It was certainly an important document. But there were things about it that I found quite odd. "This letter," I said, "sure, it's significant. It backs up her claim. I don't deny that. But the implication is, that there was some sort of dispute, no? She says, it wasn't an 'easy process.' What process is she referring to? Did she object to the adoption? I guess that's what it means."

Sylvan said he had no idea, but that it hardly mattered now. The woman was obviously Freddy's birth mother, and that was that. She had a legitimate claim under Clara's will.

"Okay, okay, but didn't you ask Sybil about the thing I mentioned? What was so difficult about the process? And what promise was she referring to?"

"Well, I did ask Sybil about these things," Sylvan said. "She claims there was no dispute about the adoption; I don't know that I believe her. She said, though, that it was hard to give him up. Well, that's often the case. I've seen this before, in my practice, maybe you have, too, Frank. I asked her about this promise, what's that all about. She said, oh, they promised to take good care of her baby, her little Frederick."

Of course, time changes people, and the letter was almost twenty years old. That the promise was simply to take good care of Freddy—somehow I doubted that. The Sybil I knew, the woman I'd met, struck me as not very motherly. Cold as ice. Tough as nails. Someone who would definitely *not* care whether Max and Kathryn were good parents. Still, maybe at the time she was a different person. Maybe giving up her baby really tore at her heartstrings; maybe that's what made her cold and calculating. A real psychological trauma.

I couldn't help thinking though, that this "promise" might have referred to something else entirely. Money? I mentioned this to Sylvan.

He said, "Don't think that didn't cross my mind, Frank. But she never mentioned any such thing; and I didn't press her. And it doesn't matter, Frank, does it? These documents, they're proof that she's Freddy's mother. No question."

"If they're genuine. The birth certificate. The letters."

"Oh, Frank, give me credit for something. Brains, for instance. Absolutely. I'm a suspicious guy. You don't last in this business unless you have a certain amount of cynicism. Not to mention my two divorces. They would make cynics out of anybody. Look: Sybil actually encouraged me, she said, 'Check them out.' She said, 'I don't mind in the least,' she knew people thought she was a fraud—you and Freddy, for example. I tell you, she's the real deal. The birth certificate: absolutely genuine. And the letters—I even hired a handwriting expert, and I somehow dug up stuff, Kathryn's signature, for example, that took some doing; but actually, Clara Fisk kept some letters, we found them in her papers, and yes, these letters are from Kathryn Lucas, no question. So: are you convinced, Frank?"

"Maybe," I said. "But, Sylvan, this is really Gideon's business, not mine. You're going to make a claim against the Clara Fisk estate, right? And that's Gideon, not me."

"Oh, Frank, of course. I know that. I'm seeing Gideon tomorrow. I'm not looking forward to dealing with that creep. I'm just letting you know. After all, Freddy's your client; and this could cost him a lot of money. So that's a bit of a blow. But there's going to be plenty left, no? For Freddy."

"True, true. And I'm glad you told me. Poor Freddy. He won't like the news."

"Why not?" Sylvan said. "Hey, it's not every day you find a mother."

"You know, Sylvan," I said. "This isn't what he wanted in a mother. Maybe a dead mother, safely out of the way, would be better than a living mother, if that mother turned out to be Sybil Glass. In other words, better dead than Sybil Glass."

If that was Freddy's wish, it would soon come true.

18

Of course, I had to report my lunch talk with Sylvan to Freddy. Sylvan had provided me with Xerox copies of the documents, and I showed them to Freddy when he came to see me, at about eleven o'clock the next morning. He was—no surprise—unhappy with this news.

"Do I have to see this woman?" he asked me.

"Freddy," I said. "You don't have to see anybody you don't want to. You're an adult, and you can make your own choices."

"Frank," he said, "do you really think she's my mother?"

I equivocated. "Well, she has some strong arguments; but I'm not sure I'm convinced."

Poor Freddy. He was obviously disappointed. "I don't want this woman for a mother. She's not what I had in mind," he said.

I didn't want to tell him, we don't get to pick our parents. But of course, in a way, a man like Freddy was free—if not to pick his parents, at least to fantasize about them. Which he did.

"Like I told you," he said, "I used to daydream about my mother. Or mothers. The two of them. Both mothers. My mom the prom queen, young, pretty, I can see her with a white dress; and her boyfriend, my dad, the football stud. They were like, I mean, sort of Romeo and Juliet, and they're dead, and all that's left is me, Freddy, the lovechild. Then there's my adoptive mom, and there she is in the jungle, dying there with the snakes and everything, and the natives, she's in this village, and she burning up with fever, and she's going to die, and her last thought was of her Freddy, back home. That's what I had in mind. I know it's stupid, but ... whatever."

"I'm sorry, Freddy. Really, though, even if this woman *is* your mother, that doesn't mean you have to have anything to do with her. You can just ignore her. Look: it's essentially Gideon's issue—that's because her claim, if she has one, is against the estate of Clara Fisk. You can stay out of it. If there's any problem, I'll handle it."

"Thank God for that. I don't want to do anything with that awful woman."

"You don't have to. Besides, you hardly know her."

"And I don't want to know her," he said. "She can just take the money, and leave me alone. I hope she doesn't come around pestering me. Maybe I should just go away someplace. I've got all this money. I could go to Brazil or wherever. Wow, there's an idea, Frank. I can hire a boat, and go up the Amazon, looking for my other mother."

"Freddy, you can do whatever you want."

"Well, I won't do that, actually. I mean, the Amazon. It's too hot there, I think. It's jungle. You could die from the heat. I was in New Orleans once, in summer, and I didn't think I'd get out of there alive, I mean, the humidity. We're spoiled here, we're in California, we don't have humidity. In New Orleans, I tell you, the mosquitos, they could eat you up alive. And I hate snakes, I won't even look at them in the zoo and bugs, cockroaches, horrible flying bugs—the place must be crawling with that stuff, I mean, that's what the jungle is like. Why they wanted to go there, God only knows. Looking for beetles and ants. Crazy. Hey, maybe I should go to the Riviera and look at the girls in bikinis, that's a better idea."

"Do it," I said, "if that's what you want."

"Hey, it's almost lunch time," he said. "Come to lunch, Frank. I'm having lunch with my friend Derek, and I'm not really in the mood. Sometimes I can hardly stand him. I don't want to talk about this mother business."

I was reluctant; but Freddy was a client, after all, and a potentially lucrative one, so I agreed.

The arrangement was to meet Derek at Il Duomo di Firenze, an upscale Italian restaurant on University Avenue, in Palo Alto. "I'll drive," Freddy said. His car was a bright yellow sports car. It was parked at a meter on the street; there was a parking ticket on the windshield.

"I never put money in these meters," he said. "I don't carry change, it's too much trouble." He took the ticket and tore it up. That was Freddy to the core.

"Freddy," I said, "you tore up that ticket, I wouldn't do that. You could get in trouble."

He said, "Oh, I've had lots of these tickets. I always tear them up. I'll pay them, eventually, it's just too much of a bother to do it right away. Hey, Frank, you're my lawyer, can you take care of it? I'll give you the money."

It's hardly my usual line of work; but I said I would try.

Derek was waiting for us, at the restaurant, in a booth. He was a striking young man—striking in every way, looks, brains, personality. He seemed completely different from Freddy. They made an odd couple. Freddy called Derek his best friend, "We're buddies," he said, "well sort of. Half the time, we're mad at each other."

Derek had dark hair, a kind of cleft chin, and striking green eyes. He wore a light blue dress-shirt, open at the neck; blue jeans, but expensive looking ones; and striking and stylish black shoes. He looked like what I think he was: a bold, aggressive, and ambitious young man. A young man on the make. I wondered if he really liked Freddy, I wondered what the basis of their friendship was. Was it Freddy's money?

"I wanted you to come along," Freddy said. "Because Derek and I were going to talk business. Derek's a law student. You know that. He knows a lot. I mean, not as much as you, Frank, he's just a beginner. But he's giving me good ideas about charities, things to leave my money to. I told you were handling my will and that kind of thing. Right now, I'm thinking of endowing stuff. Frank, you'll handle the legal end. You know, I could leave money to friends, but I decided not to."

"Hey, buddy, you don't have any friends," Derek said. "Only me. You could leave the money to me, if you felt like it."

"Oh sure," Freddy said. "I could. Only you'd want to kill me, and I can't run the risk."

Amazing how many people were discussing murder and its legal consequences. It was as if they foresaw what was going to happen. At this point, though, I added my two cents. I tried to do it with a light, half-joking tone. "You can leave your money to Derek," I said. "He won't kill you. California law tells him not to. He'd lose the money if he kills you. If you kill somebody, you can't inherit from them. So you're safe from Derek."

"Oh well," Derek said, "I'd make it look like an accident. That's what I'd do. I'd figure out a way."

"Hey, Derek," Freddy said, "I think you could actually do it. You've got the balls, don't deny it. I mean, if you thought you could get away with it. That's why I got to be careful with you, old buddy. But I'm worth more alive than dead. Like, take today, here we are this restaurant, and it's my treat, I'm going to pick up the bill; but in my will, sorry, Derek, I'm not going to leave you a dime. So you better keep me healthy and alive."

"Freddy, don't rub it in," Derek said, "you lucky bastard, you've got all this money. That's what I want, money. You can sit on your ass and do nothing, if you want to. Or make a movie or whatever, get to meet the big stars in Hollywood. I'm going to have money, too, but I have to wait, I have to work, I have to get it the hard way. That's the only way, for me. The only practical way. I didn't have a filthy rich aunt, like you did. All I've got are my brains. They got me into Stanford Law School. Someday I'll be a big shot lawyer. Like you, Frank."

I didn't appreciate the sarcasm. "I make a living," I said, feebly.

"Well, okay, but partners, the ones in the big firms here in Silicon Valley, and I guess in New York too, and other places, they make millions. I guess they deserve it, all the shit they go through. Starting with law school. Man, I tell you, it's a colossal pain in the ass."

I said, "Some people like it. I didn't mind it, actually. Some of it was boring, but that's true of all sorts of things."

"You couldn't have liked civ pro. That's civil procedure," he said to Freddy. "Nobody could like it. Prof. Hasseldorf, I swear, he's been teaching it for a hundred years and you can tell. He's just as bored as we are. If I could get myself some rich bitch, somebody willing to support me because she's hot for my body, I swear I'd do it. And I'd quit law school in a heartbeat."

Freddy asked: "You got anybody in mind?"

"Ha! Wouldn't you like to know. But, okay, yes, I've got a new girlfriend. She's great, she's really good-looking—but she doesn't have any money, that's a real drawback."

"Money isn't everything," Freddy said.

"Yeah, easy for you to talk. You're rolling in dough."

"Hey, Derek," Freddy said, "you hiding her or something? Most of the time, you're happy to show off your girlfriends."

Derek seemed to hesitate. "Well, Freddy, to be honest; it's a little awkward."

"Awkward? What does that mean? Who is she, Derek?"

He hesitated again. "All right. I shouldn't keep secrets from you, Freddy. It's somebody with, well, a connection with you."

"A connection to me? What does that mean?"

"Her name is Ella. Does that mean something to you?"

"Oh God. Not that Ella...."

"The very one. Ella Fisk-Potter. Granddaughter of that guy, Homer Fisk, who was married to your Aunt Clara."

"I knew you knew her. Recently anyway," Freddy said, "but I didn't know you were ... well, close. I mean, are you screwing her, Derek?"

"Hey, nosy, aren't you! Anyway, you won't believe where I met her."

"I have no idea. Don't give me riddles, Derek. Where did you meet her?"

"At your Aunt Clara's funeral. Honest to God. People were milling around in the funeral parlor, God those places are creepy, and I came because of you, Freddy, I knew you really liked the old lady, and now she was dead, so I thought, I'll drop in, pay my respects. And I saw this young woman, she was really striking looking—you weren't around, Freddy, I don't know where you were, talking to some of the other people or something—and I said, 'Hi, are you a relative of the deceased?'

or something like that. Not that I gave a shit whether she was or not, I was just trying to be friendly, if you know what I mean."

"And what did she say?"

"She looked right at me. Not exactly glaring, but not so friendly. And then she said, cold as ice, 'No I'm not a relative of this woman. Though maybe you could say I was. Fact is, I was her step-granddaughter, but she probably didn't know me from Adam.' I said, 'She wouldn't know anybody from Adam, she's dead after all.' And she laughed, and she asked who the hell was I, was *I* a relative or something? And I told her, 'No, I'm just here because I'm a friend of Freddy Lucas, he's the old lady's nephew. Anyway, what did she mean, step-granddaughter, what's that all about?' And she said, 'Homer Fisk was my grandfather,' and I said, 'no shit,' or words to that effect, and I said, 'Why did you come here?' and she said, 'Maybe to spit on this woman's coffin, or make sure she's dead, because I hated her.' I said, 'You hated her? Why is that?' And she said, 'She got all the money. My mother should have gotten it. My mother, she was the old guy's daughter, his only child, actually. And they had this huge fight, they weren't speaking and so on. But who knows what would have happened? Fathers and daughters, they usually make up after a while. Not this time. This bitch, this Clara person, she came along, and she seduced the old goat, and all the money went to her.'"

Freddy seemed really startled. "Wow, Derek," he said. "That's amazing. And ... well, you started dating her? Right after that?"

"Why not? Frankly, she was really something. She was fascinating. And sexy as all get-out. Like she said, her mom was Homer's daughter, Griselda. I said to Ella, 'I'm really interested, tell me all about your family, and why it happened that you mom didn't get any money.' And she told me the story. Her mother and her grandfather, they had this horrendous fight. Because of the guy the daughter got involved with, Ella's father. Anyway, Homer thought he was a gold-digger and a conman, and he probably was. But Griselda, I guess she was infatuated with the guy, maybe he took her virginity, who knows. They ran off together, actually got married, probably in Las Vegas; and that's when the old man cut her off without a penny. The marriage lasted maybe a year or two, long enough for Ella to get born, anyway. The guy, Potter, he was a real piece of work. He had other women, maybe other men, who knows, maybe animals, and he was as crooked as they come. Griselda had to pay him off to get rid of him, I guess she had a trust fund or something, anyway, in the end she was stuck with a kid, and no money. But she was as stubborn as her father. Ella never actually met her grandfather. She told me all of this stuff, all about her life and hard times, and the more we talked, her eyes were flashing and I thought, I could really go for this woman, you could almost get an erection just talking to her—if I can be blunt about it—and she said, 'Let's get out of this damn place, it was crazy of me to come, let's go someplace else' and I said, 'Okay, where?' and she said, 'My place or your place?' and I knew, when she said that, this was going to go somewhere. Maybe she liked my looks, how about that? So we went to her apartment, and one thing led to another."

"Wow," Freddy said. "You're a lucky dog. When a guy says, one thing led to another, we know what the thing was that led to the other thing, and we know what that other thing was. Probably the same night, right Derek?"

"Hey, I don't kiss and tell, Freddy, I don't ask you about your girlfriends, assuming you've got any, which I doubt. But here's the thing: where did the money actually go? Homer's money, I mean. Went to your Aunt Clara, and now it's yours, Freddy. So you kind of stole my girlfriend's money. If you and your aunt hadn't meddled with old Homer, if she hadn't gotten her hooks into the old geezer, look, maybe I'd be the rich one, I mean, because of Ella; and you'd have nothing, Freddy, you'd be a pauper. Maybe you'd even have to work for a living. Life's totally unfair. Totally."

"For sure," Freddy said. "I've got the money; so that isn't fair. But now you've got Ella, so that's unfair too."

"She's not your type, Freddy," Derek said. "For one thing, she's a hot property, and I don't think you could handle her. She's tough, too, like me. And she loves money, like me. We're two of a kind. And she has other attractions, which I won't go into here."

"It's okay to like money," Freddy said. "I mean, I like money myself. You know that, Derek. But there's other stuff, too."

"Other stuff? Like what? With money, you can buy the other stuff. You can buy happiness, don't let people kid you. Hey, Freddy, what do you want that you can't buy? Nothing."

I thought (to myself), as I sat there listening: There's lots of things poor Freddy can't buy. Strength of character for one. Better friends than Derek. And most people have a mother. You can't buy a mother. Poor Freddy: *He* can't buy a mother; but a whole army of mothers are trying to buy him.

"Anyway," Derek said, "You don't have to feel sorry for me. I'm going to make money someday; that's in the bag. When I'm a big, fancy lawyer, in a big firm, I'll be making a fortune. And I'll be a real hard-nosed boss. I'll make the associates grovel, I'll make them do all the work while I go off sailing in my yacht. With Ella maybe. "

"Is that Ella's plan, too?" Freddy asked. "To stick with you, until you get rich?"

"Maybe. But maybe she's got another plan, Freddy. One you wouldn't like."

"Yikes. What would that be?"

"How about a plan to sue the living daylights out of you? Or rather, sue the daylights out of your aunt's estate? Getting back the money that should have gone to her, or her mother, or both of them. With interest, naturally. Millions of dollars."

Here I felt I had to chime in—in defense of Freddy. "That wouldn't be an easy lawsuit," I said, "legally speaking. In my opinion, she'd have almost no chance of winning."

He shrugged his shoulder, and then laughed—a bit nervously I felt. "You can disinherit your own daughter, your next of kin? Is that legal?"

Obviously, he hadn't boned up on the probate code; and maybe he hadn't bothered to take a course on trusts and estates, or on estate planning, in law school. I reminded him that, in this country, unlike a lot of countries, you can easily disinherit a child—a wife is harder—but a child, it's duck soup.

And I told him that Homer's will, which was professionally drafted, surely took care of that detail. Freddy was quiet, which was unusual for him.

"And a million years have gone by," I said. "No way could she win."

"Well, we'll see," Derek said. "Look: I'm just reporting stuff from Ella."

As advertised, Freddy picked up the bill, but he seemed disturbed, which didn't surprise me. The lunch ended on a somewhat frosty note. We all went our separate ways.

The lunch was somewhat upsetting, for me as well as for Freddy. The last thing we needed was trouble from Ella Fisk-Potter. If she, or her mother, or both of them, actually wanted to sue, I was sure they would lose, but they might be able to force some sort of settlement, just to get rid of them.

What I didn't know, but soon found out, was that Ella Fisk-Potter had more than one string to her bow.

19

Another thing I didn't realize then—since (despite my mythical powers of detection) I had no way of peering into the future—was that I was, one by one, meeting people who were or would become likely suspects in the murder of Sybil Glass. The motive was and remained murky, to say the least. On the list, you had to put Freddy himself. Of course, I absolutely couldn't see him as a killer. One prime candidate was Lizbeth; and now I could add Ella Fisk-Potter. More on this later.

The morning after this lunch with Freddy and Derek, I had a phone call from Gideon Grambling. I had called him many times, and each time it was aggravating in a major way; but getting a call *from* the great man was an extremely rare event.

"Frank," he said, "what is it with you? Every time I get entangled with you, every time we have a client or any legal matter in common, some ridiculous, weird, and unsavory element appears to make my life difficult. I am so sorry I ever got involved with the estate of Clara Fisk. I should have known better. Of course, I knew about Homer Fisk, he was a true gentleman. I believe he was distantly related to the Getty family, and to some of the oldest families in the city, all the way back to the days of the gold rush. Fine, upstanding people, people of culture, people on the board of the opera; of course, I didn't know Fisk when he was young, though I did meet him once or twice when he was already elderly, and already married to that woman...."

"Gideon," I said, "why are you calling me? Was there something you wanted to ask me?"

"I want to know if you're acquainted with a woman named Ella Fisk-Potter."

"I haven't met her. But I know who she is."

"Frank, it's bad enough to have all these women who claim to be the mother of Alexander Lucas, but now, on top of that, this woman who shows up in my office—she somehow talked her way in, but never mind how she got there—the point is, she wants to contest the will of Homer Fisk, can you imagine, after all these years? I told her, of course, that it was out of the question, no court would allow such a thing, and she was as bold as brass, a brazen creature if I ever saw one; and she said, 'Well, we'll see about that.' I told her she was wasting her time and, in any event, I did not handle that estate, it was handled by one of the attorneys at Globus, Mervin, and Dimmering; but she said, 'Yes, but you are in charge of the estate of Clara Fisk, and that estate is made up entirely of stolen money.'"

"Stolen money?"

"Her very words, 'stolen money.' And I said, 'Young woman, I cannot allow that kind of wild accusation to be made and I would prefer it if you left, I am a busy man,' and so on. But she started talking about a section of the California Probate Code, would you believe it? And how Clara Fisk had murdered her husband and stolen the money. I felt like saying, are you out of your mind? At that point, she was muttering something about a diary, but I cut her off, and told her I would have nothing further to do with her. I suggested that she leave the premises. She did, but on the way out she said, 'Ask Frank May about the diary, he knows what I'm talking about.' All right: *Do* you know what she was referring to?"

"Maybe I do, and maybe I don't," I said.

"Frank, that kind of answer is simply intolerable. I demand an explanation. Do you or don't you know what this is all about? Whose diary? I can't tell you how much I dislike these sordid affairs. I have a reputation, I don't need to tell you about it, I've been chair of committees of the San Francisco bar, I have clientele who come from the most exclusive circles. It would be an utter disaster for me to have my name mixed up in anything sordid; and the notion that Clara Fisk murdered her husband is as sordid as you could get; and besides, it's absolutely ridiculous, not to mention that it's ancient history at best. If I could think of a good way to get rid of this blasted estate, believe me, I would, but what respectable attorney, what attorney in his right mind, would want to get involved in an estate with this sort of allegation hanging over its head? I would of course have a duty to make full disclosure...."

"Gideon, calm down," I said. "I don't think this woman has a case; and you don't think so either. My advice to you is just to ignore the whole business. Tell your receptionist not to let her in—you're good at that sort of thing."

"Well, I can do that, I suppose. But even if I can get rid of this Ella Fisk-Potter person, I can't exclude that other creature, Sybil Glass. Frankly, she seems to have at least a claim, much as I'd like to think of her as an outright fraud. Your friend Sylvan is representing her. He's shown me certain documents— he showed them to you as well, he told me that. It's a colossal headache. The whole thing is ironic. The estate itself is in apple-pie condition; Clara Fisk used the services of Shepherd Wrightman, he's with the leading accounting firm in San Francisco. The investments were sound, the records were in total order. I had reason to believe the estate would be no trouble to administer at all. I am, as you know, the executor. But now...."

"Really, Gideon, you're not listening. Sybil Glass is one thing. Ella Fisk-Potter is another. I told you, pay no attention to her. She's not going to sue the estate. At least I don't think so. She's bluffing. That's my opinion."

"I hear you, Frank, I'm not deaf, and I'm not an idiot. But you haven't said a word about this diary—what it is, and why she mentions it."

"You're right, Gideon, I haven't said anything. And I'm not going to. Confidentiality," I said, using a word that, among lawyers, has the power to shut off discussion, with tremendous effect. I made it clear I was not going to say another word about any diary. Gideon was furious, but there was nothing he could do about it. Essentially, that ended the conversation.

20

Derek had told me, or maybe warned me would be a better way to put it, that a possible visit from Ella Fisk-Potter was in the cards. This happened the very next day after my conversation with Gideon. Ella called in the morning, introduced herself, and said it was urgent. I could have pushed her off for a day or so, but I have to admit I was curious about her, and wanted to meet her. My curiosity sometimes gets me in trouble. It's like an itch that simply has to be scratched. I told myself it was best to get it over with as soon as possible. I arranged to see Ella in the late afternoon.

She was, I have to admit, a striking woman, tall, with long black hair and impressive green eyes. She looked vaguely Spanish or Italian—she had a kind of dark, Mediterranean look. She was dressed in a gray pantsuit, and I noticed rings on some of her fingers, but no wedding ring. She seemed about the same age as Derek and Freddy.

She got right down to business; there was no small talk, no pleasantries.

"Derek spoke to you about me," she said. "You're Freddy's lawyer. You know that I'm planning to file a lawsuit against his aunt's estate and since he's the main beneficiary ... well, that's why I'm here."

She added, before I could say anything, "And yes, I have a lawyer. And, yes, you'll hear from him in due course. But I wanted to come to you directly. I don't trust lawyers. I particular don't trust that Grambling person, the one in San Francisco. He's a cold, calculating, snobbish snake. I have nothing but contempt for him. Well, my lawyer will deal with him. Derek thought you would at least listen to me, and hear what I have to say."

I told her that this visit was highly irregular. I said I didn't want to be rude, but perhaps I should have told her not to come. Our interests were completely adverse to each other. I was Freddy's lawyer, and her lawsuit which was, I said, frankly quite preposterous, would, if it succeeded, cost him millions of dollars.

"Preposterous? I think not," she said.

I explained to her why I thought it was: the passage of time was an insuperable barrier; you simply can't waltz in, decades later, and overturn everything that had been done on a sizable estate. The estate had been closed for many years, and the assets completely distributed. I told her I thought she had absolutely no grounds for such a lawsuit.

"But I do," she said. "And you know I do."

"I won't comment on that. I could point out, though, that any claim you might have is really your mother's claim. And she's still living, isn't she?"

"I'm not an idiot," she said. "Don't you think I've considered that? I have power of attorney from my mother. Yes, she's alive. She lives someplace in the woods, in Oregon, with her current boyfriend; the latest in a long series of boyfriends, if you can call them that. Look, my mother never forgave my grandfather, and she swore she'd have nothing to do with him, or his money. She ran off with this guy, my biological father, he was a completely worthless jerk ... but he lasted long enough to get her pregnant. When he found out that there wasn't going to be any money—because my grandfather had cut her off—he said goodbye, or maybe I should say, *didn't* say goodbye. Anyway, he took off and nobody's seen him since.

"Meanwhile, she bounced around from this to that and whatever, making a total mess of her life. She became a hopeless alcoholic, and I was in a foster home for a while. Then she swore off the stuff, and got me back, which was, frankly, bad luck for me. Next phase of her life she turned into some sort of ridiculous religious fanatic, then she became vegan and joined a commune—a complete collection of weirdos—and there was a succession of men, one more kooky or worthless than the next. If it was up to her, I'll be honest, there wouldn't be a lawsuit. But I'm made out of different stuff from my mother. I left home—if you could call it a home—when I was sixteen, I put myself through college, I earned my own living, waiting on tables, any odd job that I could get, and all the while I thought about money. It irked me, here I was, the granddaughter, the only granddaughter, of a guy who was a multi-millionaire, and I'm washing dishes in a restaurant, I'm waiting on tables, I'm doing all kinds of miserable jobs, and I should be rich. So that's what I'm doing now: I'm trying to claim my rightful inheritance. I talked my mother into signing this power of attorney; and here I am."

I couldn't help asking, "Why right now? Why do you think you have a case?"

She hesitated a minute. Then she said: "I told you what I think of that creep, Grambling. When Clara Fisk died, I tried to get in touch with him. Wasn't easy. It was like trying to reach the Pope or something. But I'm not easily scared off. I asked him point blank, was there something in the will for me, or my mother, or both of us? He refused to say, but when the will was filed, I marched down to the court house and I asked to see a copy. Some snot-nosed clerk wanted to know what I wanted it for, and I had to tell her none of your business, it's a public record. And of course when I got it and read it, there wasn't a word in it about me or my mother. The old bitch left us nothing."

"But why would you expect something?"

"You don't know?"

"Know about what?"

"We got money over the years. Payments. Went into a bank account, in my mother's name. I got power of attorney over that, too. When the old bitch died, the payments stopped. I always assumed the money came from her. It was deposited directly, and there was something hush-hush about it; we never really knew where it came from. But from who else? It had to be her. Guilt money. Listen: we really needed that money. And now we're not getting it. That's one of the reasons why I'm doing this stuff."

I had to wonder, why would Clara Fisk make payments to Homer's daughter? A woman she never met. It could be a guilty conscience; that was certainly possible. Still, I was puzzled.

But Ella couldn't have known about the diary. She couldn't have known that Clara Fisk was responsible for Homer's death. She must have learned that from Derek. I asked her, in as innocent a voice as I could, how she came to know Derek.

"I met him at the funeral. Clara Fisk's funeral. Why did I go? I think it was fate, karma, something like that. Not that I believe in that bullshit. But it was a turning point. I was nosing around, maybe I went out of spite—at that point, I still had hopes that Clara left us money, so maybe that had something to do with it—anyway, I went. And there was Derek. He was Freddy's buddy. We clicked, him and me, right then and there, in front of the stupid coffin. Meeting him, that was crucial. Not that he's anything special. He thinks he is, but he isn't. He totally full of himself, like so many guys. You could see right through him. He was like some sort of horny frat boy. After ten minutes of talking to me, it was like his tongue was hanging out, it was like he was wearing a sign about how he wanted to have sex with me. I thought, why not? I didn't have anything to do that night. I said to myself, let's see where this goes. And that's how it started."

"And why was Derek so important to you?" I asked. I knew the answer already, but I wanted to hear it from her.

"He wasn't important at first. Just another guy. But then, it got more serious. On his part, anyway. And he told me about the diary, Clara's diary. Freddy, the fool, let Derek borrow it. And Derek told me what it said."

"Why did he do that?"

"Figure it out for yourself," she said. "I'm not going to give you an answer. The thing is, it's evidence, that diary. It shows that Clara Fisk murdered her husband. Under California law, she can't inherit. Derek told me that."

This was getting very uncomfortable. It was obvious I should not be talking to this woman; I shouldn't be making comments, I shouldn't be responding to anything she said, I should be talking to her lawyer, if I was talking to anyone, and I needed to coordinate anything I did with Freddy.

And I was wondering about something else: should I talk to Freddy about his alleged friend, Derek? It was clear to me that Derek was playing a very dubious game. Why would he talk about the diary with Ella Fisk-Potter? It would only give her ammunition for her lawsuit. And if she won the lawsuit, or got some sort of settlement out of the Clara Fisk estate, she would become a rich woman. Maybe Derek was so besotted with this woman, that he was willing to betray his friend if that would help her in her search for big money.

I told Ella that I could not continue the conversation. About her lawsuit, about the diary, or about almost anything. "I'd be happy to discuss any of these matters with your attorney, but in any event, whatever I do, I have to have my client's consent. You have to understand, I represent *him*, and I have to consider what's in his interests."

"Oh, don't give me that lawyer talk. As for Freddy, you can probably twist him around your little finger. He's a complete fool, a big overgrown baby, and you know it. And let me tell you something else: this diary—or anyway, the juicy part, the murder part—I've shared this information with somebody else. You might be interested in knowing who it is."

"Okay, tell me. Who?"

"A woman named Sybil Glass," she said.

I have to admit, this threw me for a loop. So Sybil, too, knew about the diary; knew about the strange death of Homer Fisk. Why on earth would Ella talk to her? What did she have to gain from this conversation? My brain started to whirl around like some kind of child's toy. The two women had very different interests. They had the same motive, no doubt: money. But Sybil wanted to get a chunk of Clara's estate for herself, while Ella, on the other hand, wanted to strip the estate of all or most of its money. Was she trying to form some kind of alliance with Sybil? So that Sybil would agree to pay Ella off, if Ella agreed to drop her lawsuit? Or did Ella promise to pay off Sybil, if she won *her* lawsuit, or got some favorable settlement?

Clearly, though, Ella wanted me to know something about her plans, her strategy. She was a careful, calculating woman. If she told me this or that, it was because she *wanted* me to know. But what were the things she *didn't* tell me? The things she absolutely *didn't* want me to know?

I had no answer to this question. None at all.

21

I was busy with work the next few days, absorbed in the problems of a whole slew of clients, and I almost forgot about Freddy, Sybil (his presumptive mother), and his friend Derek, not to mention Ella and the rest of that crew. I also became absorbed with a major crisis at home, this time the abject failure of the hot water heater. We use a local company for that sort of crisis; I tried desperately to reach them, and got the run-around. I left multiple messages, asking them to call back. Eventually, somebody did call back. And, yes, a man could and would come out to the house the next day, sometime between eight a.m. and noon.

I protested, of course, that nobody would be home during that time period, that we both worked for a living, which is what people do these days, and couldn't they be more specific about the *when*? Did it have to be a four-hour "window"? Of course they *could* be more forthcoming, but as usual they chose not to and since we, all of us, the whole civilized world, we're all helpless against the tyranny of plumbers, carpenters, gas and electric company workers, roofers, television repairmen, and the rest of that motley crew, who are, I suppose, themselves all rebelling against the tyranny of people who ordinarily outrank them in the social hierarchy, and who they ordinarily have to treat with deference and respect. Anyway, in the end I had to agree, rearrange my schedule, and stay home.

Some people have macro-power, like the President of the United States, and the head guy in China, whatever they call him. Some people have micro-power, repairmen very notably, maybe plumbers most of all. And, oh yes, ticket agents at the airport and, again, people who work for the Department of Motor Vehicles. They have an awful lot of micro-power. And by God they use it.

Maybe they don't live a great life. They certainly aren't rich. Maybe they have unhappy marriages. Maybe they're sex-starved. Who knows? I certainly wouldn't want to work at the motor vehicle department. And I wouldn't want to be a plumber, for example. Can anybody really love fixing toilets and mucking about with sewers? Or take roofers: people call them in after a rain storm; water is trickling through the ceiling, ruining their favorite sofa, or making a mess in the kitchen. Is it fun to climb around on the roof, especially when it's raining? Lots of these jobs are awful jobs, I think. But they have one fantastic perk: you can lord it over ordinary people, and even not so ordinary people. You can torture them with forms, with long lines, with endless delays (at the DMV), or make them cool their heels at home for hours and hours, waiting for the guy to come and fix things. And the rest of us have no way to fight back.

The hot-water heater man actually appeared at 11:45. I was beginning to think he was never coming. He said I was the last person on his list for the morning. I'm always the last on the list. Who on earth is first on the list? Anybody? I never met that guy.

But I didn't complain. I was grateful that the man came at all. And he fixed the problem. We had hot water again.

That was all to the good. Yet my karma was acting up; whatever gets bad karma going was working overtime during that period. The very next day, a plumbing issue erupted. I mentioned this before. And then came Freddy's phone call. It was just after I got to the office, exhausted by plumbing trauma. I was hardly in the mood for bad news.

There I was, listening to what I could scarcely believe. Sybil Glass was dead. Somebody had murdered Sybil Glass. Shot her to death. And her body had been found, on Freddy's own property. Disaster.

"Frank, I gotta see you," he said.

"Sure thing."

"I mean, right away, Frank. Can you do it?"

Of course I could. I would go out of my way to accommodate a client like Freddy. As it happened, I had nobody else scheduled. An hour later, he was sitting in front of me.

"I'm in deep shit, Frank," he said. "This is something I just can't deal with. Honest to God, Frank, I never go up there, you know, there's a kind of hill behind the house. It's all wild, the gardener doesn't touch it. It's like nature. This thing is killing me, Frank. They wanted me to identify the body, can you imagine? I told them I was too upset. Anyway, somebody else identified it, don't ask me any details. Frank, can you help me?"

"I'd love to help you, Freddy. But ... what kind of help do you mean? Do you mean, you'd like a criminal lawyer?"

"I think so."

"Why, Freddy? They don't think you did it, do they?"

"Frank, I don't know what they think. I'm a wreck."

I said: "Criminal law isn't my field, Freddy. Look, if you had an eye problem, you wouldn't go to a brain surgeon, you'd go to a specialist who does eyes."

"But couldn't you do some stuff, the simple stuff? I mean, do I really need somebody who's an expert? I ... I just want somebody who can go with me if the police want to question me or something. Somebody to tell them, 'No, you can't ask him that.' You know, like I see in the movies. The lawyer, he sits next to the guy, and kind of whispers about what you can say, and so on. Frank, this is going to kill me."

I told him again, this wasn't the kind of thing I was comfortable doing. I would be happy to recommend an excellent criminal lawyer. And I tried to be very sympathetic. I told him I understood his feelings, anybody would get super upset if a murder took place on their property, and especially if the victim was somebody they knew. That was only natural. And I doubted (I said) that anybody really thought Freddy was a suspect.

"I don't know, Frank. I wasn't home when they found her," he said. "I was away. Two, three days. The whole weekend. I was in Santa Barbara. Drove there on Friday ... they said maybe she was already dead when I left. Wow, doesn't that mean they think it's maybe me, Frank?"

"No, no, I don't think so, Freddy," I said. Of course, in truth I had no idea. "They just have to ask questions. That's their job. Maybe they'll find out, when they get all the medical reports, that she did die while you were out of town. By the way, Freddy, what were you doing in Santa Barbara?"

"Nothing much. Just wanted to get away, just get out of here. All this fuss, this business about Aunt Clara's estate, it's making me super nervous. Couldn't stand it. These women. And that lawyer, Gideon, he gives me a rash. I felt, I got to get some fresh air, if you know what I mean. Got in the car and drove and drove. Down the coast. And when I got there, I just hung out, you know, went to the beach, walked around, that sort of thing. I needed a break, Frank, I really did."

Freddy was a fairly incompetent liar. Even from his tone of voice I could tell: this wasn't the gospel truth. And he didn't look me in the eye when he made this little speech.

"Freddy," I said, "you're going to have to be open and above board. With the police, for sure. If you start telling lies, there's going to be big trouble. Believe me. And, by the way, that goes for me, too. You have to tell me the truth. Freddy, I'm on your side. You're got to be honest with me. And I have the feeling, you're not giving me the full story. Are you?"

"Well, not exactly."

"What do you mean, not exactly?"

He hesitated a bit. "I mean ... look, Frank. I wasn't alone. You're not going to believe this. I was with somebody. In Santa Barbara."

"What do you mean, you were with somebody? Who?"

"Okay. I'll tell you. I was with Ella."

"You were with Ella? Derek's girlfriend Ella?"

"Well, ex-girlfriend, I guess. I'll give you the whole story. I'm only human, Frank. And I'm a guy. I'm a normal guy, if you know what I mean. Ella ... she actually came on to me. Came to see me, in my house. Actually came. Rang the doorbell. Man, was I surprised. It was the morning, I was still in my pajamas. I thought it was somebody delivering something. But there she was. She kind of introduced herself, and she said, 'Freddy, can I come in, I want to talk to you?' and that sort of thing. So I said, 'Sure, sure.' I was kind of embarrassed, you can imagine. She kept looking at me, like she was giving me the once over.

"And then she said, 'I have something I want to tell you. I'm through with Derek, that's over and done with.' I mean, she told me point blank, she was dropping him like a hot potato. She said to me, 'He's not my type, not really.' So I said, 'Well, who is, Ella?' And she said, 'You, Freddy.' So I said, 'What type is that? The handsome type? The sexy type?' I mean, I was joking. She said, 'Oh, you're good-looking alright; but good-looking guys are a dime a dozen. You're different. You're filthy rich.' She came right out and said it."

"And you liked that, Freddy?"

"Well, it was honest. She didn't give me a line of crap. Hey, my aunt married a rich old creep. Homer Fisk; why shouldn't Ella throw herself at a rich *young* guy? And, like she said, I'm a presentable guy, right? I'm not ugly, I don't have warts, I don't have body odor, I take two showers a day, and I work out, I work on my abs, keep fit, hey, I'm okay, a lot of girls like me, they always did, there was one girl in high school, Megan Blitzblau, she had the hots for me. Practically threw herself at me. So why not Ella? The money is an added attraction. I mean, that's the truth, isn't it? She said, 'Look Freddy, you've got money, you can go to any restaurant you want, you can take trips, you can fly first-class, so doesn't that mean you can have all the women you want? And I don't mean sluts,' she said. 'I mean women like me.'"

I had to admit, it was a novel approach. "And you went for it, Freddy?"

"Like I said, I was in my pajamas. I swear she was ready to do stuff, on the spot. I think I was blushing, honest to God. It was like, wow, this doesn't happen to me every day, Frank. She saw I was, well, embarrassed. She said, 'Look, I'm not going to rape you, Freddy, but I want to get to know you better, if you know what I mean. Let's go someplace. For the weekend. You got any plans?' I said I didn't—which wasn't exactly true, actually, I was supposed to do something with Derek and a bunch of his law school friends, go out some place, but I knew I could cancel those guys—and she said, 'We'll go on Friday afternoon, where should we go?' And I said, 'How about Santa Barbara?' I don't even know why I said that, it just popped into my head. And she said, 'Fantastic, I'll throw some stuff in an overnight bag,' and she told me where to pick her up. So off we went."

"That's amazing, Freddy. But ... won't Derek be furious? He's your best friend, isn't he?"

"Well, I thought, I don't have to tell him. It's not like I'm going to marry her. And he isn't either. He shouldn't marry her, anyway. And, Frank, well, I mean, I did need a break, I'm kind of drifting, you know that, and I'm under a lot of stress, all this stuff about dead mothers and live mothers; and, anyway, we went, drove down the coast, and actually, it was kind of fun."

I'm too discreet to ask what the fun consisted of.

"I mean," he said, "we ate a lot, and we were in a nice place, big room, and the hotel had a swimming pool. I kind of forgot my troubles."

"Freddy, I'm glad you had a good time. But be careful. I wouldn't trust that woman. I really wouldn't."

He said: "I know that. When we got back, and I found out about Sybil.... Look: I don't want to see her anymore, I really don't. I've got to talk to Derek, he must be mad at me, by now I think he knows I went off with Ella, and I don't want to lose him as a friend. You know what I'm thinking? I'm thinking this Ella was maybe the one who killed Sybil, and she planned it in advance, and she was going to use me for an alibi. I mean, they don't know when exactly Sybil died, I gathered that from stuff they told me. Could have been before we left."

"But you said they don't know yet. And if the, uh, killing thing was before you left, okay, that might implicate Ella, but it wouldn't be an alibi for you either, Freddy. Remember that."

He looked glum. "The whole thing is just so awful, Frank. And Ella.... It seems so fishy."

"But why," I asked, "would she want to kill Sybil? What reason could she have?"

"I don't have a clue. But she's the only person I know who could kill somebody. I mean, not that she said anything, it's just that, well, I think she could do a murder, she's the type. Listen, I think she could do anything. She's kind of awesome. Too awesome for me, Frank. Maybe too awesome for anybody."

I think he was right about Ella, at least in one regard. She was not the right person for Freddy. Maybe she *did* kill Sybil Glass. But if so, why? Motive: that's always important. And I just couldn't see any motive here. In the classic mysteries, like Agatha Christie, or in the novels of Sue Grafton, or whoever, motive is really important. Motive is everything. It's all about motive. Some old geezer gets killed and there's half a dozen people who figure in the story, and as you read along, you find out everybody has a motive, everybody has some reason to kill the old guy. There's a surprise at the end, maybe a new motive pops up out of nowhere, on top of the old motives—still, they all had a motive. This guy has a revenge motive, this other guy was being blackmailed, this woman stands to get a fortune if she could get the old guy out of the way, this other woman simply must get rid of him, because he's about to change his will, and so forth and so on.

But here, with regard to Sybil Glass, it's the opposite problem. *Nobody* has a motive. I can't think of a good reason why anybody would want to kill her. Not Freddy, not Ella, not anybody. Of course, I knew nothing about Sybil's past. Maybe somebody had a grudge against her, left over from something that happened years back. But the cast of characters I knew didn't seem to have any reason to kill her. Dislike her, maybe; but kill her, no.

Still, somebody did. You couldn't get away from that fact.

22

I didn't see Freddy for a few days, and then he called me on the phone. He sounded cheerful, even upbeat.

"Frank," he said, "Derek and me, we're friends again. We had a long talk, the two of us. I mean, it was a bit hot and heavy at first; but you know, I think we both realized she's no good. I'm talking about Ella of course. She's bad news. For him, for me. We're not going to have anything to do with her. Either of us. And I said, we shouldn't let her get between us, no way, and then I gave him a great big hug, and it was all emotional, and everything's okay now. We're buddies. It's a big load off my mind."

I guess he wanted me to approve, wanted me to say I was happy for him. In fact, I wasn't. I didn't trust Derek. He was a schemer, dishonest, greedy. And Freddy was so naïve, so transparent. Derek was playing some kind of game; what it was, I wasn't sure. I wanted to warn Freddy to watch his step. But I felt I couldn't do it too openly.

"It's too bad Ella found out about your aunt's diary," I said. "Derek was the source, you know. He was the one. That's why she knew about it. And it wasn't a good idea, Freddy. Not that I'm really worried about Ella and her lawsuit. Like I told you, Homer's been dead a million years; you can't bring these things up, you can't open an estate, after all that time. And, anyway, the only evidence, if you can call it that, is an entry in a diary. That's no proof of a crime. I don't even think you could get it admitted into evidence. And your aunt, don't forget, she was never charged, accused, tried in court, or anything. There's no case."

Freddy said: "Yeah, it was dumb of me, what I did. Showing the thing to Derek. I just wanted his advice. I didn't mean for him to go blabbing to other people, especially not to Ella. Derek though, he's really smart. You have to be smart to get into Stanford, his board score is at the ninety-ninth percentile, or something like that. I wanted a second opinion, like with doctors—that's why I asked Derek what he thought, and I had to show him the diary, right? It's like, well, last year, I had this bladder problem, you don't want to hear about it, it was sort of disgusting, but I went to the Palo Alto clinic, and I saw this doctor, a real jerk by the way, and he said one thing, and I didn't like what I was hearing, so I went to another doctor, a specialist, urologist they said he was, and I got different advice. You have to wonder why anybody would want to be a urologist. Especially this second doctor, she was a young woman, I think she came from India, and here she was going on about men's bladders, and probably she examines penises and so on. Me, I thought the whole thing was not only disgusting, it was terrifically embarrassing. Maybe she gets a charge out of this, except I think most of her patients are old geezers, all shriveled up, if you know what I mean. She told me to get an antibiotic, and I was all better in two days. Anyway, Derek, he was my second opinion. Besides, wasn't he my friend?"

"Really? Was that a friendly thing to do, to tell Ella all about the diary, all about what your aunt did? The old guy was her grandfather, after all."

"Derek swears he didn't mean anything by it, they were just talking, and it sort of slipped out, and precisely because it was her grandfather, she was pretty curious, and then he felt she had to know the whole story."

"Slipped out? Do you believe that? And why did she have to know the whole story, as you put it? I don't see that."

He didn't answer. I said: "Freddy, maybe Derek isn't as much of a friend as you think he is. I don't want to poison your mind. But still ... maybe he told her things on purpose. Maybe the two of them thought they could get money out of you. Just be careful."

He listened, and nodded his head. But clearly it was a painful subject for Freddy, now that he and Derek were friends again. I changed the subject, and brought up Sybil Glass again. I wanted to reassure Freddy that nothing was going to happen to him.

But that got the poor guy all agitated. I guess it was a mistake on my part. I simply frightened him, instead of giving him assurances. He wanted nothing to do with police, investigations, trials—you can't blame him: would anybody like that sort of thing? I had hoped Santa Barbara would turn out to be an alibi, but apparently that wasn't going to be the case because the time of death was still completely uncertain. Sybil died around the time Freddy and Ella went off, but nobody could pinpoint the exact time; they have estimates, but they're not that precise. She might have been alive as they drove off into the sunset, but then again, maybe not.

I asked Freddy about what happened that day. "Okay," I said, "I want to get this straight. When you left, your house was completely empty, right?"

"Well, no, as a matter of fact it wasn't. Melanie was there, with her boyfriend Peter. They were house-sitting. They do that when I go away. Melanie's a real sweetheart, and so is Peter. Peter Chang. He's got these really strict parents, old-fashioned people, you know what I mean? At my house, they can have some privacy. So they were there. Wow, are you saying they might be suspects?"

"Freddy, I'm not the police. I don't decide who's a suspect and who isn't. I never met this Peter guy, Melanie's boyfriend. I know nothing about him."

"He's a Stanford student, like Melanie. I think he used to study computers, or maybe it was computer math. I'm hopeless with that stuff, I mean, I do Facebook and so on, but I'm definitely not a techie. This Peter, he is. Or was. Or maybe it was biology he was studying? Some science. But now it's something else, I think. He's in classes with Melanie. I don't know the guy, not really. Met him once or twice. He's nice. But why on earth would he want to kill Sybil Glass?"

"Well, why would anybody?"

"I know one person," Freddy said, "that crazy woman, Lizbeth. And Melanie told me she saw her hanging around."

"Hanging around?"

"After I was gone. I think. Listen, she actually came to the house before I left, couple of days before. Wanted to see me, I guess. Give me messages from my dead mother, or some crap like that. She rang the doorbell, but I could see her from out one of the windows, so I just didn't answer. I think maybe she killed Sybil. Like, one mother doing it to another mother. If this isn't the weirdest thing.... Frank, you know something? This is really getting me down. I'm a bundle of nerves. I got so worked up, I had this psychosomatic thing. All of a sudden. I actually got a rash, an ugly thing, it's on my butt—I can't really see it, well, maybe in one of the mirrors, if I twist myself—anyway, it itches like crazy, and I can feel it, bunch of little pimples. I just know it's because of my nerves. I made an appointment with a dermatologist, and then I canceled it, don't ask me why. I'm a wreck, Frank. I'm not sleeping much, either. I go to bed late, and maybe I fall asleep, but I get up again and it's only three in the morning or four, and I go and watch TV. What there is to watch."

Lizbeth was, I suppose, a real possibility. Maybe she had a motive, even if it was a fairly primitive one. She hated Sybil. She told me that. Did she hate her enough to kill her?

"Frank," he said, "I want you to talk to her. This Lizbeth. Maybe you can crack this thing wide open."

I tried to explain to him, patiently, that it was none of my business, really; and furthermore, that I just can't do that sort of thing. I'm not in the business of cracking things wide open. He seemed disappointed. But he accepted what I said—in fact, a bit more easily than I would have thought. I soon found out why.

23

It was hard work trying to reassure Freddy, to calm him down. I was sorry I had stirred up all these emotions which came bubbling to the surface. I asked him what he was doing about his nervous condition. I know yoga had been a flop; I mentioned meditation, but he said, no, that wasn't for him, he tried it, and it was just boring, and it made things worse. Therapy? Actually, Freddy was already in therapy, as he had told me. It didn't seem to be working.

Poor Freddy. And poor me. He had gotten into the habit of calling me on every little thing, almost every day.

In point of fact, I didn't mind that much. When a phone call goes on for some length, I bill people for the call. Sometimes, a client objects, refuses to pay, and says, "It was just a phone call." I try to explain, patiently, that time is money for me. What's the difference between coming to the office for half an hour, or haranguing me on the phone for half an hour? But some of my clients refuse to see it that way. They think they have a constitutional right to free phone calls with their lawyer. I soon learn who these people are and, frankly, I just don't bill them for the calls. If they are valuable clients, that is. I lose some money this way, but it's a loss I have to swallow. It irks me that people like that get away with it, but that's the way it is. The squeaky wheel gets the oil.

Freddy was not a squeaky wheel. He never said boo about paying for phone calls. He had, in general, a relaxed attitude toward money. He had never worried about money in his life. I suppose he was aware that money didn't grow on trees, but Clara gave him anything he wanted, and more; so his money might as well have grown on trees. And now he had his inheritance. At any rate, he never questioned a bill. From that standpoint, he was an ideal client. I would have preferred one without dead mothers, of course, or murdered mothers. But you can't have everything in life.

"Frank," he said, "I need your advice. I got a letter from Sybil Glass." This was not a phone call. He was actually in my office, "Just dropping by," as he put it.

"Good grief, Freddy," I said. "What do you mean, a letter from Sybil Glass? The woman's dead."

"I know that. She mailed me the letter the day before she died. When I came back from Santa Barbara, there was this whole murder business, and I was terrifically upset, well, you know that—there were police, and detectives, and reporters, and I just let the mail pile up, it's always mostly junk, catalogs from companies, a bunch of ads, and a lot of mail is still for Clara, you wouldn't believe how much mail, of course they don't know she's dead. She gets stuff from cruise companies, companies that cremate people, ads for walk-in bathtubs, it's creepy in a way. Anyway, that sort of mail, it goes right into the recycling bin, but I didn't even do that, I didn't look at the mail, just dumped all the stuff that came in on my desk. And then there was this big scene, with Derek, and we were hugging each other, and I was happy about that, well, you know the story, Frank, I told you all about it. And then Derek asked me if I got a letter from Sybil Glass, and I said, 'I didn't look at my mail, it's all in a pile,' and he went to my desk, and started pawing through the mail, and I said, 'Derek, what are you doing?' And he said, 'I'm looking for that letter,' and he found it, and he said, 'Freddy, we're friends now, aren't we?' and I said, 'Yeah, we're friends,' and I started saying some more stuff about being friends and so on, and he said, 'Freddy, I'm going to ask you something, something weird,' and I said, 'Okay, what is it?' and he says, 'I'm taking that letter. I don't want you to read it. I'm asking you to do what I say, it's important to me, trust me' and

I said, 'Alright, if it's such a big deal,' and he said, it was. Frank, did I do the right thing? I just gave it to him, without a peep."

"Well, what's done is done, Freddy. But what do you think the letter was about? I assume you asked him."

"He wouldn't tell me. He kept saying, 'Don't ask me. Trust me. You don't want to know, and you don't need to know.' But I couldn't help thinking about it, right? How could I not? And then I had another thought: hey, that letter was evidence, wasn't it? I mean, a letter she wrote, just before she died, it could be a real clue. Wow, maybe she says something about who killed her? I mean, no, she couldn't do that, but she might have said somebody was threatening her, or whatever. And now Derek has the letter. Isn't that concealing evidence or something? Did I do the wrong thing?"

I said: "Well, maybe you did, Freddy. Look: I don't want to make trouble between you and Derek, but this is awfully fishy, don't you think? Why didn't he want you to read the letter—it was addressed to you, after all. And another thing: how did he know about the letter? Sybil Glass wrote you a letter, and it's something Derek doesn't want you to read. But how come *he* knows about the letter? Did Sybil tell him she was writing it? Why was he in contact with Sybil?"

But Freddy had no answer to these questions. And I gathered that he didn't want to go into it. "Maybe he has his reasons, Frank. To be honest, I don't want to start in with him again. He's my friend, now. I don't want to lose him."

Some friend, I thought. But I kept discreetly silent.

24

Sylvan called me the next day. I was expecting the call.

"We've got to talk," he said. "I'm all shook up. Frank, you're used to this, this is old stuff for you—clients getting murdered. For me, it's a first and if I had my way, it'd be my last. Are you free for lunch?"

It turned out I was. Sylvan always picked the spot for lunch. He chose an upscale Italian restaurant in Redwood City, near the city hall. "I need comfort food," he said, sliding into an upholstered booth. "Italian food, it's comfort food. Pasta especially. French food, good French food, it's wonderful, of course; but you get the image of a distinguished chef—a guy with one of those hats, a toque they're called—and he carefully devises some subtle, delectable dish, with lots of ingredients. Italian food is different. With good Italian food, you think of an Italian momma, making something at home for her family. And that's what I need."

He studied the menu carefully. I ordered some kind of ravioli. He ordered the "special pasta of the day," and gave explicit instructions to the waiter about how it should be prepared.

"I'm depressed, Frank," he said, "and depression makes me eat too much. I've gained weight. Can you tell?"

I said I couldn't tell, but I was lying. Sylvan had always been, well, stocky—but he was clearly stockier than before. "Funny thing," he said, "when I'm happy, when things are going right, I eat a lot. And when I'm depressed, I eat to cure the depression. So I can't win. I better just enjoy the food. What else is there in life? Oh, I know: lots of things. Like sex. But I'm divorced, Frank, you know that. And even before the divorce ... but let's not go there."

The pasta came, and was absolutely delicious.

"Let's talk about Sybil Glass," he said. "Much as I don't want to. You know, when she came to me, I should have been more careful. But we're lawyers, Frank, we're not private investigators, well, maybe you are...."

"Sylvan, I'm not. Be serious."

"Frank, okay, you're not an investigator, but I suppose you have some special contacts with the police, or something like that."

"Sylvan, no; knock it off. I don't have any contacts with the police. I don't know anybody with the police. The last time I saw a cop was when I got a ticket for an illegal U-turn. Give me a break."

"Okay, okay, Frank. I didn't mean anything. Anyway, this woman, Sybil Glass, she came to me—I don't know who recommended her, or how she heard about me. I don't brag like that asshole Gideon, but I do have a decent reputation. Good clients. Anyway, it doesn't matter. She told me who she was, she had those documents, and frankly, I was convinced. I told you all about it. I felt this woman had a good case. Clara Fisk's will was pretty explicit, if Freddy's mother showed up alive, she was entitled to a share of the estate. And she really was Freddy's mother. That much I'm sure of."

"I'm not so sure," I said. Based on nothing, of course; but I felt I shouldn't accept this fact without question.

"Whatever. You can't argue with those documents. Birth certificate and so on. And she seemed genuine. Not that I liked her. She wasn't likable. A cold fish. There was something distasteful about her; but you're not required to love your clients, God knows they're not all lovable. Anyway, I took her on. I didn't ask her to tell me her life story, why should I? So in fact I knew very little about her. She said she wasn't from this area, but she had moved here, rented a place—she came to this neck of the woods in order to pursue her claim. That seemed perfectly reasonable to me. She gave me her address, and a cell-phone number, and that was that."

I didn't blame Sylvan for not checking further about Sybil Glass. I don't do background checks on clients; none of us do. Why should we? Still, this was not your ordinary client—a woman who comes to you, out of the blue, and makes a claim against the estate of an extremely wealthy woman, on the basis of an identity nobody knew anything about before.

"I know more now," Sylvan said. "She was a nurse, well, she had been a nurse. I suppose she had some sort of pension. But here's the thing: she had another source of income, and it was, well, kind of mysterious. She had a bank account, and somebody was giving her money, regular payments. Not a fortune, but enough to live on. I have a feeling the money came from Clara Fisk, but I can't prove it; who else could it be? Gideon might know something about this, after all, it's Gideon who's handling Clara's estate, and of course I've been in contact with him."

"Lucky you," I said.

"Tell me about it! He won't give me the time of day, the bastard. Every time I talk to him, I get the usual crap about what wonderful clients he has, members of the board of the San Francisco Opera, as if I gave a shit, and that he was not entitled to divulge confidential information. The man talks as if he was reading an insurance policy, I said, 'Gideon, try being human, we're not really adversaries here, let's cooperate.' Fat chance."

I had to smile, somewhat ruefully. Dealing with Gideon was like trying to push a giant mound of sludge up a very steep hill.

Sylvan went on: "I asked him, where did the money come from, these payments? Was Clara Fisk making them? I said, 'You must know the answer, after all, you're handling her estate, and you have access to her financial records; give me a break, Gideon.' He absolutely stonewalled me. Bunch of crap about ethical rules, and how he was on the ethics committee of the Bar, big deal, and blah blah blah. I couldn't get a thing out of him. But, Frank, it has to be Clara, though, unless Sybil was blackmailing somebody we don't know about. But here's the thing: the payments stopped. Clara died, and the payments stopped. That tells you something, doesn't it?"

I had to agree. Clara Fisk had been making regular payments to this woman. But why? There were also payments to Ella's mother; and they too stopped when Clara died. Was there some connection between these two recurring payments? Sybil had been a nurse: did that have something to do with the payments? Lizbeth had also been a nurse. Was there some connection there?

At least, I suppose, the payments to Ella's mother flowed from some sort of feelings of guilt. But why pay Sybil? Maybe the adoption was legally flawed, and Clara was afraid Sybil would suddenly rear up and claim custody of Freddy. Possible. But Freddy was now an adult, so custody could not be the issue—at any rate, not anymore. Maybe she just wanted to keep Sybil as far away from Freddy as she could? Freddy clearly knew nothing about these payments. But if this was Clara's motive, then why on earth did she put that weird provision in the will, a provision that practically invited this woman to come forward and make a claim against the estate? I was baffled by the whole affair.

Sylvan had made no inquiries *before* Sybil died, but afterwards, he had done quite a bit. And discovered quite a lot. He told me all about his discoveries. in great detail, over coffee and dessert ("The tiramisu here is to die for, Frank. Forget the calories and live it up!"). It was not a pretty story. You have to feel sorry for Freddy. I was reasonably sure Sybil Glass was his birth mother; the documents seemed totally genuine. And what was she like? Rotten to the core. She was trained as a nurse, but had been fired from job after job. Not for incompetence, but for dishonesty and vague suspicions of misconduct: the theft of valuable drugs, or money and jewelry taken from patients, and even worse. Patients did not like her, big time. Then she worked as a private nurse. That's how she got connected with Homer Fisk. As Sylvan described her, she was basically just an awful person; clever, perhaps, but without any real moral compass.

"Does she have any family? Heirs? I mean, if you represent her estate, Sylvan, you still have a claim against the Clara Fisk estate. Assuming that she's Freddy's mother."

"Well, yes; she has a brother, in Wyoming. The two of them are estranged. He hasn't seen her for years. She told me that. The parents are dead. She was married once, briefly, but that didn't last. The ex-husband died two years ago, cancer. Other than Freddy, she doesn't seem to have any children."

"How on earth did she get into the picture? And who was Freddy's father?"

"Freddy's father? No idea. Birth certificate lists him as unknown. Like I told you, she worked for a while as a private nurse, for Homer Fisk among other things. I suspect Clara was somehow involved. Obviously, she knew the woman, because of Homer, and Sybil being his nurse and all that; and I guess she knew, or found out, that Sybil was pregnant, and of course Sybil wasn't married, and probably Clara recognized that Sybil wasn't the mother type. I'm guessing Clara convinced Sybil: have the baby, don't have an abortion, go ahead with this. Probably they paid her, and then gave the baby to Kathryn and Max to be adopted. That's what I think. It makes sense. I can't prove it, though. And there's nobody around who knows the story."

"Pascal LeBeau?"

"I thought of that. I asked him about it. He says he knows nothing about the whole thing. Admits he knew Sybil, because she was Homer's nurse. The adoption? Said it was none of his business. I'm not sure he's telling the truth, but I can't force him to talk."

Again I thought: poor Freddy. This so-called mother of his had been nothing to brag about. Now she was dead and a lot of dirt about her past was coming to the surface. It wouldn't make him happy. But he never liked her, and maybe he realized she was basically no good. Would that give him a motive? A motive to get rid of this awful woman, who otherwise would be mucking up his life? You can hardly ignore your mother. I know, some people do; but it's not the normal thing.

Still, I couldn't imagine Freddy killing anybody. But what do I know? Human beings are complicated animals. You can't judge a book by its cover, and people are the most puzzling and complicated books you can imagine.

Sylvan had talked me into the tiramisu—a dessert with far more calories than was good for me. Celia would have disapproved, big time. But all of the food, including the dessert, had been totally delicious.

25

Freddy was a mess. The phone calls continued and he had also gotten into the habit of coming by unannounced.

"Frank," he said to me, in my office, where he had just dropped in. "I was around the corner, at that coffee shop, I was having coffee with Zelda, and she said I had to talk to you."

"Freddy, sure. You talk to me all the time. That's fine. I don't mind at all. But is this something special?"

"Sort of. Do I talk too much, Frank? Do I bother you?"

"Of course not, Freddy."

"Derek says I talk too much. He says I should keep my mouth shut."

Actually, Derek had a point. Freddy definitely talked too much. And not everybody was as patient as I was. Of course, other people did not charge $300 an hour for listening as Freddy rambled on. And on and on.

"What's on your mind, Freddy?"

"I love Zelda," he said. "I feel I can talk to her. She knows all about human nature, don't you think? I mean, being a novelist; she has to think about people, about what they're like. I haven't got anybody else. Well, there's you, Frank. And Derek. But I can't really trust Derek, can I? He's my friend, but sometimes I wonder. You told me to be careful. I'll do that, even though we're all buddy-buddy now."

"Zelda's a good person," I said.

"Don't get me wrong, she's just a friend," he said. "I mean, I think she likes me—and I like her—but not in that other way, if you know what I mean. Anyway: we got together for coffee and she was telling me about her problem, writer's block, and so on, and what she's doing about it, meditation, something called mindfulness, I don't think I understand it. You told me that, too; I mean, about meditation. Anyway, we were just talking, and then I felt I should confide in her, and I told her stuff, and she said, 'Freddy, I'm glad you told me. Now you better go tell Frank. He's got to know.' So, here I am."

"Okay, Freddy: so tell me. What's this 'stuff' that Zelda thinks I ought to know?"

"Frank, I'm so afraid they think I killed that woman. They think maybe I did it, then I dumped her body and ran off to Santa Barbara. I'm scared to death they'll arrest me."

"Freddy, that's not going to happen," I said. In fact, I was sure about nothing. But I felt Freddy needed to hear something optimistic. "They can't arrest you without some evidence. They don't have any evidence. You didn't do anything wrong, so they haven't got a case."

He hesitated briefly. Then he said, meekly, "I didn't do it, Frank. You know I didn't. I'm not a violent person. And she was maybe my actual mother."

"I absolutely believe you, Freddy."

"But here's the problem," he said. "I kinda told them a lie. And they caught me in it."

"A lie, Freddy? About what?"

"Well, the day before I left—that was a Thursday—I got up late; well, to tell you the truth, I didn't sleep much at all, I was tossing and turning, and having nightmares. I had seen Ella that day and ... we made plans, and I was feeling guilty about that, and nervous about a whole lot of other stuff, and I was even thinking maybe I should leave the country maybe, go to China or France or anywhere. And this woman, Sybil, maybe she *is* my mother? Like I said.... Frank, I'm rambling, I know it, God, I'm a mess."

I said, "Calm down, Freddy. Just tell me what's going on."

"Okay, well, that woman, Sybil, she didn't leave me alone, she kept pestering me, and I asked people, people I knew, not just Derek, other people, and I talked to Melanie, too, she's always sensible, and some of them said, 'You should go see her. It won't hurt. Have a frank talk with her.' I didn't want to. But then I felt, maybe I should. So I talked to her on the phone and she said things, like she was my mother and you can't reject your mother and she said she wanted to see me, and she said, 'I don't want to force myself on you.' Well, frankly, she *was* forcing herself on me, all those phone calls and so on. But then she started talking in a different way, she said, 'Why don't we meet, and talk?' I said, 'No way, I really don't want you in my house, please, I'd like you to stay away. For now anyway.'"

"That was good, Freddy. That was the right thing to do."

"Well, maybe it was. But then she said, 'Alright, I won't come to your house. But you can come here. To my place.' And … I said I would. And I did. I went there. She lived in the basement of this building, in Mountain View, somebody's house, but they rent out the basement, I guess. It had its own entrance with a doorbell, and I rang the bell, but nobody answered. And I thought, that's strange, she knows I'm coming, why doesn't she answer? And then this guy comes up to me, a middle-aged guy, and he says, 'Who are you looking for?' and I said, 'Well, the lady who lives here, but she doesn't answer, I rang the bell, and nobody answered.' And he gave me a kind of suspicious look. 'Are you her son?' he asked, and I said, 'I don't think that's any of your business.' I guess that was rude, Frank, but I didn't want to go into this whole mother thing. And he said, 'Well, I own this house, and she rents the basement, and I saw her this morning, in the yard, and she said her son was coming to see her today.' He told me he said to her, 'I didn't know you had a son.' She said, 'I do, and he lives in this area, and I haven't seen him for many years.' Then he said, 'So that's you, right?' And I said to this guy, 'Look, like I said, it's really not your business.'"

"Then what happened?"

"Don't get me wrong, Frank, I didn't say it in a hostile way; but I guess it was a hostile thing to say. I'm not usually like that, but I was upset, and I just wanted to get out of there. And this man, he was pretty hostile himself, and he said, 'Maybe it *is* my business.' 'Oh,' I said, 'why is that?' And he said, 'Well, later on, Ms. Glass called me up, and she asked me whether or not I was going to be around that afternoon.' And he said he was, he's a retired guy, and he's home most of the time. And she said she was glad he was going to be around, because she was nervous. Nervous about what? Well, this visit from her son. 'And you did come,' he said to me, 'I saw you. You were inside her apartment.'"

"Inside? You said she didn't answer the doorbell."

"Honest to God, Frank, she didn't. I told him that, and I said, 'I never was inside the place.' He said, 'You're lying. You were inside a while ago, and now you're out, and you're telling me she didn't answer the doorbell, what's going on here?' And I said, 'Look, I wasn't in the house,' but he said, 'Yes you were, I saw you. I was around in the yard, and in the front, and I looked in the window and you can see her living room, and I looked in, and I saw you.'"

"He said that?"

"I thought, wow, what is this? So I said, 'You saw somebody else, not me...'"

"And then what?"

"He grabbed me, I was actually scared. He said, something like, 'She was afraid of you, and I want to see if she's okay.' He had a key, and he pushed me in the door and there was nobody there, the place was empty; and that was pretty weird, I mean, wasn't she expecting me? And why did he think I was there before, when I wasn't?"

I had no idea.

He said: "Frank, do the police think I'm a suspect? I mean, they must have talked to this guy, I know they did; she lived there, and the police, they always check the house when somebody's murdered, I see that on TV all the time. So they must have asked him a whole bunch of questions. I know he must have told them about me, about me coming there, and how I had been in the house, and the whole thing seemed so suspicious. Frank, do I look suspicious?"

"Freddy, you're the least suspicious-looking guy I know. Honestly."

"But the police, they think everybody's scum, you know, they deal with awful people, every day, they don't trust anybody. They think maybe I killed her and dumped her body in my backyard, though wouldn't that be nuts? And then I just left it there and went off to Santa Barbara, and they know about Ella, maybe she was an accomplice or something. And I'm thinking, what, I killed my own mother? Like I was Oedipus or something. You said he didn't kill his mother, I don't remember the whole thing, it was a Greek play or something, totally boring. Anyway, these police, they don't have any idea who Oedipus was, if I mentioned Oedipus, they'd go out looking for somebody named Oedipus, arrest him for murder or whatever."

"You're rambling, Freddy. Get a grip on yourself."

"Frank," he said, "I'm sorry. I'm just all on edge. And I'm a little ashamed of myself, because I never wanted to think she was really my mother, but I did say to this detective or whoever he was, 'I couldn't kill anybody, and Sybil Glass, she was probably my mother, so why would I do a thing like that?'"

"And what did he say?"

"The guy said, 'You know what? In our business, we see people every day who kill their mothers, grandmothers, rape their children, you name it, people do it. And anyway, Mr. Lucas'—he kept calling me 'Mr. Lucas'—'we know that you never really considered this woman your mother, now did you? You hardly knew her. It's not like she's the woman who raised you and that sort of thing. Moreover,' he said—he actually said 'moreover'—'we know all about her claim against your aunt's estate. She was going to cost you a lot of money.' They must have checked with Gideon, about the will and stuff. Or somebody. I mean, they did their homework, you know what I mean? It's like they were ready right then and there to send me to the gas chamber, honest to God. I tried to be calm, you know? I said, 'Sure, she was going to cost me money, but my Aunt Clara was filthy rich. I'm going to have plenty of money, even if this woman gets a piece of it, she can have it, as far as I'm concerned, I don't need it. And it doesn't make sense, your whole story, what do you think, I lured her out here, for some reason, and I killed her, and dumped her in my backyard, and then I just zipped off with a girlfriend to Santa Barbara, how does that figure?'"

"And what did the guy say?"

"He was very calm, you know, never showed any emotion, like he was an android or something. I couldn't stand looking at him, Frank. He was downright scary. And he said, 'Look, we've seen it all, Mr. Lucas. Don't tell me what's logical and what's not. People do crazy things. So maybe you did something crazy too.' Like I said, I thought he was ready, on the spot, to pull out a pair of handcuffs and arrest me. But he didn't."

"Of course not, Freddy," I said. "He was bluffing. I'm sure of it. They don't have any evidence. And they never will. Because you didn't do anything. But if they ask you, Freddy, don't lie. Tell them everything. Tell them the truth. That you went to Sybil's house. They might know about it anyway, so be sure not to lie. And, Freddy: stay calm. Everything's going to be alright."

He hugged me after that, and left the office.

26

Of course, I knew Freddy had nothing to do with the murder. Not the Freddy I knew. But who then? Melanie and Peter: out of the question. Ella? Possible. She had the temperament. Derek? I didn't trust him; he was shifty and dishonest. And callous, I think. But what would the motive be? You don't kill somebody on a whim. Lizbeth? This seemed the most likely. No real motive there either. But she hated Sybil and she seemed, well, crazy.

Now that Sybil was dead, it was Lizbeth who bothered Freddy the most. She had somehow learned his cellphone number and called and called; she also made almost daily visits to his house. I discussed getting a court order, to force her to stay away. "Zelda has a different idea," Freddy said.

"Oh, what's that?"

"She thinks maybe if I talked to her, if I seemed friendly, she would be satisfied, and go away."

I said I had my doubts.

"Zelda said you should come along, Frank, or we should meet in your office. Or in a restaurant. Please say yes, Frank."

To say I was reluctant would be an understatement. But Freddy was the client, the good client, the nice client, the rich client, the client who paid his bills on time. And I actually liked him. We went ahead with the plan. Somehow he got in touch with Lizbeth, or maybe Zelda did, and I came out to Freddy's house and she was there, sitting in the living room. Personally,

I thought letting her in the house was a big mistake; but Freddy (and Zelda) thought otherwise.

I wasn't clear what my function was supposed to be. Perhaps some kind of buffer.

Freddy obviously had some sort of strategy in mind. No doubt it was Zelda's doing. Freddy himself was not the strategy type. "Lizbeth," he said, "tell me what it is that you want."

She repeated her standard litany: his mother's soul had entered her body, and so, in a way, she was Freddy's mother. At times she spoke quite rationally. She knew about Clara Fisk's will. It would hurt her feelings, she said, if Freddy thought she was after the money. No, no, she said. She would never take a penny of it, not a penny. Kathryn was dead, in the bodily sense. Money was no use to her. And for her, Lizbeth, the money meant nothing. After all, it wasn't *her* money. And she said, she didn't really want money. "I have a pension," she said. "I get social security money. I get a check every month. I don't spend money on anything."

She certainly didn't spend money on clothes. Or probably, from the looks of her, on food.

"I'm going to have to move though," she said. "Because of the rents. I don't mind that, either. I don't really like it here. Only... that you're here, Freddy. That's why I'm here."

"Is there something we can do for you, Lizbeth?" Freddy asked.

"Nothing," she said. "It's only this ... your mother's soul.... It's crying out for you, Freddy. I feel it so strongly. I feel this sort-of pulling, pulling, in my heart. A kind of loneliness. I know it's Kathryn. She misses you so terribly, Freddy. She has a mother's love for you, Freddy. And I feel that inside of me, now."

"I hear you, Lizbeth. And I want to believe you," he said. "But I'm grown up now. When Kathryn left me, I was six years old. Now I'm a man, Lizbeth. An adult. I can't still be a mama's boy. It's important for me to be, well, my own person."

This was Zelda's script, no doubt. And not a bad one. Lizbeth seemed to take it seriously. "But ... what about Mother's Day?" she said suddenly. "Kathryn puts great store on Mother's

Day. I know you were too little; but Max always gave her chocolates, flowers, and a beautiful card, he bought it at a stationery store, it had pink writing on it, and it was special to them, because she was, after all, a mother; they had you, their dear loving boy."

"Oh, Lizbeth," he said. "I understand."

"In the jungle, he couldn't do it," she said. "And all the years after he died, nobody sent her a Mother's Day card. I hear her, inside me, grieving. On Mother's Day, my whole body aches. Freddy, promise me you won't forget me on Mother's Day."

"Oh, no, I won't," he said.

"Max died first," she said. "The piranhas ate him. Oh, it was ghastly. Such awful little fish, with their sharp teeth. He was in the Amazon wading, you know, near the edge. And the fish just swarmed all over him. He screamed and screamed. Kathryn had to watch, it was so awful for her. Nothing left of him but bones. Can you imagine?"

Well, both Freddy and I *could* imagine; and it was an extremely unpleasant picture. I could see Freddy blanching. Lizbeth went right on: "I don't think she really wanted to live after that. She was staying in this village. Oh, and she was frightened of the snakes. All kinds of snakes. Big ones, little ones. The biggest ones, they can swallow a person whole. They squeeze you to death, and then they swallow you. And there are so many insects, swarms of them, they get all over you. And lizards, monkeys, howling all the time. And, it's an awful place; the jungle gobbles everything up, there are no paths, you get lost, completely lost. There's only the river, and it floods every year. Kathryn was in the village, like I said. She was sick, she had a fever. She couldn't speak the language."

Freddy couldn't help asking: "How do you know all this?"

I fully expected Lizbeth to say something about visions, or Kathryn's soul, or rubbish of that sort. But instead she said: "She wrote letters."

"Letters?"

"I don't know how she got them out of the jungle. But wonderful things have a way of happening sometimes, when the spirit is strong. She was so far away, so isolated, so alone; but she was still able to send out these messages. Wonderful messages. So full of details."

"Who did she send these messages to?"

Suddenly, Lizbeth was silent. She acted as if she hadn't heard my question. I asked her the question again, and again, no answer. So I tried a different tack: "What did these letters say?"

She answered in a monotonous voice—almost as if she was channeling somebody; or as if she was actually reading from a letter. "Ants. There were ants everywhere. You have to be careful. Some of them can bite you. The bullet ants. When they crawl over you, and bite, the pain is unbearable. It lasts for hours. The villagers use these ants, in rituals, testing young men, seeing if they can face the pain. And, oh, the army ants. Kathryn told me she was studying them. That was her specialty. They excited her, but you had to be careful of them. What awesome creatures they are. They're blind; but they're murderous. They crawl all over the jungle floor, millions of them, you can't count them, they never rest. They eat everything in their path. They're always on the move, nothing can stop them. They make bridges out of their bodies, and they cross over streams. And there are termites too, and thousands of beetles. And when the river floods every year, it covers miles and miles of land, and the water comes up to the bottoms of the houses, and it's full of snakes and deadly fish and crocodiles. And Kathryn, now that Max was dead, she was alone, terribly alone. And sick. That's what she told me."

It was a weird experience, listening to Lizbeth.

And you had to wonder, where did she get these letters? If they were real. Or was this just something she made up? Something she read in a book? Something she imagined?

But though I tried to probe this issue, tried to ask questions about this whole Amazon nightmare, and where her information came from, I got another disquisition about ants; this time about the little buggers that strip foliage and carry it back to their nest. They make a kind of mulch, and they eat the fungus that grows on this mulch. But I didn't care about mulch.

I was eager to get off the subject of ants, beetles, snakes, lizards, and jungle vegetation. Lizbeth absolutely would not answer anything about the source of her information.

And then, suddenly, she seemed to switch gears; she began to talk about Sybil. She raised her voice, and seemed really agitated. "I'm not sorry she's dead," she said. "She was an evil woman. She got what was coming to her. Freddy, believe me, she wasn't your mother, no way. She was a fraud. Kathryn warned me about her. One of the reasons I came here was to save you, protect you from that woman."

Did I dare ask her whether *she* killed Sybil Glass?

"I smelled danger," she said. "I knew she was up to no good. My poor boy, Sybil lied to you and she wanted you to believe her lies. But I was on to her. Kathryn sent me a message. I felt I had to warn you, tell you to be careful, tell you not to believe a word she said. So I went to the house. Your house, Freddy. There was a young woman there, and she answered the door. She said you weren't at home, but I didn't believe her. I stayed around, watching. I wanted to make sure you were safe."

When was this? It must have been when Freddy was in Santa Barbara; the young woman was Melanie, of course.

"Lizbeth," Freddy said. "I really wasn't there. I was on a trip."

She said: "There were people in the house. I peeked in the window. There was a man there, he was talking to the woman who answered the door. Who were they, Freddy? And what were they doing in your house?"

"They're friends of mine," Freddy said. "I asked them to look after the house while I was gone. They're good people."

"I saw another young man," she said. "While I was watching. He came to the house, but he didn't go in."

"That must have been Peter," Freddy said. "Peter is a friend. He and his girlfriend were the ones in the house. Her name is Melanie. Really, Lizbeth, they're the nicest people."

"This young man, he wasn't the man in the house, no," she said. "This was a different man. He didn't go in. He didn't see me. He just came to the house, but he didn't ring the bell or anything. He was sort of sneaking around. I was worried, who was he? And what was he doing there? Maybe he was some-body connected to Sybil. Somebody bad. He went to the back of the house, to the yard...."

"The yard? In back of the house? What was he doing?" I asked.

"I don't know. I had to hide, so he wouldn't see me. I don't know what he did. I was in some bushes, and then I didn't see him anymore."

"You didn't see where he went?" I asked.

"No. It's all overgrown, though there's a path I think. Fred-dy's house has a whole forest back there, you can't see where it ends. It reminds me of the jungle. I think maybe he went there. But I was hiding. And then he was gone. Or maybe he was still there, in that jungle. I waited a while, I didn't see anything; and then I went away."

Freddy and I looked at each other. I know what he must have been thinking. Who was that man? And what was he doing in the "jungle," in back of Freddy's house?

"Did you see what he looked like?" I asked her.

"It was dark. He was young. That's all I could see."

"Was he carrying anything?"

"I don't think so. I didn't see."

Lizbeth might be crazy, but I didn't think she was halluci-nating. She kept going on and on about Kathryn's spirit, and the messages Kathryn was sending her, and poor Freddy was fidgeting and hoping (I suppose) that she would finish ram-bling and go already, and leave him in peace. My mind was wandering. Who was the young man she saw outside Freddy's house? I couldn't help thinking: was it Derek?

Who else could it have been? And what was he doing there? What was he looking for? And did I dare ask him?

I realized I hadn't been listening to the conversation. Fred-dy was trying, as hard as he could, to follow the script Zelda had prepared for him. He was all smiles and friendliness. He kept telling Lizbeth how much he appreciated what she was doing, "I really do want to thank you, Lizbeth, and I'm going to make sure you get a card on Mother's Day, and on your birthday. I mean, tell me your birthday, and what sign were you born under, and we can talk from time to time. But Lizbeth, I mean Kathryn, or both of you—you know, like I said, I'm a grownup, and I need some space. I have to make my own way in the world. So ... I'm not saying, you should go away for good, but, for a while, I need, well, to be alone, so I can work things out."

Whether any of this worked, I have no idea. But Lizbeth nodded her head, and said she understood. "Now that that awful woman is dead," she said, in a grave tone of voice, "Kathryn isn't so troubled anymore. Can I come visit you sometimes though?"

"Of course," he said.

"And don't forget Mother's Day," she said. "Most of all I'd like flowers. But a Mother's Day card, that would be wonderful. And, Freddy, can I kiss you?"

He looked distinctly uncomfortable, but he said, "Yes, Lizbeth, of course." She embraced him, and kissed him on the forehead. Tears rolled down her cheeks. And then she left.

27

Soon afterwards, I left too. I went back to my office, and tried to get some work done. But the case kept creeping back into in my mind. Somebody had killed Sybil Glass. Who on earth could it be? Lizbeth? Derek? They were both hanging around Freddy's house. That was suspicious. But somebody dumped the body far in the back; and neither Derek nor Lizbeth seemed to be carrying anything or doing anything much. They certainly weren't carrying a body. Melanie and Peter were in the house. Freddy and Ella were gone already. Maybe Sybil was dead before they left. Time of death was uncertain. They simply couldn't pinpoint it to the minute. Maybe none of those people had killed Sybil Glass. Maybe it was a contract killer. In real life, I suppose there actually are hired assassins who kill for money. Still, somebody has to hire these people; they don't do it for the fun of it. Somebody has to make the contract. And that somebody must have had a motive.

Or do you really need a motive? Lots of murders have no real motive, at least not a motive in the Agatha Christie sense. Suppose somebody tried to rob Sybil, some young hoodlum high on drugs, and she resisted, and the guy shot her. Or maybe she was the victim of some insane serial killer, and she was simply unlucky: the winner of the murder lottery. You read about people like this all the time, at least in thrillers. Maybe the killer was a lunatic, like the guy in *The Silence of the Lambs*. Are there really people like that out there in the world? Apparently. But in Los Altos Hills, a posh suburb? Or Palo

Alto? Silicon Valley? World capital of nerds, yuppies, geeks, teenage billionaires?

Frankly, the whole idea of a hitman was absurd. Likewise, a crazy serial killer. Why would such a person dump the body on Freddy's property, way in the back, and cover it with leaves and dirt? Whoever did that must have known that this was a good place to stash a body.

Almost nothing about the case made any sense, no matter how long I brooded and went over what I knew, no matter how much I doodled on a piece of paper, writing names, and making little notes, no matter how often I demanded help from my brain, no matter how frequently I said: wake up, little gray cells. The little gray cells, despite all my pleas, were fast asleep inside my brain. The synapses were shut down, the little gray cells were recalcitrant; or maybe just too absorbed in other things, such as lunch, or the TV show the owner of the cells had watched the night before, or whether he needed a new pair of shoes, and whether his older daughter would do well on her PSAT.

So I came up with nothing. On the other hand, everything comes to him who waits, as they say. Not that I was actually waiting, but developments in the case of Sybil Glass—or should I say, Freddy's case—strangely enough, these developments tended to come to me, even though I did nothing to encourage them to come.

The very next day, for example, sitting in my office, the Sybil Glass case intruded on my labors. I was drafting a living trust for a client (in between daydreaming) when the phone rang. To my surprise, the caller was Dr. Pascal Le Beau. "Frank," he said, "This is Pascal. Pascal LeBeau. I think I could use your help. Your professional help."

"Of course, Pascal," I said.

"Here's the deal: it's about my granddaughter Melanie. She's got a problem and she needs to talk to you about it. Very confidentially."

I said I'd be happy to speak to her. He thanked me. We made an appointment for Melanie the following day.

Dr. Le Beau was a professional man; I didn't have to say, crudely, that my help, my advice, never came for free. I assumed he knew that my time costs money. Nor did I mention the dirty subject of an hourly rate. He would know without asking, I felt—not the precise amount, but the general principle.

I assumed she would show up with her grandfather, but instead she arrived with a young man in tow. She introduced him as "My friend, Peter Chang."

Melanie was young and nicely dressed, and she had a sweet way about her. She was hardly what anybody would call pretty. Maybe that's why Freddy never wanted to be more than a friend. Still, she was presentable; medium height and weight, fairly regular features. Her hair was dark, and rolled up into a sort of bun. There was nothing wrong with her looks, no moles and warts, no body odor. She had, to my taste, very little sex appeal, but that doesn't mean much. For most people of either gender, sex appeal is not something blatant and obvious, not something that screams out at you. It's there, I suppose, under the surface. It comes out, say, at night, when the clothes come off. Melanie seemed fairly colorless, fairly vanilla, but I could see how a young guy could find her appealing—Peter Chang obviously saw it too.

After all, who knows why anybody gets involved with this or that partner? It's a mystery no scientist has ever plumbed. One of my clients, Boris, an immigrant from Russia who owns two restaurants (they don't serve Russian food, thank God), used to wail and wring his hands about his son Vasili, "My pride and joy; and look what he's doing with his life." Not his professional life: Vasili was in medical school in San Francisco, and doing very well as far as classwork was concerned. But his personal life, according to Boris, was an utter disaster. Vasili lurched from one unsuitable woman to another. He was currently living with a woman who was ten years older than he was, divorced, and (according to Boris) she was "A disgusting creature! When she opens her mouth, you can see things stuck through her tongue, and she's fat and lazy. I said, 'Vasili, what do you see in her?' He says, 'Papa, I love her. And by the way, she's pregnant.'"

Melanie, of course, had nothing in common with Vasili's girlfriend. There was nothing whatsoever stuck through her tongue, or anywhere else visible (earrings don't count). She was the right age for Peter Chang. For that matter, she would have been the right age for Vasili. She made a good impression on me, right from the start. Her problem, if she had a problem, was that she was (as I said) fairly colorless. Peter Chang, at first sight, also seemed colorless. He wore glasses with dark rims, fairly thick glasses, and the rims were too dark for my taste. He was thin, bony, and had a receding chin. He was wearing chino pants and a light blue shirt. Everything about him shrieked: nerd. But who knows? Maybe he was a tiger in bed.

Melanie made some small talk about the weather, and then came to the point. "My grandfather said I should talk to you. About my problem. Maybe I should say *our* problem. He said you'd give us some advice."

"Well, I'll try."

"It's about this awful business at Freddy's house. Maybe he told you this, but Peter and I stayed in the house, when Freddy went to Santa Barbara. I wish I hadn't. How was I supposed to know somebody would be killed? And it was so awful, a body, lying there in the backyard! Well, not exactly the backyard, there's a big space behind the house, really huge; nobody goes there most of the time—I've never been there myself. But you know all this. I was looking forward to the weekend, and then it turned into a nightmare. I thought it would be a chance to have time with Peter. His parents are really strict. They don't know about me. I don't know what they'd do if they found out he was there in the house, just the two of us."

Peter nodded his head, in agreement. "They're really old-fashioned," he said. "They're immigrants, they don't under-stand things. I love them, I respect them, but, no way would they understand about Melanie and me. I'm supposed to marry a Chinese girl. Somebody they think is kosher. They don't know about Melanie. I'm ashamed that I can't mention her at home, can't bring her home, can't introduce her to my folks. I feel awful about that. But I really can't do anything about it. Melanie understands, she's willing to wait."

Melanie said: "We were doing Freddy a favor. Freddy asked me to housesit. Freddy never wants to leave the house empty. He has a thing about that. He thinks, what if there's a fire? Or the pipes burst, or something like that? And once, years ago, he and his aunt went to New York or some place, and the house was burglarized while they were gone. He has a thing about empty houses, ever since. So when he goes away, he likes to have somebody there. I've done it before for him. One time, he was going to LA, I can't remember why, and he was leaving on a Saturday morning, coming back Sunday night; and he asked me to stay over. I said, 'Freddy, it's only one day, sure I'll do it, but it's silly, nothing's going to happen to the house, believe me.' But he really wanted me to stay there. So I did. And, this time, I was really glad to do it because Peter and I are trying to work things out, and ... oh God, how was I supposed to know about this woman, that they'd find her dead, in the back? And the police, they asked me so many questions. I was back home by then, staying with my grandfather, and they were grilling me, it was awful! But the point is, I lied to them. I never told them about Peter. I said I was housesitting, that I did this for Freddy, lots of times, and I didn't hear anything or see anything, and that was that. I thought that everything would be okay. But when the police were asking all these questions, my grandfather was there, at least part of the time; and then later I talked to him, and he said I could get in trouble. For lying. He said, 'Melanie, you should never lie to the police. You didn't do anything wrong, so why did you tell them those lies?' I got very upset, and he said I should talk to a lawyer—and that's you. Mr. May, what do you think?"

"She did it for me," Peter said. "I didn't tell her to lie. I didn't want her to lie. I know why she did it, though, and I feel terrible about it."

"I just had to," she said. "If your parents ever found out...."

"They have to know about us, sooner or later," he said. "It's a family thing, Mr. May...."

I interrupted long enough to tell them to call me Frank. "Okay, Frank," Peter said. "I have to explain. I'm the only boy in my family. I've got two married sisters, but mom and dad pinned all their hopes on me. The son. They wanted me to be a doctor, or a scientist, a chemist, anything with science, you know? I got into Stanford, and I was majoring in biochemistry; I took all those courses, all those science courses, and I worked in a lab, doing research. Actually, Frank, I made a big discovery."

"A big discovery, Peter? What did you discover?"

"I discovered I wasn't cut out to be a biochemist. I discovered I hated it. And I wasn't really good at it. Not good enough for the big leagues. I wasn't getting top grades, and my parents were freaking out. So I dropped all my science courses, all the engineering stuff, all the math. I took introductory Russian, don't ask me why, somehow I wanted to, maybe it was fate. I like languages. I met Melanie in the Russian class. I loved the class; and I loved Melanie. Now we both want to major in Russian studies. We're fascinated with Russia. It's so big. I see it on the map, it's bigger than China, bigger than the US. It's the biggest country. And Russian history is amazing too, it's terrifically interesting. I want to do Russian studies in graduate school. I want to work on Catherine the Great. She's the most amazing woman that's ever lived; that's what I think."

Melanie gave him an adoring look. I asked him, had he ever traveled to Russia?

"I've never been there. Never. Just read about it. I want to go there. With Melanie. And I'm working hard on my Russian. I love the sound of it, all those consonants. It's a terrific language. My folks speak Chinese around the house, I understand Chinese—well, Cantonese at least—but I can't read or write Chinese. My dream is me and Melanie traveling on the Trans-Siberian railway. Days and days, looking out the window at Siberia. I want to go to all those mysterious places. I want to go to Irkutsk. Kamchatka. Dnepopetrovsk. I love the sound of those names. Those are great names. Not like the phony names around here, like Palo Alto or San Mateo—sorry, I didn't mean to insult you."

I wasn't insulted, I told him. I had nothing emotionally invested in the name of San Mateo, city or county. Or in any of those leftover Spanish names, all over California. I had never given a moment's thought to them, or asked, who was San Mateo, and why the county and the town were named after him? Or who Santa Barbara was, or why there was a town named San Luis Obispo?

"I didn't tell her to lie," Peter said again. "About that weekend. But now we're sort of stuck. What should we do?"

What indeed. I had to tell them, quite frankly, that I had no easy answer to their question. "I suppose," I said to Melanie, "you could go to the police, or whoever is in charge of the investigation, and just tell them the truth. You could explain what the problem was, and why you didn't want to mention Peter's name—and ask them to keep it to themselves. It's a little awkward, but they don't have any reason to talk to Peter's folks. They'll want to talk to Peter, since he was there at the house. And that won't be a problem, will it? Do you live at home, Peter?"

"Not now. I'm in a dorm," he said.

"So that shouldn't be a problem. You can see them at the dorm. Or the police station. Whatever. No reason to bring in your parents. Just answer the questions. Tell the truth. That's best, isn't it?"

They looked at each other. There was something in that look. Clearly, they were holding something back. I said: "Melanie, you said you told the police, you didn't see anything or hear anything. And Peter, I assume you'd say the same thing, right?"

A short hesitation. "Well, not exactly nothing," she said. "Somebody knocked on the door, it was right after Freddy left, and I thought maybe he forgot something. Anyway, I answered it. Peter was in another room, and there was this Lizbeth person, and she said she wanted to see Freddy, and I said, he wasn't there, and I didn't exactly invite her in ... and she just stood there, like she didn't believe me, and I said, 'Well, he's really not here,' and she just kept on standing there. So finally I closed the door. I think she was still there. It freaked me out a bit. And I told Peter about it, of course. But he said, pay no attention; and then a bit later on, we thought we heard a noise, and we looked out the back—there's a light you can turn on—and she was still standing there, just standing in the backyard. And this freaked me out even more."

Peter said: "I asked Melanie, 'Should I do something?' She said, 'Like what?' And I said, 'I dunno, maybe go out there and ask her to go away,' and we talked about this. But then we looked again, a bit later, and she was gone. Anyway, we think she was gone. Frank, do you think that maybe she's the one? The one that killed that woman?"

"I don't know," I said. "Could be. *Somebody* did. She seems seriously crazy. But that doesn't make her guilty." I remembered, though, how much she hated Sybil Glass. Pure hatred. No idea what lay behind the hatred—whether she knew something about Sybil Glass, or Sybil knew something about her—and what connection they had with each other.

"And I didn't say anything about Lizbeth either, when I talked to the police," Melanie said. "Not that this had anything to do with Peter; I could have told them about Lizbeth, and just kept him out of it. But I didn't say boo. I know, that was wrong. I guess I thought the less I say the better. So I told them, well, basically nothing. I told them I just stayed in the house, and nothing happened, it was all quiet, and so on. I thought, if I stick to this story, they won't bother me anymore. But this was the wrong thing to do, wasn't it?"

I didn't respond for a moment. I was thinking of Lizbeth. So she was hanging around Freddy's place, that evening, the evening Freddy went away. And that was either when Sybil died, or shortly afterwards. This was really relevant information. Still, Melanie and Peter had come to me for advice, and I had to think of their interests, and not about what the police should or should not know, or anything to do with solving the case.

Still, the two factors, I think, more or less coincided. I had already given Melanie my opinion, and now I felt more strongly than ever: she had to be honest, she had to volunteer the whole story to the authorities. Including the part about Lizbeth. I told

Melanie that she should tell them the truth—and *why* she had lied. I said I thought they would honor her confidence. Peter's parents had nothing to do with the investigation.

They seemed satisfied, and soon afterwards they left. Would they follow my advice? I had no idea.

28

I think I must have an honest, open face. I think people trust me. They *should* trust me; I *am* an honest lawyer. Many people think this is an oxymoron, but it isn't. The point is, people come to see me, and they feel they can talk to me, tell me their troubles, ask me to solve their problems—well, at least certain problems, problems that are least vaguely legal. I can't do anything for insomnia, sinus infections, pimples, infertility, or sexual maladjustment. But I do get a lot of problems that are borderline legal at best. Some of these problems are connected with these issues of murder that somehow plague me.

"You practically invite it," Celia said. It was after dinner, and she was knitting in the living room. It was a scarf for her colleague, Adam Finkel, the math teacher with the awful complexion. "You claim you want nothing to do with any of these wretched affairs, but they know you better than that. And so do I." I had just told her about Melanie and Peter.

"Honestly, I don't encourage people," I said.

"Maybe you do, subliminally," she said. "Or with body language. But can't you stay out of it, Frank? Is it really any of your business?"

"Well, in a way it is," I said. "Freddy is my client, and all of this is connected to him. I mean, this dead woman, she probably was his birth mother. She had documents to prove it."

"So what, my dear? I don't see the legal issue here."

"Murder isn't a legal issue?"

"Frank, don't play games with me," she said, putting down her knitting needles. "You know exactly what I'm talking about. Yes, murder is a legal issue. But it's not *your* legal issue. You don't do murder."

Of course she was right. She's always right. It's maddening how right she is about these things. She always gives good advice. Sometimes I even take it. At any rate, I didn't put up an argument. I changed the subject, which was easy enough. We began to talk about my older daughter and some of her friends, who seemed to us to be not exactly the kind of kids we wanted her to hang out with. As usual, of course, we talked and talked and came to no definite conclusion.

Just then the phone rang.

It was Derek, which was something of a surprise. And an annoyance. I don't like people to call me at home. And usually they don't. For one thing, clients for the most part do not know my home phone number, which is unlisted, nor my cellphone number, for that matter.

Derek sounded rather agitated. He said he had to see me, it was important: "Are you free right now, or later this evening? Can I come to your house?"

I told him, with a trace of irritation in my voice, that he could come to my office the next day. I would be happy to see him; but right now, I was busy, we had company at the house (a little white lie), and it wasn't convenient.

I certainly wasn't about to tell him the truth. The truth was, I didn't want him to come. My plan for the evening was to watch a new nature program on TV, which, people said, had fantastic shots of cheetahs and gorillas and other wonderful animals. Not to mention a segment about giraffes. I love giraffes. Those long necks, and the way they move. Big African mammals are fascinating; more fascinating than most people, definitely including Derek Schuster.

As I suspected, and later found out, it was Freddy who had leaked my phone number to Derek. I had made an exception to my rule for Freddy, who liked to call at all hours. Maybe it was a mistake to give my number to Freddy. But Freddy was willing to pay for the right to call me whenever he felt the urge. For Freddy, I was sort of a concierge lawyer.

Most of my law business (thank God) does not involve situations of crisis. For example, to take a current piece of business, I have a client, a wealthy widow, who wants to set up a trust. It's for her favorite nephew, Joshua, who calls her Aunt Minnie. He comes to visit her in her very expensive apartment, and he sends her beautiful bouquets—roses—on her birthday, on Easter, on Mother's Day, and who knows, maybe the Fourth of July, none of which her own son, Benjamin, would even dream of doing; and (she said) her daughter-in-law, whom she despises, would never think of showing any love or even courtesy to Minnie.

My practice is full of Aunt Minnies and families in general. Many of them are at least slightly dysfunctional. Almost all are at least well-to-do, or better. I'm more than happy to oblige them in any and every way; but drafting a living trust is never an emergency, and it can almost always wait until daylight, it never has to be done on Sunday, and indeed, it can usually wait a day or two, or even weeks.

Derek too would have to wait. The giraffes and the cheetahs came first.

29

I had a good night's sleep, and a hearty breakfast. The girls were on time for school, which is not something that happens every day, and they didn't even quarrel over use of the bathroom. I kissed Celia, we went our separate ways, and I headed for the office. It was a beautiful day; a fine, warm, friendly California day. Not a cloud in the sky. I indulged in a latte at the local coffee shop, and then plunged into work, on Aunt Minnie's trust, among other things. I was in a good mood. In general, I like my work. And I put Freddy and Sybil and the rest of that crowd on the back burner. Not that they stayed there.

In the afternoon, Derek Schuster came to my office. I had lunch with a client, in a Burmese restaurant. I ate too much, had a wicked dessert afterwards, and felt, consequently, a rather desperate need for a nap. This was not, of course, meant to be. I had to face Derek without the benefit of a refreshing sleep.

Derek had always struck me as a fairly tough customer. He was supposed to be Freddy's dear friend; but Derek, I felt, had only one person's interests in mind—his own. He took advantage of Freddy, manipulated him—I was sure of that. Usually, Derek seemed cocky, self-assured, a trifle brash. But today, it was a slightly different Derek who came to see me. He seemed if anything somewhat nervous, somewhat agitated.

"You talked to Freddy the other day," he said. "I want to clear something up. He told you about something that happened before that woman got killed. He had gone to see her and

159

she wasn't there. And, well, he had a conversation with some guy, the owner of the house, who claimed that Freddy *was* there. Freddy told you all of this."

"Why are you asking, Derek? What my clients say to me, Derek—you know I can't share these things with anybody else. You're in law school; you should know that."

"Look," he said, "I took legal ethics, and I know all that shit. Freddy told me the whole story. I don't need you to confirm or deny it, okay? I know what Freddy said. And I know what that guy said. About somebody in the house. The guy, I don't know his name, he said he saw Freddy. Inside the place, talking to Sybil, I suppose. And what I want to tell you is, it wasn't Freddy."

"Okay, who was it then?"

"It was me. That creep, the guy who owns the house, he peeked in the window, and he saw somebody sitting with Sybil Glass, a young guy, but all he saw was the back of the guy's head. He just assumed it was Freddy. Sybil told him her son was coming to see her. She was always saying 'My son this, my son that,' everywhere she went, I suppose, to the dentist for all I know; I guess she was trying to reinforce the idea. Spreading the word. Broadcasting the idea that she was Freddy's mother. Well, we'll see about that."

The last phrase was a bit odd, and I meant to ask him about it, but meanwhile I had a different question: "Okay, Derek, so it was you. But what on earth were you doing there? What's your connection with Sybil? Why was it any of your business?"

"Well, Freddy's my friend, my buddy, and he's, well, kind of a vulnerable guy. And rich. So here comes this dubious woman, claims she's his mother, has documents and that kind of shit—and I thought, it's my duty to my friend to find out more about her, check her out. That's why I went to see her."

Did I believe him? Absolutely not. I debated for a minute whether to call him on this. Tell him I thought he was lying. But I decided it wasn't worth it. He would just double down on his story.

"And suppose I told you," I said, "that you were seen skulking around Freddy's house, just after he left, and that you were prowling in the back. Which some people thought was pretty suspicious."

"I came to see Freddy," he said. "Then I saw his car was gone. And I saw Melanie and her boyfriend through the window. So I just gave it up, just went home."

Another lie? Told in a very brazen way. I didn't believe any of it. But why was he telling me this stuff? "Derek," I said. "You know what? I don't believe you. I have to wonder, what on earth you were doing there, at Freddy's house?"

He paused for a second. Then he said: "Alright. I was trying to find Sybil. Yes, Sybil. She wasn't at home. And I thought, maybe she's at Freddy's? And she wasn't there either. Maybe she was already dead. I don't know."

He could see on my face that I was dubious about this statement, too, and whatever else he was saying.

"Look," he said. "For the record: I'm on Freddy's side. I really am. You don't believe me. But someday I'll prove it. He'll be grateful to me. I'm trying to be honest with you. That's why I came here. To tell you I was the guy in Sybil's place. And to tell you why I was there."

"Fine," I said. "If true. But why me? Why did you come here? What difference does it make what I think?"

"Because you're important," he said. "Because Freddy trusts you, and he confides in you. And because I heard that you're, well, investigating. People say you're not just a lawyer—doing wills and that sort of shit—that's just a front...."

"Derek, what on earth are you saying? This office is just a front? For what? I'm dealing in drugs or something? Listen, I could give you a client list; you could ask those people. On second thought, don't. But look: I handle wills and trusts, I do other stuff for my clients, that's the only front this place is. Good God, where do you get this nonsense from?"

"People talk," he said. "I hear rumors. Even Freddy thinks so. You've been involved in all kinds of things. And you figure things out. That's what I hear. This woman, Zelda, she swears to it."

What could I say? Of course, I denied this utterly, but I was sure Derek didn't believe a word of what I said, any more than I believed a word of his line of guff.

People read too many mystery novels. They get the wrong idea. In many of those books, the detective is some sort of hardboiled tough guy or a fierce, hard-bitten woman who runs a private investigative shop. You would think, when they look at me—Mr. Suburbia, early middle-age, losing some of his hair, a trifle overweight, in a neat but unimpressive office, and working on wills and trusts for Aunt Minnie and Uncle Joe and God knows who else—you would think they would dismiss the idea out of hand that I was some sort of Master Detective.

But that's where the rest of the literature comes in. The books where the "detective" (so to speak) is somebody you would never think of in those terms. Miss Marple, the village spinster. Father Brown, the Catholic priest. Charlie Chan and his "number one son." In one book that I read, the "detective" was a banker. Imagine that, a banker! No doubt, among the zillions of mysteries that pour out from the presses, you can find whatever form and kind of solver you could possibly imagine: a Rabbi, an Imam, a proctologist, an orthopedist, a hedge fund operator, a pediatric dentist, a professional burglar, a certified public accountant, and who knows, maybe somebody will write a book in which a vampire or a zombie solves the crime.

Anybody, that is. Only not me. At least that's what I thought when Derek left. In a way, I was wrong. I did have a hand in the solution.

But that comes later. After Derek was gone, I sat for a moment thinking. Why had he come? On the surface, the answer was obvious: he wanted to clear up a mystery. Who was the person in Sybil's apartment? He wanted to corroborate Freddy's account. But why had he gone to see Sybil? When I asked him this question, his answer was vague and unsatisfying. He said again, that he was Freddy's friend. He was convinced the woman was a fraud, and he felt he had to see for himself, had to get to know her, try to figure out what she was after. Did I believe him? No. There was something else here.

But that day at least, I could get nothing further out of Derek Schuster. There would be answers, but I had to wait for them.

30

It was a very, very agitated Freddy that called me the next afternoon. My work on poor Aunt Minnie's trust was interrupted again.

"Frank, I've got see you. I'm going nuts," he said. But I had to tell him, there was no way I could see him that afternoon, I had clients coming in. "Can I come to your house?" he asked. I told him that would be inconvenient. But he seemed so upset, I decided to accommodate him; I promised that I would come see him at his house on my way home. "But I can't stay long," I said.

When I got there, I asked, "What's this all about, Freddy?"

"It's about Derek," he said. "Here's the story, Frank. I slept late, well, to be honest, I couldn't fall asleep last night, I tossed and turned, and then I finally got a few hours in; but it was eleven when I woke up, and I had this awful headache, I thought my head was exploding, you know what I mean? And Derek called me, and I told him about the headache, and I said, 'I can't see anybody,' so he said he knows something that's terrific for headaches, and I said, 'Okay, and bring me something to eat, there's nothing in the house.' Anyway, he came over and I made some coffee, and then the doorbell rang and I didn't want to answer it, but Derek said, 'Don't be a baby,' and I went to the door, and I opened it, and it was Desmond Fingerhut...."

"Desmond who? Is this somebody I'm supposed to know?"

"Oh, sorry Frank. Desmond is my neighbor, sort of. I mean, you know my house—it's got this huge area in the back, all wild, where the body was—and Desmond, he owns the house on the hill in back of my property. I don't know him well, he's a retired chemist or something; but he seems to be an okay guy, not like the other people around here. Anyway, he's the one who found the body. And he took one look at the two of us, and he said, 'Oh, I didn't know you were busy,' and I said, 'No, we're just talking,' but he said, 'I'll come back later,' and he was gone, just like that."

"So?"

"Well, Derek left, said he had a seminar that afternoon; and Desmond came over again. And he said to me, 'Freddy, I just came over to talk, tell you how sorry I was about all the stuff going on—but I have to ask, who was that guy you were talking to?' I said, 'His name is Derek Schuster, he's a friend.' And Desmond said, 'What kind of friend?' And I said, 'You know, just a friend.' And Desmond said, 'Look, I don't want to say anything out of line, but I saw that guy prowling around.' I said, 'What do you mean, prowling around?' And he said, 'Well, before I found that woman's body, I saw him in that area. There's a part of it I can see from my house. And he was there, looking for something. Did he tell you about this?' And I said, 'No,' and he said, 'Well, it's suspicious. I just thought you'd like to know.' Frank, what should I do?"

"I really don't know, Freddy," I said. "Just be careful. I don't think you can trust Derek. I know he says he's your friend, but some of his behavior seems awfully strange."

"Frank," Freddy asked. "You don't think he killed that woman, do you?"

I told him I had no idea. Actually, things pointed in two contradictory directions. Certainly, you couldn't rule out Derek as a suspect. It did seem that he had some sort of connection with Sybil; maybe they were working together. But on what? And for what purpose? To squeeze money out of Freddy? Yet, assuming this was true, how would Derek profit from Sybil's death?

I tried to cheer Freddy up, as much as I could. I told him the police were surely hard at work on the case and that they were certain to figure out what had happened. Of course, I made this up; I had no idea what was going on. Fortunately, I was able to change the subject. Freddy was, after all, my client, and he was in the process of inheriting a great deal of money. Not without complications, of course. And one of these complications, I pointed out, was Sybil Glass and her claim to a portion of what would otherwise be Freddy's money.

I explained it all, in clear simple language. I also went over some of the details of the probate process, and Freddy's rights under his aunt's will, and I raised the issue of Freddy's own will, and talked about some of the possibilities. Freddy nodded. Of course it went in one ear and out the other.

I left Freddy's house, and drove on home; I was late for dinner, which was a source of some familial aggravation. But fortunately, the family storm blew over, and relatively quickly.

When I thought about the case—and, despite Celia's good advice, I couldn't keep it from crowding into my brain—it seemed clearer and clearer to me that Derek Schuster was somehow crucial to the whole affair. He had to be considered a prime suspect.

I wasn't the only one who thought so. I had a surprise visitor the next day: Ella Fisk-Potter. She came unannounced, in the afternoon. I had been talking to a client; she waited until the man left, then came in and demanded to speak to me.

"People talk about you," she said. "They say you're an important player. In this mess. They say you're trying to figure things out behind the scenes. And don't give me your usual 'I'm just a lawyer' shit. I know better."

I did give her what she called my "just a lawyer" shit, a bit stronger than I do ordinarily. The disclaimer had the usual effect it has on people: absolutely nothing. Proving a negative of this kind is simply impossible.

"Whatever," she said. "Have it your way. I know that bastard, Derek, has been talking to you. You can't trust him as far as you can throw him, believe me. He poisoned Freddy's mind against me. Told him all kinds of shit. Believe it or not, I actually liked Freddy. I thought he was sweet. I had a good time with him. Okay, he's rich: is there anything wrong with that? You'd think having money was some kind of disadvantage, for God's sake, like having body odor, or weighing 300 pounds. Sure, I liked Freddy's money, but I liked Freddy, too. And that bastard, Derek, when he got through talking to Freddy—and Freddy is like a baby, he believes everything that guy tells him— what was the result? Well, you know what it was. Freddy dropped me. Dumped me. Just like that."

"Look, Ella," I said. "That's up to Freddy, isn't it? It's none of my business, as you certainly realize."

She ignored this comment completely. "I just want you to know," she said, "that that guy is playing a dubious game. I know you're on this case...."

"Ella, how many times do I have to tell you I'm not?"

"You're Freddy's lawyer, right? He's relying on you. This guy, Derek, he was in cahoots with that woman, Sybil. I don't know exactly what they were up to, but nothing good, I can promise you that. He spent time with her; did you know that? Went to her house. They were thick as thieves. Then I think something happened, they had some sort of argument, maybe about money; and he killed her. Maybe he didn't plan to kill her, but he did it. And then he decided to pin the thing on Freddy. So he dumped the body in that area, in Freddy's backyard; well, it's not exactly a backyard. I guess he did it after dark. Maybe he planned to have somebody find the body. Maybe he tipped off that mushroom guy. I don't know. All I do know, is, this is Derek's work."

"I hear you, Ella," I said. "But what do you want *me* to do? It's not my affair."

She raised her voice; she was clearly angry. "It *is* your affair. You're Freddy's lawyer."

She had a strange idea of what lawyers do for their clients. The conversation went nowhere. I tried to mollify her, as much as I could. She wanted me to go to the police, to make a fuss, to get Derek arrested, thrown in jail. Of course, I couldn't agree to anything of the sort. Finally, she left the office—quite unsatisfied, I suppose.

Why had she come? Did she really think Derek killed Sybil Glass? Or was she trying to shift attention away from somebody or something else? Herself, maybe? I had to agree with her about one thing: Derek Schuster was playing some kind of dubious game. Was he double-crossing everybody? And if so, why?

31

I hardly had a chance to catch my breath after Ella left, when I had another visitor, also unannounced. It was Melanie. She asked, politely, and in a very quiet voice, if I had time to talk to her, and said how sorry she was about barging in, but she was nearby doing some shopping and she really needed to talk.

I couldn't help thinking how different she was from Ella. How much more likeable. I wrote her off as a suspect. Of course, if this was a novel by Agatha Christie, that would be all the more reason to be suspicious. The obvious people are never the ones who did it.

"I need your advice again," she said. "Something's come up. It's about this wretched business, this awful murder. And I know, you think I should go to the police. But … it's the same old problem. I don't want to drag Peter into this, and I'm afraid, if I go to the police with anything, anything at all, they'll start asking more questions; they'll want to know why I didn't tell them any of this before, and…"

"Melanie," I said, "I gather you didn't do what I told you, about telling the truth—telling the police about Peter—and explaining things."

"I meant to," she said, "exactly like you told me. I really meant to. I'd tell them about Peter, and why it was an embarrassing situation and I'd mention this woman, Lizbeth. But something came up since then, and … well, it's maybe different now."

"Different, Melanie?"

"Well: there's this man, he's the neighbor, Desmond Fingerhut. He was the one who found the body. Looking for mushrooms, you remember, that's why he was there, in that part of the grounds. Well, the local paper, the *Palo Alto Gazette*, the other day they were running a story about the murder. They don't have a murder very often around here, especially not in Los Altos Hills, it's a really wealthy town, nothing much happens there. So, they've been covering the murder, running stories about it, and they had an interview with Mr. Fingerhut, and he told his story—how he was looking for mushrooms, and so on, and he found the body. And in this story it says the body was covered with leaves and dirt and so on, and it was wrapped in a plain white bedsheet. That's something I didn't know about before."

"What didn't you know about before?"

"About the bedsheet. When Peter and I came to the house, we just brought overnight bags, and we brought the bags into one of the guest rooms. It's a big house. Anyway, I always stay in this one room, upstairs; and there were no sheets on the bed. I didn't think anything about it at the time, but in the past, whenever I came, the bed was made up, sheets, pillow cases, and so on. I know the house inside out, so it didn't bother me that the sheets weren't on the bed. I didn't think anything of it. I just went to the linen closet, took out two sheets, and made the bed myself. But now.... You see what I'm thinking."

"That those missing sheets ... is that the point? That they're the ones that the body was wrapped in? Were some sheets missing from the house?"

"How could I tell? I mean, there's a linen closet, and it's got towels and pillowcases and lots of sheets, but, naturally, I never counted them. Now it strikes me as peculiar. The bed wasn't made. The pillows were on the side, on top of a dresser. I mean, at the time, I didn't give it a thought. But now, because this man said the body was wrapped in a sheet, I couldn't help thinking—I know it's an awful thought—but it just struck me, was that woman killed in Freddy's house? After all, her body was on Freddy's property. But if I told this story, about the sheets, wouldn't that get Freddy in trouble...?"

"Freddy? You can't possibly think he had something to do with this," I said.

"Oh, no, no, no. Of course not. Not Freddy. I don't know what to think. But this is important, isn't it?"

I had to admit it was and I wasn't sure what to say to Melanie. I hesitated for a while, then I said: "I don't think you have to talk to the police about the sheets. After all, it's just a vague idea; maybe the bed just wasn't made. You don't have anything concrete to go on. I still think you should talk to the police, but, in my opinion, you don't need to say anything about these sheets." She nodded her head in agreement.

Actually, I don't know if this was good advice. It was safe advice. I must say, what she said about the sheets was intriguing. Maybe the murder *did* take place in Freddy's house. Maybe the murderer had been *in* the house at some point. Gently, I nudged Melanie into telling me more about that fateful day. When had she actually gotten to the house? And was Freddy there at the time?

She said: "I don't remember the exact time we got there. I met Peter downtown in Palo Alto, he had his car, and his overnight bag. Peter doesn't live at home; he's in the dorms. Anyway, we had coffee, and a sandwich, and then we drove to Los Altos Hills, to Freddy's house. I think it was about eight o'clock. Freddy was waiting for us to come. I guess we were a bit later than expected. That woman, Ella, she was already sitting in Freddy's car. It was after dark. Freddy was at the door, and we went in. I gave him a hug, and then he said a few things, something about the microwave oven—that it wasn't working, I don't remember exactly—and then he and Ella drove off. And that's all. Until that woman, Lizbeth, showed up, but that was later on. Me and Peter watched TV, and went to bed."

"You didn't see Derek, by any chance?"

"Derek? No. He didn't come by, as far as I know. I mean, he didn't come in the house, or ring the bell. Why do you ask? What does Derek have to do with this?"

"Maybe nothing. There's a rumor he was seen around the house, or on the property. Just forget I mentioned it."

"But what are you saying, Frank?" She had a worried look on her face. "Do you think Derek had something to do with this? "

"No, no, really, Melanie. Just forget what I said, really."

"Well, I can't forget it. And ... do you think ... the sheets, does that mean something? Frank, it's a horrible idea. I mean, if this woman was killed in Freddy's house.... Is that what this means? But wouldn't the police know about this? I mean, they would have some evidence, they must have gone over the house, for fingerprints or something."

"Melanie, in all honesty, I have no idea. I have no pipeline to the police, really."

I calmed her down, repeated my advice, and sent her home. Then I called Freddy. I didn't mention the sheets. "Freddy," I said, "I've got to ask you a question. Tell me what you did that day, you know, the day you went off with Ella, and ... that woman was killed. I need to know."

"Why, Frank? Did I do something wrong?"

"No, no, Freddy. I'll explain later."

"Well, I got up late, and I had some coffee, and then I went to this exercise class—I'm taking an exercise class—it was noon, I think. I can't stand that class, I'm going to quit it, the teacher, Reggie, gives me a pain.... Oh—I'm rambling again! Anyway, what did I do next? I went home, I put some stuff in a small suitcase, and then I went to meet Ella."

"What time was that?"

"I don't know. Maybe three o'clock. I went to her apartment."

"Okay, and then what happened?"

"Frank, do I have to give you a blow-by-blow description? I mean, do you need to know what we did in her apartment? Really."

No, I didn't need to know. He was blushing. I suppose they had sex. Or maybe not. Maybe they watched the daytime soap operas. Or played monopoly; it didn't make any difference. I just needed to know where he was, and when. "When did you leave the apartment?"

"Frank, you're getting me nervous. What is this all about?"

"Later, Freddy. Just answer the question."

"Well, about six o'clock, we went and had dinner. Do you need to know where?"

"No, I don't, Freddy. So the house was empty between three and ... well, when did you go back to the house?"

"Melanie was supposed to come with her boyfriend at around seven thirty, or eight. We got to the house at, oh, maybe ten to eight. I don't remember exactly. Ella stayed in the car, I went in, got my stuff, and just then Melanie drove up. She was a little late, I think. And that's that. We said goodbye and left. I was driving—or was Ella driving? I can't remember. Frank, you're getting me very nervous. What is this all about?"

I wondered, how much should I tell Freddy? I didn't want to make him even more nervous. "Freddy, I'm just trying to figure some things out. The house was empty for, oh, about five hours, give or take?"

"So what, Frank? What are you driving at?"

I felt myself somewhat boxed in. I decided to be honest with Freddy. I told him about Melanie and the sheets.

"Oh, God, Frank. Wow. No, it's not possible. You mean to suggest that woman was killed in my house? That's crazy. How would she get in? And whoever killed her, how did he get in? I don't know anything about these sheets. A woman comes once a week, her name is Gabriela, she's Mexican, she changes the sheets ... I don't pay any attention. Maybe she forgot to put sheets on that bed."

"Had somebody been using that bed?"

"Nobody. It's a guest bedroom. I mean, Melanie and Peter use it. I don't pay any attention to the sheets. Should I ask Gabriela, when she comes? It's hard to communicate with her, she hardly speaks English."

"No, don't do that, Freddy. Let's leave Gabriela out of it. And just forget the whole thing. I can see, there's nothing to it. Just a silly idea; I can see it doesn't make sense."

"Frank, if somebody killed that woman in my house, in that bedroom or wherever, I swear, I'll move into a motel. My nerves are on edge as it is. My therapist says...."

I interrupted Freddy at that point. I had no interest in what his therapist said. I repeated, more forcefully, that the whole question of the sheets was a red herring; nobody was killed in his house. I made the point that the police, if they thought the murder took place there, they would have been combing the place for clues. They didn't do that, so clearly they didn't think so; and I told him I was sorry if I had made him nervous, and that he should forget the whole affair of the sheets.

He said he would try.

"It's nothing, Freddy," I said, "it's really nothing." I stressed this point. I think he was, finally, convinced.

But I, on the other hand, wasn't.

32

I didn't expect any particular fallout from my conversation with Melanie, so imagine my surprise when the next unexpected and unannounced visitor turned out to be Melanie's boyfriend, Peter Chang. A few days had gone by. He came by in the late afternoon, and rather timidly knocked on my office door.

As it was, I was about to leave; I had my jacket on, a briefcase in hand, and I knew Celia would be furious if I came home late. She was having guests for dinner. She had invited one of her colleagues to join us. This was a relatively new addition to the faculty, a woman who taught Spanish classes. She was, Celia said "Very attractive—she's from Spain, originally. She's divorced, and awfully nice. I was thinking Adam might like to get to know her better." Adam was, of course, Adam Finkel, the math teacher with the horrible complexion; Celia never gives up trying to find him a life-partner, or at the very least, some sort of romantic interest. She had also invited Cindy Dobbins, the daughter of one of our neighbors. Cindy was in her late 30's. She was recently divorced (no children), and had moved back in with her mother and father. I had no idea what she did for a living, but she was another candidate for Adam. All this, of course, was going to be utterly futile. Adam was sweet, but hopeless when it came to women. Celia, however, refused to abandon the struggle.

Moreover, I had been told to stop by the grocery and buy vinegar for the salad dressing. "Make sure it's balsamic, Frank,"

I was told. "Don't just buy the cheapest vinegar. Get good vinegar. It makes a big difference."

"Do you have a minute?" Peter asked. "I'd like to talk to you; it won't take long."

I told him I was on my way out, and in something of a hurry. I imagine he thought I was on the way to court or something serious in the legal department. I was certainly not about to tell him I was in search of balsamic vinegar. He asked if he could walk with me to my car. I'm sure he would have preferred to sit down in my office, but I had orders from higher authority, and I had to obey.

Downstairs, when we walked out the door to the street, he said to me, "I know Melanie came to talk to you the other day."

"She did," I said.

"I know I can't ask you what she said. I know it was confidential."

Actually, Melanie and I had talked about her suspicions—the matter of the bedsheets. Surely that was not a secret from Peter. He was, after all, the other half of the team that ended up on top of and between the bedsheets on that bed; I imagined that he too had noticed the bed was unmade, and probably he helped put the sheets on.

"Why are you bringing this up, Peter?" I asked. We had reached my car. He hesitated for a minute.

"Because ... because something is going on."

"Excuse me? Something is going on? What do you mean, Peter?"

He looked as if he was on the verge of tears. "She means a lot to me, Mr. May...."

"Please call me Frank."

"I love her. I know we have problems, but she's ... she's everything to me. I never was so involved with anyone before, any girlfriend I mean. You have to understand that. I think about her night and day. And now ... now, oh God, I don't know what's wrong. She didn't appear in one of the classes, a Russian class, we were doing verbs, and she had been very excited about the verbs. She loved the verbs. And then she just wasn't there. I called her, and she said she was about to call me herself, she had something to say to me. I asked her about the class. She said she was dropping it. I asked her, 'Why, was it the verbs? They're awfully hard. But I thought you loved the verbs.' She said, 'No Peter. It's not the verbs.' Then she said: 'Peter, this is hard for me, but I have to tell you, we can't see each other anymore. We have to break up.' I begged her, I pleaded with her, I asked her what I did wrong. She said, 'You didn't do anything wrong. Please, Peter, it just has to be this way.'"

I have to admit I was surprised. "She didn't explain things?"

"She wouldn't. She refused. She was crying, I could hear that. But I couldn't get anywhere with her. She just said, over and over again, 'It has to be.'" And then he asked me: "Could it have something to do with what she talked to you about?"

"I can't see how," I said. I kept thinking of those bed sheets, but why would that make a difference to her relationship? Had something else happened?

"Also," Peter said, "there's something more. Maybe I shouldn't talk about this. I tried to go to see her, I thought, I'll go to her dorm. But I was, oh, about a block away, and I saw her, standing by the front doorway. She wasn't alone. She was with that guy, Derek Schuster. They were talking, talking, and they seemed to be all involved. Then they both starting walking away, I followed them and they walked off the quad, off the main campus, and got into a car, I guess it was his car, and they drove off."

"Peter," I said, "I don't know anything about all this, and I don't really know them that well, but if you're thinking she dropped you to take up with him, I seriously doubt it."

"I don't know what to think," he said. "I'm just so upset.... I was hoping you could tell me something that might, well, explain why she did this."

"Me? Why me?"

"Because she went to see you. And it must have been about something important. Please help me, Mr. May."

But of course I had no real explanation. I had no idea what had gone wrong between them. Or what was bothering

Melanie. Or why and how Derek Schuster was involved. I said something bland, like, "Maybe things will work out, just be patient." To tell you the truth, the balsamic vinegar was uppermost in my mind. I got in my car and drove away, leaving poor Peter standing on the curb with a devastated look on his face.

The main thing was that I reached home, in good time. And it was exactly the right kind of vinegar—exactly what Celia wanted.

33

The dinner, as I predicted, was not a success. Not that it was a total failure: the two women guests, who had never met before, seemed to hit it off; and the meal itself was delicious. I hope the vinegar played at least a supporting role. Everybody praised the salad.

On the other hand, neither woman seemed the slightest bit interested in Adam, who hardly said a word the whole evening. It was clear to me that Cindy avoided looking at him directly, because of his awful complexion, although she sat across from him at dinner, and was ostentatiously polite. Celia, in the post mortem, as we worked together in the kitchen doing the dishes and scouring the pots, admitted the evening was failure, as far as her plot to fix up Adam was concerned. "But other than that," she said, "it wasn't half bad." She said she really liked Cindy, and hoped they'd become good friends.

For me, the dinner was a welcome break from problems at the office—not to mention the nagging affair of Sybil Glass. But after we finally finished cleaning up, and the dishwasher was humming its little tune and doing its job, and I finally found myself in bed, I couldn't help thinking about that case. And I couldn't help thinking, too, that Derek Schuster, somehow, was the key to the mystery. Or one of the keys at least. He seemed to crop up everywhere. Sometimes I even imagined he might be the actual killer. I had no clue as to motive. But I distrusted the man; to me, he had a mean, ruthless streak. He was the sort of person who might, given the right opportunity, and the right frame of mind, find it in its heart to kill somebody. Provided there was something in it for him.

But what on earth could that be?

I had a restless night, even though I was terrifically tired. I tossed and turned and finally got out of bed, read a magazine, and then, when I finally fell asleep, I overslept to compensate. I dragged myself into the office in mid-morning and found, to my surprise, a message on my answering machine from none other than Derek Schuster. He left a number, and I called him back. He asked if he could come see me, and of course I agreed. I couldn't imagine what he wanted to talk to me about.

When he appeared, he sat down and began talking, without any preliminaries or small talk. "I want to clear up some stuff," he said. "I don't know what people have been telling you. Freddy for one. Maybe Melanie. I don't know who else. I know I've got a big problem. Bad optics, if you know what I mean."

"Actually, I don't."

"This woman, Sybil Glass. People are saying I had a relationship with her. I don't mean sex or anything like that. I mean, some sort of business arrangement; I don't know how else to describe it. They think I was in some sort of alliance, trying to get money from Freddy, or his aunt's estate, or whatever. But that just isn't true."

I didn't know what to say.

He said: "She wrote a letter to Freddy. I know you know about that letter. I didn't let Freddy read it, I took it, and I destroyed it. Tore it in pieces and flushed it down the toilet. Did you talk to Freddy about the letter? About what it might have said?"

"Derek," I said, "what I talk to Freddy about is, frankly, none of your business."

"Okay, I get it," he said. "Whether or not you talked to Freddy, you must have suspected what was in the letter. So I'm going to tell you pointblank. It was a warning to Freddy, it said, 'Don't trust Derek Schuster. He's a false friend.' It accused me of, well, betraying him. Said that I had gone to see her, Sybil that is. Said that I tried to hook up with her, financially speaking; I wanted a piece of Aunt Clara's estate, and I promised to help her get the money."

"That's what was in the letter and what you saying is, it wasn't true? Is that it?"

He said: "Exactly. I know things look that way. Like I was playing up to her, for some dastardly reason. Betraying Freddy. Behind his back. Look: I did go to see her, and I did pretend to be, well, on her side. That day in particular, when the guy who owns the house—you know the story, how he told Freddy he saw Freddy in Sybil's apartment and of course he didn't, what he saw was me. I'm telling the truth. I was there, I was talking to her. She told me Freddy was coming to see her later, in an hour or so. I told her not to let him in, to go out, just don't be in the flat when he comes. She wanted to know, why should she do that? I gave her some kind of cockeyed reason, and I said, 'Look, trust me: I want to talk business.' She said, 'What sort of business?' And I said, 'Business about the estate.'"

"And she agreed to that?"

"Well, she was cautious. I said to her, 'You're Freddy's mother, you really are; I know that, I know you've got documents and I believe you, but show me your stuff.' And she did, the birth certificate and the rest of it. I told her, I could give her good advice, I could show her how to handle Freddy. I said, 'You can't really expect him to throw his arms around you,' and all that stuff. 'I'm a law student, I know something about these things, estate planning, wills, and so on; I can help with the estate, but above all, I can help you deal with Freddy.'

"Well, she was suspicious. She said, 'Aren't you supposed to be Freddy's friend?' And I said, 'Yeah, I am, I'm his friend, probably his best friend; but I want to be your friend too. Freddy, well, he's got to be handled, and I can do that, you know? Can't blame him for being, well, cool to you.' She said, 'You know, I really am his mother,' and blah blah. And we talked, and then we went out and had lunch and talked some more. She was as cool as a cucumber. All she wanted was the money, of course. Didn't give a damn about Freddy. Some mother. I made her think I was interested in the money too, and that's why I was willing to help her. I thought I convinced her, but I guess I underestimated her. She was a shrewd, cold-blooded bitch; in the end, I think she saw through me. That's why she wrote that letter. She decided it would be better to ditch me, and get Freddy on her side. That's what happened."

"How did you know about the letter?"

"I'll get to that point; just be patient."

"Alright, Derek. But tell me this, why *did* you go to see her? You say you weren't really on her side, but doesn't it look that way?"

He looked straight at me. He paused for a minute, and then he said, "I know it does. That's what I want to explain. I never trusted her. I was sure, I felt it in my bones. There's something wrong here. This woman is a fake. She can't possibly be Freddy's mother. It doesn't make any sense. She's a fraud, an imposter—I don't know how she does it, and there were those documents, but something about the whole thing smelled bad—and I decided I was going to prove it."

"Prove it? How?"

"With modern science. When I was talking to her, buttering her up, I had an ulterior motive. What I really wanted from her was a sample of her DNA; it was the only way I could prove she was a phony. She had a cup of coffee in the restaurant and when she went to the bathroom, I stole the cup. I also took a tissue she used, and whatever else I could get my hands on, so that I could have all this stuff checked out. And I did the same with Freddy; I got samples of his DNA. That part was easy."

"And you did this ... why?"

"Look, you don't believe me, I can see it, you think I'm a skunk, a false friend. But I really was trying to help Freddy. I really was. And I had a hunch. Who was this woman? What was she up to? And, like, where had she been all those years? Suddenly she pops up and says, 'Hello, I'm your mother'—what kind of shit is that?"

"Well," I said, "as a matter of fact, I don't think it's that all mysterious. Did you know Clara Fisk was paying her off? She was getting regular payments, in her bank account. That's maybe what kept her away; she was always just interested in money. Then, Clara died, and she didn't make any provision for

Sybil, there was nothing in the will, and so the money stopped. Maybe that's when she figured, now's the time to make my move."

"I didn't know about those payments. Even so, I still think there's something funny going on. The lawyer, the one who's handling the Clara Fisk estate...."

"Gideon Grambling? Is that it? You're working on behalf of Gideon Grambling?"

"Not exactly."

"Is that a yes or a no?"

"I'd rather not say," he said.

I didn't press on the point. It seemed quite dubious to me. I suppose I could check with Gideon; I made a mental note to do so. "Well, what was the result of the DNA test?" I asked, "How did it turn out?"

"That's what I came to talk to you about. And when I tell you, you'll finally believe me. That I'm a good guy. That I'm Freddy's friend. And you'll tell him that."

"Derek, don't beat around the bush," I said. "What were the results of the test?"

"I double-checked everything," he said. "I didn't take the first results as conclusive, no, I wanted to make absolutely sure. And now I am."

"Well," I said, "out with it: what did you find?"

"What I suspected all along. The results are conclusive, Frank. Beyond a shadow of a doubt. That woman was not Freddy's mother. She has no genetic connection with him whatsoever."

I was staggered at the news. For a few seconds, I was speechless. Then I said, "No joke Derek: you're really sure, I mean, do you realize what you're saying?"

"Frank, it's certain. One hundred percent. The DNA doesn't lie. This is science. I'll show you the reports. This woman was not Freddy's mother. She's a total fraud."

"Okay, okay, I believe you, Derek. I suppose I have to. At least, when I see the proof...."

"You'll see it. I guarantee it."

"But then where did she get these documents? This birth certificate—look, it shows that a boy was born on the day Freddy says is his birthday, it lists Sybil as the mother, father unknown. And ... she had other proofs. A letter from Kathryn, Freddy's adoptive mother, addressed to Sybil—and it thanked her for turning over her baby, and so on. I mean, what does all that mean?"

"I have no idea. The birth certificate, maybe it's a forgery. I can check on that. Or maybe she stole this from somebody else, who knows? The letters, well, maybe they're fakes. Who knows who wrote those letters? From the moment she came here, I thought, this woman is out for the money, plain and simple. She's an impostor. And I was right."

"Did you tell all this to the police?"

"No, but I'm going to. And, Frank, I left out part of the story. About the letter. The day before she died, she said she wanted to talk to me. I went to see her. She said she had been thinking about our conversations, and she didn't want to have anything more to do with me. And she said she knew what I was up to. She was a shrewd cookie. Maybe she realized I had gotten some sort of sample, and was checking her out. I tried to deny it, but she saw right through me. So then I said, yes, alright, I know you're not Freddy's mother; and I'm going to expose you. She said, cool as a cucumber, 'Well, what do you want, money? I won't give it to you.' And I said, 'No, I don't want money.' Then she said, 'Well, suit yourself,' and she repeated that she was Freddy's mother and she had the documents and so on, and I said, 'Oh? DNA doesn't lie.' And she said she didn't give a damn about DNA, 'You think that's proof? Labs make mistakes all the time,' she said, 'and I can prove my case, I can even get witnesses, people at the hospital when Freddy was born,' and so on. 'He's my son. Freddy's my son. He's always been my son.' I said, 'We'll see about that.' And she said, 'I think you had better go.' And I went. And that's when she wrote the letter. She sort of hinted she was going to warn Freddy against me.

"But if I tell all this to the police, I'm afraid they'll think I killed her. Because she *was* killed, and the police think it happened that very day, maybe later that afternoon, right there in her place—I think they found some evidence, I don't know, maybe blood traces or whatever—and then somebody took the body and dumped it at Freddy's. But I didn't kill her. I swear I didn't. Why would I do that? I could show the world that she was a phony. I didn't need to kill her."

I told him I believed him. But did I? No, he didn't need to kill her; but maybe his story wasn't totally on the up and up. Maybe he left out something important: maybe they had this confrontation, and it got hot and heavy, and somehow the argument became physical and she ended up dead. Derek Schuster was still my number one suspect.

But the mystery had gotten even deeper. If Derek was right, Sybil Glass was not Freddy's mother. But *somebody* was; and how did one explain the birth certificate, and the letters? It just didn't make sense to me. My head was in a whirl.

There's an old saying, "the darkest hour is just before the dawn." The mystery of Sybil Glass was very dark indeed. But as a matter of fact, it was going to be solved—and very soon. And I was destined to play an important role in the drama.

34

But at the time, there I was, sitting in my office, trying to absorb the news I was getting from Derek Schuster. After I got over my initial shock, I asked him: "Does Freddy know this? About the DNA?"

"I haven't told him yet," he said. He wanted me to do it. He said things were a little rocky again between him and Freddy. I asked him for the lab reports, and he produced them. They seemed authentic to me, although, by this time, I was willing to doubt my own birth certificate and everything else—even my own existence. I remember some science fiction movie I saw, in which there were these lifelike robots, they looked like people, and the robot company or whoever implanted memories in them, so that the robots actually *thought* they were people. After seeing that movie, you begin to doubt everything, and you begin to say to yourself, am I really human at all? Me? Could I possibly be an android?

Some of my clients—I'd be quite willing to believe they're androids. Myself, personally, I have to believe I'm really human. But maybe Sybil Glass was an android. Or even Freddy. But then I thought, no, not Freddy. Nobody could make an android that acted like Freddy. It was beyond robot science. And what would be the market for a Freddy-like android?

At any rate, I called Freddy, armed with the documents, and said I had to see him. He came to the office, I sat him down, and I told him what Derek had imparted to me and I showed him the lab reports. His first reaction was skepticism:

"I don't know about any of that stuff. Is Derek sure? I mean, is it really proof?" I told him I thought it was. I said, "I'm not an expert, Freddy, and of course, we have to have all of this checked out; but it looks pretty convincing to me."

"Wow. This is really something," he said. "But, Frank, why did Derek do this? Why did he go around, getting samples, and all of that stuff? Why was he so sure she was a fake? I didn't like her, he knew that, but so what? Who says you have to like your mother? Derek is hardly on speaking terms with his own mother, I met her once, and I could see why he couldn't stand her, she was an awful person. This Sybil, she said she was my mother, and she had that birth certificate, and all those other things, the letters, and so on. Why was Derek mixing in? I never asked him."

"He says he did it out of friendship. He wanted you to know he's a true friend."

"Yeah. Whatever. Look, I don't know, Frank," he said. "Derek and I, we've been friends, sure. I used to tell him my troubles, I thought we were really close. But lately, I just don't know what to think. He's done a lot of funny stuff. Like that business with Ella. I mean, supposedly that's all over, for both of us. But still, there's a part of me that, well, finds it hard to forget what he did. What do you think, Frank?"

I didn't know what to think. Meanwhile, Freddy seemed depressed, which was not surprising. The whole affair was getting him down. Perhaps he had gotten used to the idea that Sybil Glass was his actual mother. Even a dead mother was a mother. "But I never liked her," he said. "I guess I should be glad that she's not my mother."

And he *was* glad, I felt; but in a way, it unsettled him too. Left him, as it were, hanging in midair. If Sybil Glass was not his real mother, then who was?

35

And who killed Sybil Glass? Lizbeth? I really didn't think she was the one. Derek? I had my suspicions. Derek himself, when he talked to me, voiced his own theory. "I think it was Ella," he said. "I think she did it because of the money. I think she thought, this woman is rapacious, she'll find a way to take all of Freddy's money, he'll have to accept her as his mother, and who knows what will happen then? That's one of the reasons I was trying to expose Sybil Glass."

I had said to him, "I thought Ella and Sybil were more or less allies."

"Well, they were once," he said. "But maybe they had a falling out."

None of these theories appealed to me. But I couldn't help thinking and thinking about the case. It was constantly on my mind.

I did what I often do when I find myself boxed into a corner. I took my problems home—to Celia. I wanted her advice.

"Naturally, you want my advice, Frank," she said. "You're like a little boy; when you get in trouble, you come to momma."

"I'm not in trouble, my dear," I said. "I just want to share stuff with you, get your view of things. You're really great at giving me advice. Don't think I don't appreciate it."

She knew better, but she did listen carefully. One piece of advice, which I could have anticipated, was to sit tight, mind my own business, and do nothing at all. Do not go to the police, for example. You have no real information, all you have is idle speculation, which is basically worthless. You don't have any actual evidence about Lizbeth, or anybody else.

"And besides, Frank," she said, and her voice now had a familiar tone of disapproval. Twenty years of marriage, and you get to recognize that tone. "You don't actually *take* my advice. You're incorrigible. You've gotten all involved again. No matter how often I warn you, you simply will not stay out of these wretched affairs. And you lie to me...."

"Celia, dear," I said, "I do not lie to you."

"It's a question of definition," she said. "Maybe you don't tell an outright lie. It's not what you tell me, it's what you don't tell me. I never get the whole story. I just get dribs and drabs."

"Fair enough," I said. "But now you'll get the whole story." I told her everything I knew. And didn't know. "The whole thing is a puzzle. Okay, this woman, Sybil Glass, she lied to me. You're right, people lie; they lie all the time. But documents, they don't lie."

"What documents are you talking about?"

"Well, Freddy's birth certificate. Or the letters that Sybil had. Or Clara's diary."

"Anything can be faked," she said. "Anything. Experts can tell if these things are fakes. And you're no expert, Frank. That's another reason to mind your own business."

I promised to mind my own business—but I pointed out that Freddy and his affairs *were* my business. I can't quite wash my hands of this matter; Freddy often comes to me for advice and I'm not about to discard him as a client; okay, I said, I won't play detective. I think Celia understood; she was, however, still skeptical about my promises.

"And remember one thing," she said. "Take that birth certificate. Suppose it wasn't forged. Consider that possibility."

"But what would that mean?"

"You figure it out," she said.

But I couldn't. Wild ideas flashed through my mind. Maybe a woman in the hospital gave birth to a baby, and Sybil Glass stole the baby, and had it recorded as her own. Such things do happen. They're rare of course; but they happen. Not that I believed this for a minute. Still, what Celia said did, subconsciously, start a process—and one that in the end proved fruitful.

Meanwhile, Freddy came by the next day. As he often did. "I'm a mess," he said. "After I talked to you, I was really depressed. It was awful. But now I'm feeling a little better, Frank. You know, I'm kind of happy that awful woman wasn't my mother. But who *was* she, really? And how did she get involved."

"Freddy, I have no idea."

"I know something about Sybil Glass," he said. "Derek told me. Don't ask me how he knows so much. Maybe he has some connections with the police. She was a nurse...."

"I knew that, Freddy.'

"But she was an awful nurse. She worked for hospitals, but she kept getting fired, because she did bad stuff, I'm not sure what. Maybe she even killed a patient. She never had a husband I guess. Maybe she never had a baby. But it's all so weird. I mean, the birth certificate. The date, it's the day I always thought was my birthday. Aunt Clara made a big deal out of my birthday, we always had cake and ice cream, and once we had a clown, with balloons, and she invited other kids. And the birth certificate says the baby's a little boy, and his name is Frederick. Not Alexander, but Frederick. Is that why they call me Freddy, instead of Alexander? Frank, it's driving me crazy. And maybe the police think I killed this woman, to keep her from getting my money."

"Oh, nobody could think that, Freddy."

"The police can. They think everybody's scum. Frank, I wish you could help me. I wish you could do what people say you can do."

I knew that was coming: another plea to Frank May, the great but secret sleuth.

"I'm desperate, Frank. Zelda says you're good at this. You could get me out of all this trouble, Frank. You could figure out who killed that blasted woman. Oh lord, how I wish you would do that. I'd be eternally grateful."

"Freddy, I would if I could," I said. "But I'm really afraid it's beyond my powers."

Funny thing though: it turned out that I did exactly what Freddy wanted. I actually solved the damn case. And fairly quickly.

Meanwhile, I didn't blame Freddy for having these mood swings. I didn't blame him for feeling bewildered. I felt bewildered myself. I had been sure Sybil Glass was Freddy's birth mother. She had what seemed to be ironclad proof. And yet, apparently, she was a fake. Which raised more questions than it answered.

I had lunch with Zelda the next day. I had been in touch with her, off and on. We were friends, after all. And she had taken a real interest in Freddy. She said she'd been "trying hard to help him. He's a good soul, and these are tough times for him, as you can imagine."

Zelda was another one who was firmly convinced I was investigating "the case," as she put it. She had confidence (she said) in my detective skills; and she was absolutely sure I would soon solve the mystery. I could never talk her out of this fantasy. And she wanted to "play a role, too," as she put it. Wasn't there some way she could help?

"I'm a romance novelist, Frank, you have to remember that. I love learning about people, finding out their stories. That's where I get my inspiration. I mean, I write about olden times and so on, but people are people, even in the 18th century—even pirates were people—and I like to find out about people, that's where I get my ideas."

"You know any pirates, Zelda?"

"Oh, Frank, you know what I mean. Of course I don't know any pirates; but I get these notions, from talking to people, and I just translate those people into pirate-people."

I wondered what people had inspired Zelda during her vampire phase and her zombie phase, but of course I didn't ask. And I really had no job for Zelda. We had fun anyway, chattering away at lunch. I was perhaps a bit indiscreet: I told her all about my conversation with Derek, and what Derek had told me about the DNA.

"My goodness," she said. "I would never have guessed. But, Frank, are you supposed to talk about these things? I thought everything people said to you was confidential."

"Everything clients say. Derek was not my client."

Zelda was terrifically excited by the news. "Imagine! She was a fake after all. I tell you, Frank, I just love it," she said. "Oh, it's wonderful what they can do today, with science. You can check out your DNA, and you find out all sorts of things. Do you know, Frank, I had myself checked, with one of those companies, it's called 'X and Y and All the Rest'? You give them a sample, and they dig into your past, it's all there, in the DNA, all your ancestors, all the way back to the stone age, I suppose."

Myself, I couldn't care less about ancestors. But Zelda, like many other people, was enthralled by genealogy. She said, "The things I learned. I always knew a little about the Valdez side, those people, they came from Spain, well, originally. My great grandfather moved to Mexico. They lived in Chiapas, and then they moved to Mexico City, and then over the border into Texas. I've got such a mixture in my blood, Frank, no wonder I became a novelist. I have some North African blood. I can close my eyes and see it: it's way way back, in the middle ages, maybe it happened in Spain, maybe Cadiz or Granada, and there's this wild, impulsive man, he's a Berber, one of the Berber tribes-man, and he swept into Spain from the Morocco side, and he seduces a Christian girl; maybe it was a nun, like Sister Santa Cruz in my novel."

"Couldn't it be the other way around, Zelda," I asked. "Why is it always the man, seducing the woman, and he's some sort of romantic figure and she isn't. Sure, maybe your ancestor was a Christian guy, a white guy, and he seduces some Arab woman, sleeps with her, and that's the story, or maybe it was the other way round, this woman seduces the guy. Or maybe it was just an ordinary love story, two people meet, and they get together."

"Oh, I suppose. But I like it the way I picture it; who knows what happened way back then anyway. And of course in Mexico, these things happened, too, these love affairs. I can imagine this Spanish soldier, one of the conquistadors, and he's totally smitten with this Aztec princess—her family was slaughtered by the Spaniards, and she's destitute, even though she was a princess, and along comes this soldier, handsome dog, he's lonely, and so far away from home—so they become lovers. But that's not all. Frank, would you believe it, my mother or somebody in the family tree, they had some Eastern European connection, and that showed up, too. One of my forefathers, I can just picture it, he came from Mongolia or someplace like that, maybe it was Attila the Hun himself, I can imagine him on horseback, they come roaring into this village, and everybody is screaming, the Huns burn the village to the ground, they kill the men, but here's this young woman, she's hiding, she's trembling with fear, and here he comes, he's a giant of a man, he carries a spear, he's a devil on horseback, wearing these fur things, and he gets down off his horse and takes her, brutally."

"Zelda, what are all these fantasies about? All of those brutal men; why can't you imagine somebody kind, gentle, a real caregiver? That's more what *you're* like, Zelda, maybe your ancestors weren't soldiers or Attila the Hun, maybe they were just nice people, people in love, with ordinary families."

"You're probably right, Frank," she said. "But there's no romance in that. And I need romance for my books."

"You can put Attila the Hun in your next novel, Zelda," I said. "Meanwhile, let's have dessert."

I couldn't help thinking, as we had coffee and cake, about some of my clients who had also checked out their DNA. One client in particular, a youngish man, Zachary Finch, who struck it fairly rich in the computer business. He had lived with this woman, Samantha, for ten years. Lo and behold, she became pregnant and gave birth to a child, much to Zachary's disgust. He said, "I wanted her to get rid of the kid, I'm not the fatherly type, but she refused." They had never actually gotten married ("I don't believe in marriage," he told me), and the birth of the child was the last straw for Zachary; they split up, and it was not a friendly break. He was totally convinced that the little boy, Samantha's baby, was not his biological child; consequently he refused to pay child support. "She was horsing around with this guy, Andy—he got her pregnant, and they thought they could fob the kid onto me. But I'll be damned if I'm going to spend my hard-earned money on this brat. Let Andy pay."

Indeed, Samantha and Andy had been having a hot and heavy affair; she even admitted it. But she insisted the baby wasn't Andy's. They had always been "super-careful." And, unfortunately for Zachary, she turned out to be right. It was Zachary's child, not Andy's, and he had to pay through the nose to get rid of his legal obligations. Meanwhile, his company went bankrupt and most of his millions melted away like snow in summer. I lost him as a client; he moved to Boston. I was secretly glad. I had always found him totally repulsive: arrogant and selfish to an astonishing degree. Samantha, I must say, was not much better.

Meanwhile, I had enjoyed the lunch. It was, I felt, an interlude. Of course, in my opinion, Zelda had told me nothing that could be counted as progress toward solving the mystery. Yet, in fact, at the very end, she made a point that resonated with me. Two points, actually. The first was about Lizbeth. Zelda, it seemed, had been checking up on her.

"I know you were annoyed that I made you talk to her," Zelda said. "But she's important, I think." Zelda told me that Lizbeth and Sybil, both nurses, had worked together in the past. And their paths crossed at one important point: the house of Homer Fisk. Both of them, at one time or another, or even simultaneously, had acted as private nurses in the Fisk household.

The second point was about Derek. Zelda was walking me back to my office. Zelda was still voicing astonishment at my news. "That Sybil," she said, "I was sure she was really Freddy's mother."

"So was I," I said.

"I guess Derek didn't think so," she said. "I wonder why. It doesn't seem in character. Maybe he just wanted to prove she was Freddy's mother, beyond a reasonable doubt, as you lawyers say. Well, the joke's on him."

The joke, I'm afraid, was on all of us.

If it was a joke. But Zelda's comment started boring into me. Why, indeed, was Derek so interested in the issue? What game was he playing? He told one story; but it was impossible for me to believe. What on earth was Derek up to, and why? Ultimately, these questions produced some very fruitful answers.

36

But first I had to talk to Sylvan Platt. Sybil Glass had been Sylvan's client, and I wondered if he knew about this latest development. I asked Sylvan if he was free for lunch. He was. We arranged to meet at his favorite Japanese restaurant, on El Camino Real, in Palo Alto. "It's one of the best places in the whole area," he said. "Japanese businessmen all go there, when they're in town. They know it's authentic, not some phony American imitation of Japanese food."

At lunch, I broke the news to him. Clearly, this was a big surprise; and of course a shocking one. Someone (I didn't specify who) had actually done DNA testing, on Freddy, and on Sybil Glass, and the tests were dramatic and conclusive. Sybil Glass was not Freddy's mother. She had no genetic relationship with him whatsoever.

Sylvan was aghast. "My God, Frank, I can't believe it," he said. "All those documents ... are you sure? Have you seen the lab reports?"

"I have. And I have copies."

"I've got to see those reports. I mean, they can make a mistake, can't they? Anybody can make a mistake."

"I'm sure that's true, Sylvan. But it's probably not a mistake. I'm assuming it's absolutely true."

He said, "Frank, this is terrible. For me, at least. Here I thought I had a client with an excellent claim under the Clara Fisk will. I was reasonably sure she was going to come into big

196

money. Either get a share of the estate, or some really nice settlement. And meanwhile, she'd pay me big fees. Then she was killed, and I'm supposed to be handling her estate. That was too bad; but that didn't kill her claim. And now it looks as if there isn't going to be an estate. Bummer. But you understand, I have to be absolutely sure about this, Frank. I have to see the lab reports."

"Of course, Sylvan. I had the same reaction. I mean, it affects my client, Freddy Lucas. It means this woman's claim is bogus. For me, though, it has the opposite effect; it's more money for Freddy."

"Yes, but Freddy was always going to inherit a shitload of money. For Sybil, and me, though, this is disaster. Well, for me, at any rate. Sybil's dead."

Bad news, and indeed news in general, never affected Sylvan's passion for food. "It's my food karma, Frank," he said, "I mean, the fact that we're eating here, in this wonderful Japanese restaurant. I try to eat Japanese, when I get bad news. It's purer than other cuisines, simpler, more subtle. Some people think it's bland; but it isn't. Japanese food doesn't scream at you. Not like Korean cuisine, or Mexican food. Japanese food, well, it calms you down. I mean, classical Japanese food. Not tempura. That's not real Japanese food; they got it from the Portuguese, did you know that?"

Actually, I didn't.

"Sashimi, on the other hand, that's food for the soul," he said. "You know what? I should have doubted that woman from the beginning. There was always something wrong there, something that just didn't seem right. For lunch once, I took her to this very Japanese restaurant, we were sitting almost exactly where we're sitting right now. She claimed she loved Japanese food, but there was something about her, the way she ate, that seemed wrong to me. Hey, she didn't even use chopsticks. I observe these things carefully. She was ... hiding something, holding something back.... And I had to pay the bill; she didn't have much money, she said. Frank, she's a total loss to me. I didn't charge her, because she said she couldn't afford it, my fee would come out of the millions she would get from the Fisk estate. Oh well, live and learn. But how did she pull this scam? She had that birth certificate and so on."

"Sylvan," I said, "I have no idea. It's a mystery to me. One thing I thought about: maybe this woman wasn't really Sybil Glass. Maybe Sybil Glass was Freddy's mother, but this woman wasn't Sybil Glass. She just took on Sybil's identity. You read about such things. After all, did any of us ever *see* Sybil Glass? I mean, the real Sybil Glass? The Sybil Glass who gave birth to Freddy? Do we have a picture of her? Is there anybody here who would recognize her?"

Sylvan said, "Nice try, Frank. But as a matter of fact, there are people who did recognize her. Pascal LeBeau, for one. He knew her from her nursing days, when she was taking care of Homer Fisk. That Lizbeth woman, for another; she's completely nuts, but not *that* nuts. She used to work with Sybil, after all. Lizbeth said Sybil wasn't Freddy's mother, and that turns out to be true, but she never even hinted that she wasn't Sybil Glass. Though I wonder how she knew Sybil Glass was a fake as a mother."

I wondered about that myself.

"Also," Sylvan said, "Sybil had a family. We all do. You know, when she died, I realized, okay, she's dead, but she's still worth millions, you know, from Clara's estate. So I thought, I'll probably have to manage her estate. She didn't have a will. At least not that I knew of. Anyway, she told me a little bit about her family, not much—she was pretty close-mouthed about everything—but I did know she had a brother, Erastus, a guy living in Cheyenne, Wyoming; he does something with horses. Maybe everybody in Wyoming does something with horses. Anyway, this Erastus, he's a married guy, four children. Converted to Mormonism. He flew out here, and I met him. A total jerk, but that's not the issue. Anyway, he said Sybil was estranged from the family, said he hadn't seen her in years. Wouldn't go into *why*. Just said she was a 'dyed-in-the-wool sinner, a bad person.' Anyway, he identified the body, in the morgue or wherever. It was definitely his sister. He refused to pay for burial costs, by the way. I told him there might be money in the estate, which surprised him, but seemed to make an impression. He told me he was the next of kin. Actually, I thought Freddy was the next of kin, but Erastus had a legitimate claim. Since Freddy was legally adopted, I think he couldn't really inherit from Sybil; I'd have to check that out. Anyway, that's all meaningless now. But when he was here, I asked Erastus if he wanted me to manage Sybil's estate, and he said yes."

"Sylvan," I said, "I'm awfully sorry. You're a great guy, and I was rooting for you, in a way. I know we were kind of on opposite sides, though not really. Freddy didn't begrudge the money Sybil would get. He couldn't care less. He didn't like her, but he thought she was his mother and she'd be entitled to her share. And there's so much money in the estate, we thought, okay, it's not worth fighting about. In any event, Freddy's not the fighting type."

"Sybil's estate isn't worth a nickel now, of course. There go some of my pipedreams. I was salivating over the fee. I was thinking of flying to France, and having meals in all the 3-star restaurants, you know the ones in the Michelin Guide. My only consolation is that I get to call up that awful person, Erastus, and tell him there's no money after all. I wish I could do it face to face. Do you know, Frank, I was actually checking on flights to Paris, and reading up on some of those restaurants? I knew it would be a year or more before I could cash in, but the thought of those places was giving me wonderful thoughts. Now all I have is heartburn. Oh well."

"Treat yourself, Sylvan," I said. "Go on the trip anyway. Life is short."

Later on, during dessert (in another restaurant), Sylvan discussed a couple of his cases. Sylvan handled a lot of family law—divorces, very notably, as well as estate planning. He mentioned one of the matters he was dealing with, as particularly interesting. "This one's a doozy, Frank. Hotly contested divorce. And here's the wrinkle, it's like your Freddy situation. A kid with two mothers." And then he told me how it was that this kid had two mothers.

Then he stopped short. He looked at me. I looked at him. An electric light bulb flashed in his brain; and in mine. "Are you thinking what I'm thinking?" he said.

I was. I told him I would follow up on this. Was this the key? I came back to the office excited.

37

I had a plan. A plan of action. I thought I understood some things that, well, explained a lot of the mystery. And the more I thought about it, the more I imagined that I knew—maybe—who killed Sybil Glass; though not necessarily why.

One key fact was the character of the late Sybil Glass. She was, by all accounts, a truly awful human being. Nobody seemed sorry she was dead; some people were downright gleeful. Freddy felt somewhat guilty about her; and massively confused. But he was also experiencing a kind of relief.

Before I could make my move, I had another one of those unexpected visits. This time it was Lizbeth, of all people. She seemed somewhat altered. Her look was less crazed; she was more neatly dressed and in general, more lucid.

"I wanted to stop by and thank you," she said.

"Thank me? For what, Lizbeth?"

"For being so kind and helpful to Freddy. It's meant a lot to Kathryn. And I also wanted to say goodbye. My sister is here, and she's going to take me back to her home, in Yreka, that's near the Oregon border, it's a lovely place, and she has room for me."

"That's nice of her," I said, a bit lamely.

"My sister is a very nice person, you're right about that," she said. "And I know I'll be happy there. There's a bakery there, the Yreka Bakery, and I realized that this name is the same, backwards and forwards, and I thought, that's a sign, this is the place for me. It's a new phase of my life. Kathryn ... Kathryn's left me. She's happy now. Her soul is at peace."

I mumbled something. She went on: "I think it might be because that awful woman is dead. Now Kathryn can go back to where she came from. Her job is done. Kathryn's job. And my job is done, too. Everybody knows now that the woman was lying. Imagine, claiming to be Freddy's mother. She just wanted Freddy's money. She'll never get it now."

Yes, Sybil will never get any money. Because, among other things, she's dead. At any rate, Lizbeth seemed genuinely happy ... pleased with herself. "I have to go now," she said. "My sister's downstairs, in the car. We're leaving right away. We're going to drive up the coast. It's a beautiful drive. But I wanted to come to see you. I said goodbye to Freddy. And now you. And I want to give you a hug." Which she did.

After she left, I started wondering: did she know about the DNA test? And what did she mean when she said her job was done? Exactly what was that job? And what was Kathryn's job?

At one time, I had thought, maybe she—either in her own right, or as the soul of Kathryn Lucas—had been responsible for the death of Sybil Glass. I didn't think so now.

38

Despite what people say, I can't actually solve mysteries. I'm not Sherlock Holmes. I have no powers of deduction. But some mysteries have a way of solving themselves. And sometimes, oddly enough, I do play a role. It's because, unlike the police, I know the actual people, the cast of characters; and this is always important. And sometimes, in some strange way, the case gets solved because of something I do, or something I've done. Or something I learned, from talking to people.

I had by now some vital information; and a plan of action. One piece of information concerned Ella Fisk-Potter. Ella had this wild idea about attacking the will of Homer Fisk. She dreamed about getting Freddy's money. Freddy was pretty relaxed about money, but he certainly didn't want to lose it all.

"Wow, Frank," he had said to me, when we discussed Ella's claim. "You say I shouldn't worry about her, but I can't help it. I mean, if she got all the money, I'd have to get a job or do something awful like that."

"I don't think it's an issue," I said. "I keep telling you, she can't win. Anyway, Freddy, have you ever stopped to think, maybe you're be better off without the money."

Maybe that was mean of me to say. Freddy said: "Oh God, Frank, that would be a fate worse than death. I don't even want to think about it. I'm not qualified to do anything. What kind of a job could I get? I couldn't even be a security guard or something like that. Who would hire me?"

I told Freddy, over and over again, that he had nothing to worry about. It's true that there's no statute of limitations for murder. Even if fifty years have gone by, you can still be convicted of murder. If you have an auto accident, you have to sue within a certain time and if you don't, you're out of luck. But murder is different.

"Does that mean," he asked, "that if Clara was alive, they could arrest her for killing her husband? And then she couldn't get his money? Which would mean I wouldn't get it either?"

I said, "Whoa, that's a stretch, Freddy; like I told you, nobody's going to know, unless we publish that piece of the diary, and we're not going to do that, we promised we wouldn't. Second, even if the news got out, I don't know what would happen, I don't think Ella could prove anything. Third, Clara *isn't* alive, so she can't be convicted, whether she killed anybody or not. So just sit tight, Freddy."

Freddy, I'm afraid, was not capable of sitting tight; he was definitely not the type. Nor was he the type to keep his mouth shut. He's not alone in this. If you tell something to a friend, and say: this is a secret, don't tell anybody—first of all, you've already told somebody, let's call him Mr. A. And Mr. A will surely tell at least one other person, Ms. B, though usually, Mr. A. will tell Ms. B that it's a secret, don't tell anybody else, and then of course Ms. B will tell just one person, Mr. C., and in the end the whole world knows. We know that Derek spilled the beans to Ella. And maybe it went from him to Ella, from Ella to Sybil.

So Ella was a chain in a link: A link that concerned the diary. And Ella connected, somehow, with Sybil. Did all this have something to do with Sybil's sudden death?

This and a number of other things were rattling around inside my brain. Waking up the little gray cells, perhaps. Making the light bulb go off.

And the final stimulus was Derek Schuster.

Freddy had asked me out for lunch at another Italian restaurant on University Avenue, in Palo Alto. When I got there, somewhat late, Freddy had already arrived. He was sitting in a booth, and Derek was with him. He and Freddy were apparently again on good terms. For how long, I wondered. I watched Derek carefully during the meal: I saw how subtly he flattered Freddy, how he tried to convey a message, through his tone of voice, his body language, his demeanor, a message that he (Derek) really cared about Freddy. He put his arm around Freddy once or twice, he smiled at him, he laughed at Freddy's jokes, he indicated, as plainly as he could, that Freddy was some kind of wonderful guy. All of this struck me as, well, exaggerated. Contrived. Somewhat insincere. It brought back to me, quite forcefully, all of my suspicions about Derek.

It goes without saying that Freddy picked up the bill. Afterwards, I went back to the office. Derek said he and Freddy were "going to hang out." I asked Derek, didn't he have classes that afternoon, and he said, "Yeah, but they're really boring. Intellectual property. Who gives a damn. I'm taking a break."

A client was due to see me, but the client canceled. I had plenty to do, but I found myself leaning back in my chair and thinking about details that, in my mind, were starting to add up. But especially about Derek. Derek's DNA caper had been a major development. Of course, it made the puzzle of Sybil Glass even more impenetrable: who was she really, what was she up to, where did she get the documents, and were they fakes or not? Thanks to my lunch with Sylvan, I thought I knew at least some of the answers. But the puzzle of Sybil Glass had driven out of my mind another, lesser puzzle: why was Derek so involved? Why did he go to all this trouble? What was his game? He said it was because of Freddy, that he wanted to help Freddy. He said he did it out of friendship, or out of the goodness of his heart. But I never believed that. I knew Derek Schuster. There was, I felt, very little goodness in his heart. The lunch reinforced my suspicions: this is not a trustworthy guy. This is not really Freddy's dear friend. Then why is he doing this?

And why had he been so sure, in the face of all the evidence, that Sybil Glass was a fraud?

And another little fact, that I had almost forgotten. Sylvan, who was Sybil's lawyer, had in his possession letters written to Clara Fisk. Where did he get those letters from? Presumably from Sybil. But where did *she* get them from? From Kathryn herself, according to Sybil. But was that true?

Sybil Glass. She had worked as a private nurse. She had been, at one time, a nurse for Homer Fisk. Living perhaps in the house. Clara knew her, of course. And somebody had been paying her money, all those years. We presumed it was Clara.

Paying her for what? Did Clara think Sybil was Freddy's mother? She must have thought so; otherwise, why pay? But we now know that Sybil was *not* Freddy's biological mother. Was Sybil blackmailing Clara? Because of the murder of Homer Fisk? Or for some other reason?

I turned all of these things over in my mind. I didn't know Clara, of course; she died before I ever met Freddy. But I did know Derek Schuster. And then, suddenly, the light bulb lit up. A lot of things came together. My conversation with Sylvan, for one. And then I did something very much out of character—something bold and presumptuous (which is definitely not me). I picked up the phone, and made a phone call. The person I called was at home. I asked a few questions.

I didn't get answers, not then. Instead, the person said: "I'd better come see you. I've been meaning to. We have to talk." We fixed a time. I remember that afternoon. Brilliant sunshine outside. A real nice day, cloudless, a pitiless blue sky. Completely normal, in every way. Outside, the usual street noises. And someone sitting across from me, in my office, with a slightly crooked smile.

I asked a couple of questions. And then he said, "Go no further, Frank. I know what's on your mind. You don't have to play games. Look, I'm way ahead of you. I know what you're thinking. And yes, I do know more than I let on. Lots more. I know who killed Sybil Glass. How do I know? Because it was me. I killed her. And I'm not sorry I did. And I'm going to tell you all about it."

39

I stared at the man sitting across from me. Sitting upright; straight as a ramrod. An old man, thin, with a white moustache and a slight tremor. Again I noticed he was carrying a cane. Despite his age, and his obvious ill health, he exuded a kind of strength, determination, mental vigor. I was looking at Clara's old lover, Homer's cousin, Dr. Pascal LeBeau.

"And you were right, Frank," he said. "I was the one who got Derek Schuster to check the woman's DNA. I couldn't do it myself—I couldn't go to Sybil Glass, she never trusted me. I thought, Derek, he's just the one. I paid him to do it. I knew all along, of course, that she wasn't Freddy's mother. That's why I launched that campaign."

"Not Freddy's mother? But how did you know?"

"It's a long story," he said. "If you've got time, I'll give you all the details. It's a kind of confession. I'm afraid I've made a mess of things."

"Look, Pascal," I said, "I don't want to hear it if you're telling me secrets that I'm supposed to keep."

"Don't worry," he said. "I don't care whether this is confidential or not. I'm going to tell the same story to the police. Well, not really the same story; I'll doctor some of it. But I'll tell them about Sybil Glass. Look: I'm old, I'm sick. I don't care if they arrest me. What difference would it make? By the time this business goes to trial, I'll be dead or as good as dead. I don't regret anything I've done, not really. But things have become too complicated. I'm starting to cause trouble for people I love. Melanie, for one. I love her. She knows that I'm involved.... She doesn't know the whole story, but she knows some of it. And it's been bad for her. She broke up with her boyfriend, and it's all because of me."

"Because of you, Pascal?"

"Oh yes. Because of me. You know, this boyfriend, Peter, he comes from a very traditional Chinese family. They would never approve of her, I think, under any circumstances, but they might come around in the end—except that, when this stuff comes out, about me, that would be the absolute kiss of death. Granddaughter of a murderer? No way. I'm dragging her into a mess, that can't be helped, but I don't want to make trouble for Peter, and Melanie didn't want to either. This Peter, he's a good boy, he's got good values, and I'm sorry this is happening. And I'm making things hard for Freddy, too; and I don't want that. I love Freddy. He's like a son to me."

I stared at him. I didn't know what to say.

"I have to explain about Sybil," he said. "Why I killed her. For one thing, she knew too much about me. She knew something that might surprise you. You see, I killed Homer Fisk. It wasn't Clara at all. It was me. Clara and I were lovers. We were always lovers. Always. And Homer found out. He was furious. Old and sick, half dead; but still, he was furious. He threatened to get a divorce. He would have made things really difficult for Clara. I decided to get rid of him. We pretended it was a mercy killing, but it wasn't. Well, not exactly. I mean, he was really sick, his life was a misery, he was better off dead. We talked ourselves into thinking he really wanted to die. Maybe he did. But maybe he didn't. At any rate, he never asked to die. He never asked us to put an end to his misery. I just did it.

"But let me tell you about Sybil Glass. I blame myself for a lot of things. Not for killing her; the world is better off without her. She was a truly awful woman. Greedy, dishonest, cruel, money-mad. No, I don't blame myself for killing her. I blame myself for ever having had dealings with her. I should have known better. But let me explain. She had been Homer's nurse for a while, private nurse. He fired her—we fired her—she was stealing stuff, she wasn't taking good care of him, she had to go. We didn't know much about her past—at the time. She was working for an agency, and she no doubt lied to them. She had been fired from at least one hospital. There were suspicions about her, stealing drugs, neglecting patients, maybe she even killed a patient, who knows. Then, as a private nurse, she cheated some old lady out of her savings. But I think you know some of this stuff about Sybil.

"Oh, and by the way, that woman, Lizbeth, she also worked as a private nurse. She wasn't crazy then, and that's how she got to know Sybil. And Lizbeth hated her, for good reason. Lizbeth was an honest nurse, a caring nurse, and she detested Sybil, who was mean and dishonest, everything Lizbeth wasn't. Poor Lizbeth was always pretty neurotic, and she got more and more unhinged, but that was later on.... Sybil was awful to her, truly awful.

"Anyway, Sybil, when she worked as a private nurse, was the same rotten person she had always been. But we didn't know this at first. Then, as it happens, things got rough for Sybil; her past caught up with her, and she was desperate for money. I think there was a warrant out for her arrest, not in California though. We had the goods on her, anyway, about the stealing: she took some of Clara's jewelry. I knew it. I thought that made her vulnerable. I thought we could put the screws on her. I was a damn fool to think so. To think I could outsmart her. That was stupid of me. I thought if I dangled money in front of her, and also threatened to expose her, turn her over to the police, I thought this would keep her under our thumb. She would do what we wanted, to stay out of jail, and to pocket some money. Boy, were we wrong.

"Here was the problem. Kathryn and Max, they wanted a child—they were desperate for a child. They couldn't have children. But they didn't want to adopt. I should explain. Max was downright sterile, and Kathryn, well, she was fertile, but she had a medical condition; she couldn't carry a child, it could kill her. I won't go into the details. I suggested hiring a surrogate. I thought this was a great idea. Kathryn's eggs would be implanted in another woman, and the woman would carry the child for nine months, and give birth to the child. Genetically, it would still be Kathryn's child, of course. She'd be the biological mother. Sybil would be the womb mother. I thought this would solve the problem. I was sort of blackmailing Sybil. I thought it would work.

"So we arranged to pay Sybil a nice chunk of money. Kathryn supplied the eggs. And it worked, in the sense that Sybil did become pregnant—with one of Kathryn's eggs. These contracts, you know, for a surrogate mother, they're illegal in some places; but not in California. In California, they're perfectly legal. Anyway, the deal was, she would give up the baby as soon as the baby was born, and the birth certificate would list Kathryn and Max as the parents. But Sybil—God, to think I ever trusted her—she was as crooked as a three dollar bill. She gave birth a couple of weeks prematurely, that was a bit of luck for her, but in any event, she had figured out a way to cheat us. She left town, she just plain disappeared. Kathryn and Max were frantic, they didn't know where she was. She went to Fresno, where nobody knew her. She was basically in hiding. And she gave birth there. Sybil was listed on the birth certificate as the mother—look, she was the one who gave birth, after all. She recorded the father as 'unknown.' The baby, of course, was little Freddy.

"Then Sybil came back to town, baby in hand, and broke the news to Kathryn and Max. Told them she had given birth, and that *she* was the legal mother. Of course her plan was to get a lot more money out of them. She threatened to give the baby up for adoption, to another couple. Said she had these people all lined up, and they were willing to pay big bucks. Maybe this was just a bluff, but they panicked; they gave her whatever she asked for, thousands and thousands of dollars, which I suppose Clara supplied, and then they took the baby, and went through a formal adoption process. So, yes, Freddy did have two mothers, but not the way he thought. Sybil was his womb mother, and Kathryn was his biological mother. And his adoptive mother too. I think they would have told Freddy, eventually, explained things to him, but they never had a chance. They disappeared while he was still a child.

"Oh, one detail: Lizbeth. She worked, for a while, as a nurse for Homer, I guess you know that; and she was a kind of nanny for Freddy, but he wouldn't remember her, because he was so little at the time. Kathryn was very fond of her; she was eccentric, but she wasn't unhinged as yet. I'm sure the letters from the jungle were authentic, or at least parts of them. Kathryn would have tried to write to Lizbeth, and to Clara. I guess Lizbeth stole them, or got them somehow. She loved Kathryn, and she loved Freddy. Of course, they had to let her go when it became pretty clear that she was out of her mind. As I said, Freddy was very little at the time. Kathryn gave Lizbeth money, I think, after she got rid of her. I don't know the exact details.

"Back to Clara. Of course, Clara knew the true story. But she never told Freddy, even when he grew up. I think she just didn't want to. Let him think Kathryn and Max were his adoptive parents, what's the harm? Her will ... it wasn't as crazy as it seems. It was foolish, though, but in a way I guess she didn't realize that it could be misunderstood. And it was true that she never gave up hope. To her, the will was not the least bit ambiguous; her niece was Freddy's adoptive mother, but she was also his biological mother. She never imagined that Sybil would appear on the scene, she hadn't been in contact with Sybil for more than twenty years—and she didn't know that Sybil had been in contact with me. She thought Sybil had no rights anyway, since she wasn't the real mother at all. And Sybil, of course, she didn't care about the baby. She had not one iota of feeling for the baby she carried for nine months. She only cared about the money. She never had the slightest urge to see Freddy, meet Freddy, find out what Freddy was like."

He paused, and he mopped his brow. I sat open-mouthed, listening. Then he went on:

"Kathryn and Max paid her off. They made regular payments. When they disappeared, Sybil came to me and demanded money. I paid and paid, all those years. It wasn't Clara who paid; it was me. I had the money, and it was worth my while to pay, if only to keep her out of the picture. But when Clara died, I decided, this had to end. I didn't have long to live myself and I warned her, no more money. That was another mistake on my part. She wasn't going to take that laying down, no, not Sybil.

"As I said, that was a big mistake. But I felt: enough was enough. For years, she had been sucking money out of me, and now it was time to stop. So, again, I underestimated her. Underestimated how devious she was, how cruel, how intent on getting rich. The smell of money intoxicated her. The will, unfortunately, gave her a perfect opening. That's when she came back, and put in her claim: she was Freddy's mother, she said, and she was entitled to millions from Clara's estate. It wasn't hard to make that claim. She was the womb mother, after all. She had a birth certificate, which said she was Freddy's mother. She had a bunch of letters from Kathryn. Some of them had language that could help her cause. She edited them carefully, to bolster her case.

"And she had another plan, another scheme. Something else to pressure me with. She knew, or thought she knew, what had happened to Homer Fisk. I'm not sure how she found out. Maybe she overheard a conversation between me and Clara. She certainly knew the family situation. She knew I had been Clara's lover. She was a nurse, after all; she knew enough about Homer's condition, and what had happened, to feel pretty sure that Clara and I had gotten rid of him. Of course, she had no proof of anything. And I was the one who did the dirty work. It wasn't Clara. Maybe Clara was an accomplice, technically. I don't know how the law defines these things. Anyway, I did the actual killing.

"Clara and I, we loved each other. Always. And yet, after Homer died, well, that was the end of the relationship, for a time. We felt we couldn't marry, and we couldn't live together. At least not right away. It would raise too many suspicions. So we ... drifted apart. After a while, well, we resumed, more and less, our relationship—but never openly—and mostly we were just very good, very intimate friends. Clara loved me; and I loved Clara. She was terrified that the truth would somehow come out. I think she was frightened of Ella and Griselda. I think they made noises, from time to time, about suing Homer's estate. We paid Griselda some money. I told Clara there was nothing to worry about. But she was frightened. She wanted to protect me. She wrote that fairytale about the way Homer died. Well, part of it was true, the sex part, actually; but I was the one who killed Homer, not Clara. So why did she write that stuff? It was supposed to be a kind of insurance. She made Freddy promise not to produce that part of her memoirs, unless he absolutely had to. I guess she was worried that the police would somehow learn the truth, from Sybil maybe, and they might come after me, but if they did, Freddy could say, 'Hold on, it was Clara, not Dr. LeBeau who did the bloody deed, and here's proof' and meantime, of course, Clara would be already dead.

"Anyway, I guess she felt, and correctly, that she was at least morally guilty of killing Homer, even though I was the one who actually did away with the guy. And she wanted, above all, to protect me. Wanted to protect me from prison, and also to protect my inheritance.... I guess she didn't realize that she was jeopardizing Freddy's inheritance.... I'm not sure what she was thinking,....

"Well, Clara was dead and Sybil was now on the scene. I told her to get lost; I said I'd pay her, if she insisted, but I wanted her to go away. She demanded a huge pot of money, more than I could manage, and she said, besides, if I didn't pay, she would just go ahead and make the claim against Clara's estate. She had the birth certificate, and the letters. She said, 'I don't even need your money, I'll prove I'm Freddy's mother, and I'll get a slice of the estate.' I think she intended to do both things, squeeze me for money, and squeeze the estate as well. I just couldn't have that. I paid Derek to get the DNA info—it would prove she wasn't the biological mother—but I was afraid that wouldn't be good enough, she could argue that a womb mother is a real mother.... I don't know what the law is; I don't know whether she would have had any rights. But above all, I wanted to spare Freddy. I love the guy. I don't know what he thinks about me, but that's what I think about him. Clara loved him, and I love him too. And I didn't want that horrible woman ruining his life. She was the last person in the world Freddy needed as a mother.

"So that was the situation. It was bad. Sybil was threatening to expose me, and maybe Clara. There was no end to her wickedness; she was willing to team up with that Ella person, and cause all kinds of mischief. I just couldn't have it. I didn't mean to involve Freddy, like I told you, Freddy's like a son to me. I told her to clear out, I told her she wasn't going to get a penny and that two could play at this exposing game. 'You're not really Freddy's mother,' I told her. 'We can prove that with DNA.' But she just laughed at me. She said, I'm his womb mother, wouldn't that count? It got heated. I ... I threatened her, I had a gun; look, I didn't mean to kill her, but ... let's not go into that. What's the point of rehearsing all those gory details. She ended up dead. I hadn't planned it, but it happened. Where was this? At my apartment. You think I'm sorry? I'm not. She was no good, she was rotten to the core. And she was a threat to all the people who are dear to me. And to me, too, as a matter of fact.

"Well, there I was with a dead body. What was I going to do with it? I had a problem. I wrapped the body in a blanket, which I took off my bed, and I carried it downstairs, and put it in the trunk of my car. I drove around wondering what to do with this thing. I came by Freddy's house. I thought maybe he was gone already. Nobody seemed to be home. I parked in the driveway. It was dark already, pitch black, a moonless night. The house was dark, too. I could see that nobody was there. I rang the doorbell and nobody answered. I thought Freddy might have gone off already. I have a key to the house. I've always had a key.... Clara wanted me to have a key. I haven't used it much in recent years, but anyway I had this key. I went into the house and took some sheets off one of the beds, plain white sheets, and I wrapped the body in those sheets, I wanted to keep the body wrapped up. But not in the blanket, because I was afraid the blanket could be traced to me. Why not just dump the body in the bay or somewhere? Frankly, I don't know. I'm a pretty cool customer; but I didn't want to have to look at the body. I wasn't thinking clearly, to tell you the truth. Getting rid of bodies is not exactly my usual line of work.

"Freddy's property, you remember, it's in Los Altos Hills. It's a huge piece of land; there's the house, and a large hill, completely wild, in the back. A couple of acres. Densely wooded. Nobody ever goes up to that part of the property. I thought the body would be safe there, at least temporarily. I went up the hill, with a flashlight, and I stashed the body. I covered it with leaves and twigs. My plan was to dig a hole and bury it. But I didn't have a shovel, and I didn't have the time. I wasn't worried. As I said, nobody goes there. I hid the body as best I could. Then I drove off.

"I thought nobody would find the body, not for a long time anyway; and maybe they never would; or they'd find it a year later, after I was dead, and the whole thing would blow over. Derek was a problem—he came by the house, and he saw my car. He was suspicious of something. Maybe he saw me come back, get in my car and drive off. I don't know how much he knew or guessed. When Freddy came back, Derek hid somewhere on the property. Melanie and Peter came to the house, and Freddy left; later on, after Freddy was gone, Derek went up the hill.... I'm just guessing about this; maybe he had a flashlight, but he didn't find anything. I mean, it's a big area, and it wasn't obvious. I think if he had found the body he might have made trouble for me; but he didn't.

"That nosy neighbor, though—the one who was out looking for mushrooms. He found the body. That's the sort of thing you never expect. Who would have thought somebody would be mucking around there, just for some stupid mushrooms? But life is full of little tricks like that.

"Melanie: I feel guilty about her. I know she talked to you about the sheets. Melanie, she's got her own place, in the dorms, but she spends a lot of time with me, and she often stays over. She's a keen observer, and she noticed the blanket was missing from one of the rooms. She totally freaked out. I think she put two and two together. That's why she broke it off with Peter; she was afraid of what was coming, she was afraid there'd be a big scandal, and she didn't want to get him involved. And she knew that I had some connection with Derek; she saw me with him, maybe; and I'm pretty sure she talked to him about that whole DNA business. I think she found out that I paid him to do it. All of those things made her uneasy. Unhappy. She's really worried, and I don't want that. I'm going to sit down and talk to her. Explain myself to her. Ask her for forgiveness.

"And then I'm going to go to the police to tell them my story. Not the whole story. Not about Homer's death, for instance; we'll skip that part. They'll never suspect anything about that and if it comes up, well, there's that fake memoir, we can drag that out. I think we can buy off Ella. I'm figuring there's not going to be any problem with Clara's estate. Basically, what I'm going to tell the police is that I'm responsible for Sybil's death. Maybe I'll say it was an accident. We were arguing, and the gun went off. Whatever. They can arrest me, I honestly don't care. I'll plead not guilty, I'll get a smart criminal lawyer, we'll claim, like I said, that it was an accident, or maybe heat of passion or something. Whatever the lawyer advises. And the whole thing will drag on.... I'll be dead anyway; I've got congestive heart failure, and a bunch of other things. Look, I'm a doctor, I know the score. I'm not worried about the criminal justice system, it's the least of my worries right now.

"Anyway, that's it. That's my story."

He was finished. I sat there speechless, fumbling with my hands. "You're shocked," he said, smiling. I had to admit that I was. I had more or less decided he was involved. I had figured he was the one who hired Derek, paid him to get the DNA. I had guessed, after my conversation with Sylvan, that Sybil was maybe a surrogate mother; I have dealt with that situation in my practice, once or twice. In any event, I expected that Dr. LeBeau could give me some answers. But the full story, in all its details—I never expected that. Now I asked him: "What do you want me to do?"

"Absolutely nothing," he said. "Be nice to Freddy. The rest is up to me." And then he got up and left. I noticed the tremor; it seemed even more obvious than before. He walked slowly, but deliberately, using the cane.

I never saw him again.

* * *

Of course, that wasn't the end of the story. Yes, the police did arrest Dr. Pascal LeBeau, and the charge was first degree murder. But it was hard to make that stick. Pascal was right: he never went to trial. He managed to get himself released on bail—very unusual for a murder case. He pleaded not guilty. Nolan Thom was his lawyer. They argued that Sybil's death was an unfortunate accident, and that the doctor panicked and took the body and stashed it where it was found. Of course, the authorities didn't believe him, but it hardly mattered. He died at home, about seven months later. He left most of his estate to Melanie. I saw her once or twice after that. Alas, the affair with Peter Chang didn't survive the turmoil and the bad publicity. Melanie was the one who insisted it had to come to an end. I don't think it was Peter's doing. I suppose they'll find somebody else, each of them. They're young, after all.

Derek Schuster: well, by now he's a member of the bar, I suppose. Working for some big law firm, making money. I lost sight of him. Somehow, I doubt that he'll find happiness. I don't think he has a vocation for happiness; he's too selfish.

Nobody ever found the slightest trace of Max Lucas—the Amazon jungle keeps its secrets. Some of his colleagues named two new beetles after him. One was a form of glowworm, the other was a leatherwing beetle, whatever that is. I'm told these were two very distinctive beetles, and now they carry Max's name. It's nice that there are beetle-lovers in the world, seeing as there are hundreds of thousands of beetles, in all shapes and forms, and the rest of us in the world care nothing at all about beetles, except insofar as they munch on our crops and cost us money.

Nobody named a new ant species after Kathryn, and her death, like her husband's, is something of a mystery. But her skeleton, unlike his, was discovered (and identified), buried near some tiny village, deep in the Brazilian jungle. Some tropical disease probably carried her off. Freddy found the news upsetting, he told me, "though really, I never knew her. I've got a picture of her, but that's about all. I always knew she'd never come back." Poor Freddy had, in this way, lost both of his mothers—they were the same person, of course, but now it was a sure thing. Freddy would never have a real mother.

Meanwhile, I lost Freddy as a client. "Not that I'm not satisfied with all the stuff you did," he said. "I never thought I could really get close to a lawyer, not even Derek—well, he's not a lawyer yet. But Frank, I really appreciate you, I've loved talking to you, and I think I actually love you as a person. I'm going to give you a great big hug."

Which he did. But he had decided he was going to move on, change locations: "I need to get a life," he told me, "I need to make something of myself." He put his house on the market, and sold it "for a zillion dollars," as he put it, "not that I needed the money," and then he moved to Los Angeles. I did fix him up with a living trust, managed by a bank; I was always afraid he might squander the money. But there was plenty of it to squander. Freddy told me he wanted to go into the movie business. He said, "I've got money, maybe I can be a producer? I don't know what producers do, but it's something to do with money, isn't it? I love Los Angeles, that's where I'll go. I want to meet starlets, models, you know, really beautiful women. I'm rich, they'll go for me."

I never found out whether he in fact had luck with starlets and models. But I have a friend in Los Angeles, a former client, a doctor at UCLA (a professor of dermatology) and this friend, Richard, knew Freddy. He treated Freddy for a mysterious rash on his butt, and Freddy took a liking to Richard, who kept me up to date on his doings. About a year after the move to LA, Freddy Lucas got married. He married a woman some ten years older than he was. Freddy had rented a luxury apartment, near the ocean, in Santa Monica, and he had the habit of eating breakfast at a restaurant nearby, overlooking the Pacific Ocean.

That's where he met his wife, Goldie. She was working as a waitress in the restaurant. Waiters and waitresses in Los Angeles are, for the most part, show business wannabes. They are waiting and hoping for the big break; in the meantime they wait on tables, because the rent comes due every month. Goldie was part of this army of wannabes. Actually, she may have given up by then. Like the rest of the wannabes, she had never found the key to success, never got that break, the lightning never struck. Her only gigs were occasional ads on television. In one, she had a feature role: dressed demurely, she discussed a diet formula, designed "for women reaching that special stage in life," in other words, menopause. The product, she said, was a sure-fire path to a slim and attractive body. In another ad, she looked at the camera, and admitted she was suffering from diabetes; but now she, like all other sufferers, could get relief, "with no injections; just a simple pill twice a day. Just ask your doctor if he thinks you could benefit from Maziloprom." After this recommendation, there was, as usual, an interminable list of possible side effects. Tort lawyers are responsible for that sort of thing. They tell the makers of Maziloprom that, unless they come clean about side effects, they'll be crippled with lawsuits. I've seen the ad on TV. If I ever get diagnosed with diabetes, I intend to avoid this drug like the plague.

Freddy's wife, according to Richard, was rather plain: she was somewhat overweight, looked her age, and had irregular teeth. What she saw in Freddy was pretty obvious: money. But maybe I'm being unfair. Freddy isn't bad-looking. He's young. And he's genuinely nice. Useless, yes; lazy, yes; but fun to be with, and extremely good-natured.

My friend wondered, though, what Freddy saw in *her*, in Goldie. "It's a mystery to me," he said. "Freddy says she's awfully nice, and I suppose she is. But still."

It wasn't a mystery to me. Freddy may have talked about starlets and models—and I'm sure he lusted after starlets and models—but what he really wanted was a mother. Not a womb mother, not an egg mother, not a dead mother, but a live, functioning mother, a warm, buxom, caring mother, and maybe Goldie fit the bill. Freddy was bound to fall for this kind of woman, despite the extra pounds and the irregular teeth. That was Freddy's destiny in life. Aunt Clara had been sort of a mother, and Freddy missed her a lot. After she died, many women stepped up to fill the role. But Sybil Glass was definitely not what he really wanted, and Lizbeth absolutely not. Still, maybe all those wannabe mothers had an impact; maybe they kindled the desire in him to have a real mother at last, or at least a mother figure.

Of course, I was sorry to see him go. While it lasted, he was a wonderful client—he was rich, he was interesting, he was pleasant; and he paid his bills on time. I have fond memories of Freddy, and I wish him a long and happy life with Goldie, his mother figure. My informant tells me, by the way, that she's pregnant with twins.

About the author

Lawrence Friedman is a professor of law at Stanford University. He teaches courses in American legal history and law and society. He is the author of *A History of American Law*, *Crime and Punishment in American History*, *The Human Rights Culture*, and *Total Justice*, among other works.

In recent years, Friedman has published *The Big Trial: Law as Public Spectacle*, which vividly recounts famous cases in history and their media coverage of the day, and *Impact: How Law Affects Behavior*. He has also published *Dead Hands: A Social History of Wills, Trusts, and Inheritances*, a subject which is the backbone of Frank May's (fictional) practice.

Visit us at *www.qpbooks.com*.

www.ingramcontent.com/pod-product-compliance
Lightning Source LLC
Chambersburg PA
CBHW051644260626
47170CB00004B/1326